THE ANGEL

A Grand and Batchelor Victorian Mystery

M J Trow

CRÈME de la CRIME

This first world edition published 2016
in Great Britain and the USA by
Crème de la Crime, an imprint of
SEVERN HOUSE PUBLISHERS LTD of
19 Cedar Road, Sutton, Surrey, England, SM2 5DA.
Trade paperback edition first published
in Great Britain and the USA 2016 by
SEVERN HOUSE PUBLISHERS LTD

British Library Cataloguing in Publication Data
A CIP catalogue record for this title is available from the British Library.

ISBN-13: 978-1-78029-089-8 (cased)
ISBN-13: 978-1-78029-572-5 (trade paper)
ISBN-13: 978-1-78010-812-4 (e-book)

Typeset by Palimpsest Book Production Ltd.,
Falkirk, Stirlingshire, Scotland.

ONE

I t wasn't often James Batchelor had the house to himself, but just sometimes he could persuade Matthew Grand that the Muse must take precedence over finding lost dogs and other footling pursuits. Today was such a day. When he had first had the news of the death of Charles Dickens he had, like most of the English-speaking world and a decent proportion of the rest, been stunned. Yes, the old boy wasn't a spring chicken and yes, he had been ill on and off for a while, as reported in the *Telegraph* but . . . dead? It didn't seem possible that that great heart had stopped beating, that there would be no more deaths to wring men's withers, no more ghosts to haunt their nights. Batchelor had been working on his Great British Novel for some time and it wasn't going well. It seemed to him that every time he imagined a plot twist which would make his fortune, so it would appear in some weekly sheet and he would have to begin again. He had stopped talking about his opus; the walls clearly had ears. Grand reminded him sardonically from time to time that this happened to him because he couldn't actually write for taffy, but Batchelor maintained a lordly silence and retired to his little garret under the eaves whenever he got a moment.

Their new housekeeper, Mrs Rackstraw, had words to say on the subject of the garret, and some of them were fair enough, as Batchelor agreed when he was feeling generous. She rightly pointed out that there were many rooms much more congenial on the ground, first and even second floors. So why did she have to haul herself up another flight of stairs every time she needed to speak to the young gentleman? The best houses had bells for that sort of thing. Her cousin Mildred's eldest knew of a parlour maid in Stoke Newington who never had to put her foot to the floor unless her particular bell rang. Mrs Rackstraw had no truck with his answer that he couldn't write except in total solitude; when she was in a proper bate, as her friends called it, or an apoplexy, as her doctor tended to refer to it, she would go so far as to spit. But

she could cook like an angel, cleaned the house as if the devil
himself were after her and – perhaps most importantly – she hated
and abhorred cats with an unusual fervour. Grand and Batchelor
had not disliked Mrs Manciple, their previous housekeeper but
one, but in the end her cat obsession had reached a level that no
normal household could sustain. After she was carted away to the
Colney Hatch Asylum, where she still lived in the lap of luxury,
courtesy of Matthew Grand, it had taken them months to find
homes for all of her pets. They seemed to be self-sustaining; as
soon as three went to good homes, another had four kittens. But
eventually they were all gone and, after a brief sojourn with a butler
and a chef in charge, during which time they both gained a stone
– or, rather, Batchelor gained a stone and Grand gained fourteen
pounds – they found Mrs Rackstraw, who had many failings, but
suited them most of the time.

Happily, on this beautiful June morning, marred only by the
fact that Dickens was still dead, Mrs Rackstraw was in a moder-
ately good mood. In anyone else it would have looked like a foul
temper, but Batchelor was used to her little ways, so ignored
most of the crashing, banging and foul oaths that preceded her
up his little winding stair.

The door to the garret crashed back, leaving a deep gouge in
the plaster behind it. Why they kept having it repaired, Batchelor
never knew – it would only be there again in a few weeks.

'There's a sailor downstairs wants you.'

Batchelor looked up, another golden phrase dribbling from his
brain, another gem forever lost to posterity, like King John's
jewels in the Wash. 'I beg your pardon, Mrs Rackstraw. Did you
say a sailor?'

'That's what I said,' she said, taking another step into the room.
The climb had made her a little breathless, so she did no more. 'I
asked him his name, like you always say I have to, though for the
life of me I don't know why I bother. They always says it again
when you come in. Or say it's personal and none of my business.
I asked him his name and he says "Tell him I'm a sailor." So
here I am, telling you. There's a sailor downstairs wants you.'

'Does he want to consult us professionally?' Batchelor was
excited. A sailor could have any number of intriguing problems
he needed them to solve. Missing cargo, perhaps. Piracy on the

High Seas. Embezzled naval funds. Man overboard – now, that *would* be a challenge worthy of their mighty intellects.

'Don't know,' Mrs Rackstraw said, and Batchelor almost heard the unspoken 'don't care'. 'He'd go to the office, wouldn't he?'

Sometimes the woman came out with bursts of logic, and in this case she couldn't be faulted. Batchelor got up. There was clearly no way in which this present puzzle would be solved unless he went downstairs and confronted this sailor. 'How old is he, Mrs Rackstraw?' he asked, his foot on the second stair from the top. There would be little point, after all, in going downstairs to interview some cabin boy or other lowly seafarer. Time, in the largest city in the world, was money. And Grand and Batchelor had a fixed price for their services that was hardly, as Grand would say, bargain basement.

'Ooh, I dunno,' she said, pursing her already very pursed mouth. 'I'm no good on ages . . . forty? Fifty? Sixty? Could be anything.' She turned on the stairs and looked up at Batchelor. 'He's a bit . . .' she waved her hand in front of her face, vaguely sketching in details. 'Blobby.'

'Mrs Rackstraw! That's not a polite way to describe our guests.'

'No, but you wanted to know . . .'

They were now on the landing of the first floor and Batchelor raised an admonitory finger. 'Ssshh! He'll hear us.'

'No, he won't,' she said, crossly. She didn't use so much breath going downstairs, so she could give her temperament freer rein. 'I put him in the drawing room.'

'Even so . . . blobby, you say?'

'Yes.' She screwed her face up at him. 'Like a . . . what's that animal?' She set off down the final flight of stairs. 'That animal, you know the one?'

By now Batchelor could hardly wait to meet his visitor. A sailor who looked like an animal. He was almost sure he could actually include such a creature in his Great British Novel.

Mrs Rackstraw reached the drawing-room door first and flung it open with her customary élan, remembering the animal as she did so. 'Gorilla!' she cried and stepped back.

The visitor half rose from his chair with commendable calm following her rather unusual introduction and turned to his host.

'James!' he said. 'You look well. It's good to see you again. How is the writing coming along?'

Batchelor covered the distance to the man's outstretched hand in three enormous strides. Everything fell into place. The carefully Macassared hair, the Savile Row suit, the air of the swell, the nose; especially the nose. It wasn't a sailor who looked like a gorilla at all. 'Mr Sala!' he said, shaking his hand enthusiastically. 'Mr George Sala! How can I help you?'

Mr George Sala's smile vanished instantly. 'Dickens,' he said.

'Yes.' Batchelor nodded solemnly. 'Tragic. Tragic. You worked for him, didn't you?'

Sala bridled a little. '*With*, dear boy, with. To me, he was everything. In him I have lost all that I most revered and loved.'

'Oh, George,' Batchelor shook the man's hand again, 'I had no idea. That's quite beautiful.'

'Yes, it is, isn't it? It'll be in the *Telegraph* tomorrow.'

'Ah, you've done the obituary,' Batchelor realized. 'Who better?'

'Who indeed?' Sala sat down without invitation. 'But that's not why I'm here. I'm writing his biography – *A Life Like No Other*. Like it?' Sala looked down with an expression of what he assumed was modesty on his face. 'Just a working title for now, of course. Like it?'

'Love it,' Batchelor crooned. Ever since he had been a boy reporter on the *Telegraph* he had crept in George Sala's shadow. Everything that Bachelor had done or hoped to do, George Sala had been there already.

'But that's not why I'm here either.'

'God!' The door flew open and a large American burst in. 'Can this city get any hotter? I'll swear the sidewalks are smoking . . . Oh, I'm sorry, I didn't realize . . .'

'Matthew,' Batchelor extended a hostly arm. 'You remember George Sala?'

Sala had subsided back into his chair on Batchelor's entrance and didn't get up now, merely waving a lazy hand vaguely in Matthew Grand's direction. 'How's that woeful country of yours, Mr Grand? Got over its teething troubles yet?'

George Sala had witnessed those teething troubles himself. He had covered the Civil War for the *Telegraph* and, if his expense account at Washington's Willard's Hotel was a *little* on the outrageous side, he *had* stood in the trenches of Vicksburg and held the hands of dying boys at Shiloh. Matthew Grand had done that too, except that they had been his boys, from the Third Cavalry of the Potomac, and he had had to write the sad letters to their wives and mothers.

'I believe we're only eighteen hundred years or so behind you now,' Grand smiled. 'Is this a social call, Mr Sala?'

George Sala could be as sociable as the next man when the mood took him, but today was not one of those days. He flipped a card from his waistcoat pocket and held it up while Grand took a seat, loosening his tie and peeling the collar from his neck. 'It says here,' the doyen of journalists said, '"No stone unturned."'

It was one of Grand and Batchelor's calling cards, announcing to the world that they were 'Enquiry Agents', working out of number 41 The Strand, with their private address on the back for good measure. 'Yes.' Batchelor shifted a little uneasily and cleared his throat. 'It's not my best work, I admit. Somebody in America suggested it when we were there last and I, perhaps a little foolishly . . .'

'Don't do yourself down, James, my boy,' Sala said. 'You see, I have a stone that needs to be turned. And it may be that you gentlemen are the ones to do it.'

'Can you be a little more precise, Mr Sala?' Grand asked.

'Very well.' Sala leaned back in his chair, allowing his girth free rein and letting the morning sun dazzle on his gold Albert. 'I will cut to the denouement. Charles Dickens was murdered.'

Miss Emmeline Jones sat at her desk as always, alert and ready for the sound of the love of her life approaching up the stairs. She had a lot of work to do because she had gradually, by means of bullying and genteel intimidation, managed to get rid of almost all of the other office employees, particularly any who were younger and more obviously attractive than she was herself; a long list, as Miss Jones was spectacularly plain and the conventional severe hair fashion of the old decade did her no favours. The gorgeous ringlets had gone and the bun ruled everywhere. But in her favour she had loyalty, efficiency and the neatest handwriting to be found the length and breadth of the Strand, so she knew her place with Chapman and Hall was secure.

Frederic Chapman – or Young Mr Frederic as he was always called, despite clear evidence to the contrary – ran the publishing house in the Strand with a benevolent hand and he was not famous for his work ethic. He made no bones about the fact that he was simply born into the job, having taken some of the reins on the death of his cousin's partner, Edward Hall, and then total control when said cousin retired. It wasn't a hard life but it was lucrative, thanks in the main to the fact that they had had Charles Dickens on their books on and off for over sixteen years – and sixteen years of Charles Dickens's output was a lot of books. Elizabeth Barrett hadn't done the company any harm either, and for some reason which Young Mr Frederic couldn't quite fathom, her work still sold in enough numbers to take his wife on her annual holiday to Spa, with all the trimmings.

But then, the previous Friday, Miss Jones had entered her beloved's office with dire news. Charles Dickens, that great writer but, more importantly, that great earner, was dead. She would never forget the look on Frederic's face when she told him the news. She wanted to fly to his side, to press his head into her bosom and give him succour. But, instead, she had stood still just inside the room as he went as white as ash and then gave vent to a string of epithets she had never thought to hear coming from those heavenly lips. When he had recovered a little, he had taken up his hat and cane and gone home, instructing her to close the office as a mark of respect. A black bow was to be tied to the brassware. And that, followed after a brief pause by the slamming of the street door, was the last she had heard of him.

A note had been delivered to her lodgings on the Sunday, carried by an urchin grinning from ear to ear at having been given a sixpenny piece for his trouble, telling her to call a meeting of the editors, sub-editors and copy editors in his office, Wednesday next at eleven o'clock, sharp. Oh, and the young idiot should be there as well. She had given the task her full attention and had managed to find most of them. A few had been last seen in various public houses and chop houses, drinking to speed the soul of the dead author on its way to that great scriptorium in the sky, and were not expected to emerge for a day or so. But she had started the grapevine twanging and she was fairly confident that everyone would be there at eleven o'clock, sharp.

She sent a note to the young idiot, too, although she was careful to address it more respectfully to Henry Merivale Trollope, Chapman's partner in the firm.

Her head came up like a questing beast sniffing the air as she heard the street door open. With it came the sounds of the Strand; hawkers calling, carriage wheels rumbling and hot, tired cab horses shaking their harnesses at the flies which hung permanently around their heads. The month was only just beginning and already the heat was beginning to tell on London and on everyone who had to pound its streets. When Miss Jones was a girl, it would have been next to impossible to work this near the river because of the smell. But that clever little engineer Mr Bazalgette had worked his magic and built The Embankment, which effectively moved the Thames further away. Nowadays there was the odd waft on a very hot day and it was this that broke into the room now as Frederic Chapman came in.

No one knew of Emmeline Jones's passion, except perhaps the post boy; all of the editors, sub- and copy; the woman who 'did' and brought their tea; and Mrs Chapman, who found it all rather hilarious. Frederic Chapman, however, remained in the list of those who didn't know, and so barely noticed the frisson of excitement that set the wattles under the hairy chin of his secretary and amanuensis shaking.

'They here, Miss Jones?' he barked.

'Most of them, Mr Frederic,' she simpered.

'The young idiot?'

'Not as yet,' she said. Then her ears pricked up. Someone had let the street door go with a crash and was bounding up the stairs. No editor ever had that amount of energy, drinking to the shade of Dickens for the best part of five days straight or no. 'But I think that may be him now.'

Chapman had just enough time to step out of the way when the door banged open with as much fervour as the street door had banged closed, and Henry Merivale Trollope burst in. 'Em,' he carolled, 'Fred, sorry I'm late, dears. Horse collapsed on the bridge – heat stroke, poor thing. Made me think, have we got anyone who is a horsey writer? I don't mean looks like a horse, of course, although . . .' He cast his eyes up, scanning some faces in his mind. 'No, we haven't really. Elizabeth Barrett Browning looked like her dog, of course, but she's no longer with us . . . umm . . .' He came back to the here and now and looked at the two faces before him and grinned. 'Sorry, letting my enthusiasm get the better of me again.' He pulled a sad face. 'Here to pay our respects, of course. Charles Dickens, of course. Dear Charles. Very sad. Sudden. I say, I heard a story at my club . . .'

Chapman took control of the situation, as far as anyone could when the whirlwind that was Henry Trollope was present. 'If you would go into the board room, Henry, I believe you will find the staff assembled there . . .' He raised an interrogative eyebrow at Emmeline Jones, who nodded. 'And some sherry and biscuits?' Again, she nodded.

Trollope rubbed his hands together. 'Splendid. Oh, I say, Em . . . you've not put the funny glasses out, have you? The ones with the thick bottoms, the ones that're supposed to fool the authors that they've had a full measure?'

Miss Jones drew herself up. '*I* have not put out any glasses, Master Henry,' she said, frostily. 'Mrs Halfbrackett will have doubtless done what is necessary. Would you like me to call down and find out?' She reached for the speaking tube by her desk. 'I can't promise she will answer – you know how she can be.'

'No, no, don't trouble the old trout. I'll find out soon enough. I'll go through and have a chinwag with the lads. I'll tell them you'll come through when you're ready, shall I, Fred?'

Frederic Chapman closed his eyes and murmured, 'That would be just splendid, Henry. Thank you.'

Trollope pushed open the door into the board room and was greeted with cries of delight. He might not be very popular with Miss Jones and Young Mr Frederic, but with editors of every colour, he was a great success. Not only was there the chance that by sucking up to him they might get access to his old man – his father had, after all, bought him a one-third share in the company as a coming-of-age gift – but he was also a lot of fun; not something they had seen much of working for Chapman and Hall before his arrival.

Gabriel Verdon, the most senior editor, patted a chair next to his. 'Come and sit here, Harry,' he said. 'Any gossip today?'

'I'd better sit up there,' Trollope said, regretfully pointing to the head of the table. 'Sad day, all that.' He worked his way up the table, patting shoulders as he went. 'But that doesn't stop me sharing a bit of tittle-tattle. Got to be quick. Freddie is having a bit of a spoon with Em but he won't be long.'

The editors guffawed, the sound rolling like thunder into the outer office.

Chapman looked at the door, his nostrils quivering. The man was a menace. Coming to work was no reason for hilarity, especially on such a sombre occasion. Did the guttersnipe have no respect for dear Dickens at all? One would almost think that the young idiot enjoyed himself: preposterous! 'I should join them, Miss Jones,' he said, looking down at her. She was no oil painting, he had to admit, but she was a sane thing in a mad, mad world. 'If anyone wants to see me, tell them to come back tomorrow.'

Miss Jones nodded brightly and made a note on the large pad on her desk. Her pencil squeaked across the page – 'Tell any callers Mr Frederic busy.' But she knew she wouldn't have to tell anyone; perish the thought, but all their callers came for Master Henry these days.

British hotel rooms – like this one in Tavistock Square – weren't a patch on those in New York, New York, that Beulah would attest, and she did it loudly and often. Henry had got used to her over the years and hardly heard her any more as he carried on with what he felt he did best, which was writing. He would agree, if asked, that the lighting could perhaps be improved, but he had pushed the little table over to the window and was getting on famously; the dappled sunlight filtering through the trees was very pleasant, and surely even Beulah would have to agree that the view of the little railed garden full of perambulating nannies and their charges was a vast improvement on that from their own sitting room at home, which was a brick wall not three feet away.

'I said, Henry, I said . . . Henry? Are you listening?'

His pen didn't falter. 'Indeed I am, Beulah my love. The bed here isn't as soft as the ones in hotels in New York and you don't think they wash the comforters very often. You've just found a long blonde hair.'

She tutted. 'If you hear me, Henry, I say, if you *hear* me, Henry, why don't you answer?'

He put his pen down carefully and turned to face her. 'I didn't know there was an answer, my love,' he said, patiently. 'Why don't you go for a little walk in the garden over the way there, while I finish this?'

Beulah leapt up, to the extent that she ever made any sudden movements. She had always been a bit top-heavy – in fact, Henry, in expansive mood when out on the town with his fellow journalists, had been known to remark that that was the main reason he had married her – but now, with middle-age creeping on, she had a bust like a roll-top desk which made her a little circumspect. She stood over Henry now, roll-top heaving indignantly. 'Do you mean to tell me, Henry Morford, that you expect me to go outside alone – me, a woman, alone in . . .' she took a deep breath and lowered her voice to give it proper gravitas, '*London*?'

Her husband sighed. He looked at his writing, half finished or less. He looked at his wife, looming over him like a shop awning. He looked outside at the sunshine. He looked at the nannies, tripping through the gardens, and he made his decision. 'Well, Beulah,' he said, smiling up at her. 'When you put it like that.' He got up and shrugged into his coat. 'Get your bonnet on and we'll go explore a while. Time we got the lie of the land, I'd say.'

Dimpling with pleasure, Beulah tied her bonnet beneath her chin with a jaunty bow. 'Oh, Henry,' she said. 'You spoil me, you really do. And don't forget, we're bound to meet some local colour – cusses who grind knives and sell trinkets, that sort of thing. It'll be good for your writing, Henry, I say, Henry, it'll be good for your writing.'

'Beulah,' he pecked her on the cheek, 'you're always thinking of me. It's not many wives would come all this way just for a dream.'

'Aw, Henry,' she linked her arm in his. 'But if it comes off, we'll be in clover. I say—'

'Yes,' he smiled, cutting her off in mid-flow. 'Clover is right, my love. Clover is just the right word.'

Beulah beamed. If her Henry, great writer that he was, thought it was the right word, then right word it was certain to be!

'Gentlemen! Gentlemen!' Frederic Chapman rapped the table with the end of his pencil but to no avail.

'I say, chaps,' Trollope murmured. 'A bit of hush for the guv'nor.'

The editors all turned as one man to gaze on their employer. Chapman hated it when they did that; he could almost see their avid thirst for words, like a bottomless well before him. 'Well, gentlemen,' he said, 'as you know, today is a very sad occasion. We meet here to pay our respects to that great writer and great man, Mr Charles Dickens, who, as you know, departed this vale of tears peacefully last Thursday, at his home, Gads Hill.'

Trollope turned his snort into a cough and looked down into his lap. That wasn't exactly as he had heard it, but if it made the old man happy, who was he to argue?

'The world will mourn him, gentlemen, as will we.'

'He's left a void; that much is certain.'

'We shall not look on another like him, not in our lifetime,' Gabriel Verdon was sure.

'He trod on my foot once. I'll never polish that boot again.'

After that eulogistic flurry, the room fell silent. Inevitably, it was the young idiot who broke the silence. 'John,' he looked earnestly at the solid, square-looking man in the corner, 'you knew him better than any of us. How's the biography coming along?'

John Forster raised his whiskered head for the first time. 'Sala,' he said and lowered it again.

The editors at their respective levels looked at each other. '*George* Sala?' Chapman found his voice first.

Forster nodded. 'I have it on good authority that the blighter has taken it upon himself to write a Life quicker than any of us.'

'Preposterous!'

'Unthinkable!'

'Unreadable, that much is certain,' Gabriel Verdon was convinced of that.

'Dickens barely knew the man.'

'Gentlemen, gentlemen,' Chapman called them to order again. 'We are all missing the point here. The master will indeed leave a great void. John will write a masterpiece of a biography and no one will read Sala. But the point at issue, gentlemen, is that Charles Dickens left unfinished business. *Our* business depends upon it. I can sum it up in two words, gentlemen – *Edwin Drood*.'

TWO

'I think he was losing the plot, you know.' James Batchelor put down the latest instalment of *The Mystery of Edwin Drood* and stared at the empty fireplace.

'Hmm?' Matthew Grand had his nose buried in the *Telegraph*, wondering if *Magic*, Captain Osgood's yacht, had a hope in Hell in the America's Cup next month.

'Dickens,' Batchelor explained. 'His latest opus – forever unfinished now, I suppose – *The Mystery of Edwin Drood*. Not much of a mystery, really. Uncle Jasper did it.'

'Did he?' Grand looked up. 'How do you know?'

'*Please*, Matthew,' Batchelor chuckled, 'I *am* an enquiry agent.'

'Of course you are.'

'So, it's not just that the "who" in "whodunit" is as plain as the nose on George Sala's face, it's that about a third of the book is written in the present tense.'

'Is that illegal?' Grand wondered aloud. He had been in England for less than five years and he knew they did things differently over here.

'It should be,' Batchelor told him. 'Reads appallingly. I'm surprised at Dickens; I'd hoped for more. How did you get on with the burial details?'

'Well, I couldn't get into the abbey for the crowds.'

'He was a national treasure, however you look at it.'

Grand nodded. He remembered Abraham Lincoln's funeral, with strangers crying and hugging each other. Everybody wanted to touch the casket, pat the white horses, collect the petals that floated down in the April sun. Four men claimed to have laid the pennies on the dead president's eyes. Barbers in Washington made a fortune selling locks of the great man's hair that had been nowhere near the great man's head. 'It wasn't that simple, though,' he said.

'What wasn't?'

'Well, it seems Dickens wanted to be buried in a village called Shawe, the church of St Peter and St Paul.'

'No, no,' Batchelor shook his head. 'His adoring public wouldn't have allowed that.'

'Exactly. The authorities from Rochester Cathedral were round to the Dickens place like rats up a pipe. Said they'd already dug the grave.'

Batchelor looked at him. 'That was a little premature,' he said, 'or am I mixing my authors?'

'Time was,' Grand reminded him, 'you'd have given your right arm for a word from Dickens. According to you, the sun shone out of his—'

'Yes, but that was before this.' Batchelor waved the paper at him. 'Chapters Ten to Twelve.'

'When's the next instalment due?'

'Thirteen to Sixteen should be out next month, but perhaps that won't happen now; without the end, there seems little point. But I have to admit, Matthew, I'm disappointed. It's just not up to his usual standard.'

'The obituaries said he hadn't been well.'

'So you think George Sala was wrong – about the murder, I mean?'

Grand shrugged. 'You know the man better than I do, James,' he said. 'You tell me.'

'"No stone unturned",' Batchelor murmured, staring again into the blackness where the fire roared in darker, cooler days. 'He seemed pretty adamant.'

'And he *did* pay us a retainer.'

Batchelor snorted. 'Notice how pale he turned, though? The man would rather have his teeth drawn than draw a cheque, I fancy. So, how did Dickens end up in Westminster Abbey?'

'Dean Stanley.'

'Who?'

'Arthur Stanley, Dean of Westminster.'

'You've met him?'

'No, I've spent most of the day in the various bookstores around the church—'

'Abbey,' Batchelor corrected him.

'Right. If you want to find out local details, ask the store clerks. Most people wanted to chew my head off on Gladstone's Irish policy. One of them couldn't understand why we weren't

backing the Prussians by invading France. And don't get me
started on Mr Forster's Education Act.'

'But on Dean Stanley . . .?'

'On Dean Stanley, they were as one. He's a Helluva nice cuss,
who would never suggest that England's greatest writer should
be buried in his ch . . . abbey, but he knows the very place, right
between Handel and Sheridan.'

'Perfect. So,' Batchelor crossed to the brandy decanter and
poured for them both. He raised his glass. 'To the detecting game,
Captain Grand.'

Grand raised his glass too. 'To the detecting game, indeed,
Mr Batchelor. The only game in town. Now, what have we got?'

George Sala was a great story teller, no one would deny him
that. In fact his detractors would go further and say that everything he wrote was a story, no matter how factual it was meant
to be. But he was so wound up in the toils of the tale of a dead
man that he went backwards, forwards and sideways randomly,
so that in the end Batchelor's notes, taken during his discursion,
looked like the ravings of a madman. While everything was fresh
in his mind, Batchelor had retired to his garret and rewritten it
all in an attempt to make it seem like sense. But even then there
were so many gaps and bits of nonsense that he was sure that
he had got the wrong end of the stick more than once.

He now planned to read it all out to Grand, who was invited
to interrupt whenever he thought Batchelor had gone wrong, as
he remembered it.

'I'm sorry, James,' Grand said before the reading even began.
'At times I wondered whether the man hadn't come straight here
from some opium den or somewhere. He was . . . well, I can
only use the word incoherent.'

'Sala does have a habit of using twelve long words where
one short one would do,' Batchelor agreed. 'I've cut all that
out where I can.'

'That's a mercy,' Grand said, leaning over and tugging the
bell, the only one that linked to the kitchen. 'Brandy's good when
you have work to do, but shall we have a snack as well? I'm as
hungry as a hunter.'

Batchelor sighed. They had both managed to lose the excess

weight caused by their brief employment of a gourmet chef, but Grand had been left with a taste for canapés of an evening. Sadly, Mrs Rackstraw had never quite got the knack, and she usually produced a cheese sandwich, cut into small squares. She was an excellent plain cook, as her references all attested, but with the emphasis very much on the plain.

In answer to the bell, there was a thunder of running feet in the hall and the housekeeper burst in as though the hounds of Hell were at her heels. 'Yes?' Then, 'Sir?' There was something about her timing that added insolence to injury whenever she spoke.

'Umm . . . yes,' Grand said, ignoring the slur. 'Could we have some canapés, do you think? Not cheese-based, if possible.'

The woman stood there, still swaying with the violence of her entry, but didn't speak.

'So . . . that would be marvellous, thank you,' Grand smiled and turned back to Batchelor. After a moment or so, the door slammed, and the running feet were heard to disappear down the corridor. The slamming of the green baize door completed the picture.

'Shall I wait . . .?' Batchelor was loath to begin when she would be back shortly with a tray of something unidentifiable. With cheese out of the question, it was doubtful that she would have anything else she could squeeze between two bits of bread.

'No, no,' Grand said, waving a hand. 'Let's get going. We can't hang around waiting on the help all the time. When did Sala's story begin? I could hardly tell even that, honestly.'

Batchelor shuffled his papers and tapped them into neatness on the table. 'I don't know when *Sala*'s story began, but I have started with the finding of the body. Dickens, as you probably know, did all his writing in a small summerhouse in the grounds of Gads Hill, which everyone refers to as the chalet.'

Grand threw up his hands. 'There you are, you see; I have already learned something.'

Batchelor was aghast. '*Everyone* knows that,' he said.

Grand made a decision and leaned forward. 'James, before this all begins in earnest, can we come to a consensus? I won't keep on telling you it was news to me, if you don't keep telling me that everyone knows that. Is that agreed?'

Batchelor was sulky, but agreed. He took a deep breath. 'So, on the 9 June last, Dickens's housekeeper, Georgina Hogarth, known as Georgy, went to the chalet.'

The door crashed back. Mrs Rackstraw deposited a plate of toasted squares of bread oozing something brown. 'Canapés,' she remarked.

'And they contain . . .?' Grand wasn't sure he wanted to know, but couldn't help but ask.

'Dripping,' she said. 'You said you didn't want cheese.' As an explanation it left a little to be desired, but she swept out anyway, giving him no chance to pursue the matter.

Grand looked at them from every angle and finally popped one gingerly into his mouth. He chewed with his eyes closed and then opened them, smiled and mumbled through the mouthful, 'They're good.'

'Of course they are,' Batchelor snapped. 'I had dripping toast practically every afternoon of my life until I left home. Now, do you mind if we get on?'

'Not at all.' Grand slid the plate nearer to him. 'Do you want any of these?'

'No. As I was saying, Georgy went to the chalet and found Dickens there, dead in his chair.'

'What time was this?' Grand interrupted through his next mouthful.

'Er . . . mid-afternoon . . . ish. She screamed the place down and several of the staff from the house and grounds came running. It strikes me as odd.'

'Why? Most women scream when they find someone dead. It's kind of in their bones; dead body means scream. Spider, scream. Mouse, scream.' Grand was unashamedly polishing off his dripping; most English food left him cold, but this he liked. His remarks were short and pithy so as not to interfere with eating.

'I agree. But it appears that George Sala – this could get confusing, this George, Georgy confluence. I'll call George just Sala, shall I?'

Grand nodded.

'So, Sala said he got the impression that she wasn't just screaming that a dead body was in there, but that anyone at all was in there. Her reaction, according to the gardener who saw her open the door, was just too immediate. Dickens's body didn't look unpleasant or even very dead. He was just sitting in his chair. For all she knew, he was just asleep.'

'So, is that why Sala came to us?'

'Partly. But wait. If you remember, Sala said that Dickens had complained of exhaustion and of being unable to sleep for several weeks. But when he tried to find someone to whom Dickens had spoken on this subject, he could find no one. It was all just supposition and gossip *after* the event. The doctor gave the cause of death as a severe stroke. But you could say that about many deaths which have other very well-attested causes. You may as well say he died because he stopped breathing, or because his heart stopped.'

'Did Sala find out why she went there?'

'Pardon?' Batchelor thumbed through his notes.

'If she was surprised to see him there, why did she go to the chalet?'

'I expect she was just going to tidy up or something. She *was* his housekeeper, after all.'

Grand looked thoughtful. 'Have I imagined it, or is there a rumour going around about Dickens and his housekeeper?'

Batchelor was shocked. 'I think you must be thinking of Wilkie Collins,' he said, on his dignity. 'That's well known.'

Grand set his lips and shook his head. 'Nope. I definitely remember hearing it about Charles Dickens.'

'Thackeray. Apparently—'

'James.' Grand had had enough. 'If Thackeray once lived with his housekeeper as man and wife he certainly isn't doing it any more. Even I, unlettered colonial though you think me, know that he's as dead as a nit. But if it upsets you we will agree that yes, Georgina . . . what did you say her name was?'

'Hogarth.'

'Any relation?'

'Yes, she's his sister-in-law.'

Grand's mouth moved as he tried to work it out. 'Whose sister-in-law?' he had to ask in the end.

'Dickens's of course. Who else are we talking about?'

'For a moment there, the artist. But that doesn't matter – I didn't know she was his sister-in-law.'

'Yes. His wife lives apart from him these days,' Batchelor grudgingly admitted, 'and her sister runs the house.'

Grand said nothing and his expression was so bland that Batchelor could have struck him.

'I will admit that there are rumours about Dickens and the odd actress, but I am sure they are just ill-natured gossip. He loved a pretty face, apparently.'

'There were no actresses there, I'm assuming. In the chalet, with the dead body.'

'No. He was by himself. Sala apparently was there within the hour – they sent a post boy, Isaac somebody, on a fast horse to various key people, and of course he was a great comfort to Georgina on her loss. Some of the children were there of course, Trollope . . .'

'That is a bit uncalled for. Some people don't have much respect for actresses, but they deserve a bit of respect, nonetheless.'

'What?' Batchelor was puzzled for a moment. 'Oh. I see. No, Trollope. Trollope the author.'

Grand shook his head.

'The Barsetshire novels?' He looked at his friend, who was still in the dark, and wondered whether to tell him about the dripping on his lapel. 'No. You'll just have to take it from me that Anthony Trollope is a leading author. Not as great as Dickens, of course . . .'

'Of course.'

Batchelor continued, 'But a great friend of the family, according to Sala. Dickens's doctor, Dr Beard, stayed to speak to the family, and Sala managed to take him aside and ask him a few pertinent questions.'

'Which were . . .?' Grand was getting a little tired of George Sala already, retainer or no retainer.

'He didn't say. But he did say that Dr Beard was extremely circumspect in his replies.'

'Doctors are,' Grand observed. 'Especially when one of their patients has been found unexpectedly dead.'

'Yes. I agree with that at least. But Sala . . .'

Grand had finished all the dripping and was bored. The discussion was going nowhere, George Sala, in his humble opinion, was just building up his part, hoping to be able to write himself into the last chapters of his biography of the great, dead, Dickens. It was time to wrap this up. 'So, James, if I may. Dickens is found dead in a place in which he spent a lot of time. He wasn't stabbed, shot, throttled or otherwise done away with.'

'As far as we know.' Batchelor couldn't help the addition.

'As far as we know. He had been working like a demon, had complained of exhaustion, and lived what we must agree to call an unusual private life. How old was he?'

'Fifty-eight.'

'Not a bad innings, as you English chaps say. A bit too young to just drop dead, I suppose, but I really can't for the very life of me work out why Sala thinks he was murdered.'

Batchelor tidied his papers once more and marshalled his thoughts. 'It isn't very obvious, perhaps,' he said. 'But . . . but he was willing to part with money and that isn't like him. And he came to us because Dickens had our card on his desk. Why would he have that unless he was thinking of engaging us? And why would he want to engage us unless he was in fear of his life?'

Grand walked over to Batchelor and took the notes from him, sliding them into a drawer. Batchelor took the opportunity to flick the globule of dripping off his friend's lapel and into a dried-flower arrangement gathering dust on the table. 'Come on, James,' Grand said kindly. 'Time for a walk to clear our heads. Because you know why Dickens had looked out our card, don't you? Hmm. Now, don't you?'

Batchelor smiled and buttoned up his coat. 'Because he'd lost his cat?'

'You know it!'

THREE

Piccadilly was murder that day. The world and his wife had come up to Town for the Season and demure young ladies were being chaperoned along the pavements, past window shoppers and flower sellers. Dray horses steamed and sweated, clattering over the cobbles and dipping their velvet noses into the green-scummed troughs.

James Batchelor had found number 48, a large town house tucked a little further back than the rest, and he was grateful that it stood on the shady side. The heat rose from the stones and leather-clad tradesmen puffed out their cheeks and tried not to swear for fear of offending the gentility that swarmed around them in frothy gowns and under fussy parasols. City gentlemen, up West for any number of reasons, regretted their top hats and starched collars, looking with envy at the cravats and boaters of visitors from the country.

'Do you have an appointment?'

Batchelor swept off his low-crowned derby and said, 'No.'

'Then I can't see you.'

'I am not a patient, doctor,' he explained, sliding out his card. 'I am an enquiry agent. You *are* Dr Beard?'

'I'm Frank Beard, yes,' the doctor nodded, plopping his pen into an inkwell on his desk. 'And what exactly is an enquiry agent?'

'A private detective,' Batchelor told him. He hadn't taken to Dr Beard and he sensed that the feeling was mutual. The man had clearly been blond once and was now pepper and salt. His eyes were a clear blue, hawk-like astride his beak of a nose.

'I see.' Beard pursed his lips and pressed his fingers together on them, looking his visitor up and down. 'I thought such people were creations of fiction,' he said. 'Something from the pen of Mr Collins, perhaps.'

'No, sir,' Batchelor stood his ground. 'I can assure you I am a creation of fact.'

'Clearly,' Beard sneered. 'Well, what do you want? I have a very busy schedule.'

'The late Charles Dickens,' Batchelor said. He was still standing in the man's opulent study because he had not been invited to sit.

'What of him?' Beard's eyes narrowed above the pince-nez.

'Can you tell me the cause of death?'

Beard sat upright. For a moment he toyed with ringing his bell and summoning help, but the only help to reach him quickly was Mrs Le Tissier, his secretary, and Beard knew that, formidable though the woman was in the ordinary scheme of things, she'd be no match for Batchelor if things got ugly.

'Yes and no,' he answered.

'Er . . . I'm sorry.' Batchelor was a little thrown. 'I don't follow.'

'Because I am a doctor, yes, I can tell you the cause of Mr Dickens's death. But precisely because I am a doctor and dear Charles was my patient, no, I cannot. Surely, Mr . . . er . . . Batchelor . . . in your line of work you must have come across the phrase "doctor–patient confidentiality"?'

'I have,' Batchelor nodded, 'but it doesn't help.'

'Forgive me, sir,' Beard was on his dignity, 'I was not aware that it was my lot in life to help you. If you are ill, consult your own physician. Otherwise . . .' and he reached for his pen again, 'I wish you good day.'

'Is it possible,' Batchelor decided to take the bull by the horns, 'that Mr Dickens was murdered?'

Beard sat up again so slowly that he dropped the pen, ink spattering over his pages. 'Murdered, sir?' he repeated. 'Murdered? What the devil do you mean?'

'Surely, doctor,' Batchelor said, 'in your line of work you must have come across the phrase?'

'Get out!' Beard was on his feet. 'Leave this instant or I shall call the police.'

Batchelor ignored the threat. 'The obituaries said a stroke,' he said.

'Well, there you are, then.' Beard was still on his feet, white with fury. 'Your question is answered.'

'No, it's not,' Batchelor persisted. 'You see, I used to *be* a journalist, Dr Beard. I know the hacks who write this stuff. They can be, shall we say, ill-informed?'

'Ill-informed by whom?' Beard demanded to know.

'Oh, that's the question, isn't it? Have you spoken to the Press, doctor?'

Beard rang his bell furiously and a bombazined Gorgon appeared at Batchelor's elbow. 'Mrs Le Tissier, this . . . gentleman . . . was just leaving. Could you show him out?'

Batchelor raised his hands. 'I can find my own way.' He smiled at her, while being careful to avoid her basilisk stare. He had no time to be turned to stone today, not with a murder to solve. 'You've been help itself, doctor.' And he was gone.

'Mrs Le Tissier.' Beard sat down, crumpled up the stained page and started a new one. 'Have that dim-witted lad from the back stairs take the letter I am about to write round to Scotland Yard. He is to give it to Adolphus Williamson in person. And I shall expect a reply.'

When he and Batchelor had tossed the coin that morning to see who went to see the doctor and who went to see the housekeeper at Gads Hill, Grand was pretty sure he had been the winner. After all, the doctor was bound to be a much harder nut to crack than a grief-stricken young woman; Grand had quite the track record when it came to grief-stricken young women, even if it was only a lost cat they were mourning. He had asked Batchelor, the Londoner born and bred, how he would set about getting to Gads Hill, and his reply had not really been very heartening.

'If I were you,' Batchelor had said, 'I wouldn't start from here.'

Grand had been in no mood for levity, so he had simply jammed on his hat and left the house in something of a snit. The cabbie had been more helpful and had deposited him in quick time at Charing Cross Station, from where, he was reliably informed, he could get a train to Higham. He was no stranger to railroads, of course, but he still enjoyed the English trains and their stations. The lines were not wide and windswept and straight as a die for hundreds of miles like they were back home. They were narrow, winding and parochial; in a nutshell, just like the English roads, but steel-shod. The stations in London, on the other hand, were built like palaces. He stood back against the cross and held on

his hat as he tipped his head back to take in the front of the station
– who but the British would hide a train station in a building that
looked so very like a hotel? He realized, and not for the first time,
that he loved this country.

That mood passed as soon as he got inside. The queues seemed
to snake around and disappear into some hellish tangle in the
middle. Children screamed, hawkers cried their wares, and at one
point Grand was almost trampled to death by the unwavering
crocodile of a Thomas Cook Temperance Tour, led by a determined-
looking bald gent whose expression suggested that he was very
much in need – perish the thought – of a stiff brandy and a good
long lie-down.

But eventually Grand had his ticket and had found his platform
and had even found a seat on the train. He unfurled his *Telegraph*
and prepared himself to read Sala's eulogy, without coming over
bilious. The train puffed and heaved and there were various
incoherent cries from the platform and then a series of crashes
getting louder and louder until suddenly a porter materialized at
Grand's elbow, wrenched open the door and then slammed it
again with an almost manic vigour. Grand's ears were still ringing
when, with an extra-large lurch, the train was on its way.

The journey was slow to the point of tedium, and Grand gradually came to understand just how much stopping a stopping train
actually did, even in a journey as relatively short as his. He
watched the station names trundle past and felt a little homesick.
Where he came from – and you could take the boy out of Boston
but you could never take the Boston out of the boy – stations
were generally named after an event, usually a massacre of some
kind, or some very minor local personality, usually run out of
town on a rail the day after the tape was cut. Somehow Erith
and Belvedere just didn't get his imagination racing. Somewhere
south of the former, he felt himself drifting off to sleep and did
nothing to prevent it.

He was woken by a gentle poke in the ribs and struggled
upright in his seat. He had slid sideways at some point in the
journey and was leaning on the shoulder of an elderly gent who
very politely helped him up.

'I do apologize,' Grand muttered. 'Dropped off for a moment,
then.'

'Please,' the elderly gent said, 'it's no trouble. But I noticed you had a ticket for Higham in your hatband and that is where we come into next. About five minutes, as long as there is nothing on the line to prevent us.'

Grand did his best to look wise. He knew all about that kind of thing. Buffalo. Arapaho. The things that prevented travel in the West. He shook his head. No, perhaps neither of those; not in Kent. He held out his hand, which was sweaty from being trapped under him for so long, but too late now. 'I'm Matthew Grand,' he said.

'Are you from America?' the elderly gent said. 'How terribly exciting. My daughters would just love to meet you. Would you like to join us for lunch? I'm sure Cook could stretch to one more.'

'Thank you,' Grand said. 'That's very kind.' He had had meals stretched by cooks before and they had little to recommend them. 'I need to get to Gads Hill and I'm not sure how long—'

'But my dear fellow! How very serendipitous! I am the rector of St John's and Gads Hill is on my way. Let me at least offer you a ride in my brougham. If things have gone to plan, it should be waiting for me outside the station.'

It was at this point that Grand noticed the dog collar and rather clerical garb. He wasn't in the habit of taking rides from strange old men, but surely this was kosher, if he could mix his religions for a moment. He smiled and nodded and the elderly gent was ecstatic. 'And lunch?' he asked again. Then, his brow darkened. 'You are not from the . . . Press?' He said the final word as though it were the deepest obscenity.

'No, no, goodness me. Not at all.' Grand hoped he had not protested too much.

'That's wonderful. Poor Georgina and the family have been positively *bombarded* by the Press, in the grounds, night and day. One even got in – a ghastly sort, who claimed to be a friend of the family.'

'George Sala?' Grand, though loyal to his clients as a rule, did so hope it was.

'Eh?' The rector was startled. 'Oh, no. No, Mr Sala is a delightful person, we've met on numerous . . . but wait? Not a pressman, surely!'

Grand pointed to his newspaper, by now rather battered. Even so, Sala's by-line was clearly visible.

'I'm shocked. He never said.' The rector was still shaking his head when they reached the station, just a single platform, Grand was pleased to note, without a queue in sight. A pile of hampers was leaning precariously on a boy pushing a hand trolley, and an almost comatose guard held out a lacklustre hand to take their tickets.

'I'm the Reverend Moptrucket,' the vicar suddenly said, turning with his hand outstretched again. He smiled and nodded. 'A ludicrous name, I am the first to admit. My poor daughters struggle beneath it but, as I always say to them, with luck they will soon be able to change it.' He laughed. 'My poor wife, God rest her soul, suffered for twenty years as Mrs Ernestine Moptrucket, but she was pleased to know she brought hours of innocent amusement to our neighbour, Mr Dickens. I believe at one time he asked if he might use the name in one of his tales, but my lovely wife was too unassuming to accept such a plaudit.'

Grand was speechless. He had heard some jim-dandies back at home but this one had to take the biscuit.

'My name is Reginald,' the rector added. 'I wouldn't usually be so informal with someone I had just met, but I do try and avoid Moptrucket as much as possible.'

'I do understand,' Grand said. An idea was forming in his head. 'Were you very great friends? You and Charles Dickens, I mean.'

'Not *very* great, perhaps. No, no, I wouldn't say that. But we were neighbourly, you know. Yes, very neighbourly. Oh, look,' he suddenly said. 'There's young Isaac, the lad who does up at Gads Hill. I think we can squeeze him into the brougham; save his legs.'

Grand's eyes began to take on a cunning gleam. 'Really?' He looked at the rather unprepossessing child who was coming now out of the station, no longer encumbered with the baskets. The boy was not much more than thirteen or so and was walking with a jaunty air, as well he might, having divested himself of the hampers. He had spots, carroty hair and freckles to match across his nose, and an open expression which made Grand, used to the Alsatia urchins, smile to see. He turned to the vicar. 'May I take you up after all on your kind invitation?'

'My dear fellow,' the man said, bouncing on his toes with joy. 'It would be our absolute pleasure. And look – there's the brougham. Isaac!'

The lad looked round and slouched over, his previous jaunty air rather dampened by the proximity of the clergy. 'Yus, vicar,' he mumbled, flattening down a recalcitrant lock of hair with his hand.

'Can we take you in the brougham up to the house? You must have had so much work to do since your master died.'

'It's been a fair bugger, vicar,' the lad said, clambering happily up alongside the driver.

Grand waited for the typical clerical response to the boy's gaffe, but the vicar simply laughed. 'A simple soul, Isaac,' he said. 'But no malice in him. None at all.' He gestured to the vehicle. 'After you, my dear chap. After you.'

Grand got in, but not without a calculating glance at young Isaac, sitting happily up on the seat. He was prattling away to the driver and Grand's day began to take on a very different shape. Very different indeed.

Grand was optimistic by nature, but even he was not ready for the Misses Moptrucket. There were four of them altogether, ranging in age from a dimpled little creature of about sixteen who giggled and blushed a lot when faced with a big, handsome American, up to the eldest, a rather languid girl of twenty. But the Reverend Moptrucket was not being overly hopeful when he said that they would all marry and slough off the handle nature had dealt them – he could see in his mind's eye that the youth of the parish were probably already forming an orderly queue.

The food was also excellent, and if the cook had stretched anything, it didn't show. Grand found himself looking around the table and smiling fondly; if this family was also made up of inveterate gossips, his day would be complete. He chuckled to himself, thinking of Batchelor having to lock horns with a recalcitrant doctor, the journey forgotten.

As the last mouthful of featherlight sabayon disappeared, Grand sat back with a sigh. Dripping on toast was all very well, but that meal had been just perfect – he pushed thoughts of press-ganging the cook back to Alsatia with him and addressed the vicar. 'That was a wonderful meal, Reverend Mo . . . sorry, *Reginald*. Your cook is a marvel.'

'Indeed she is,' the vicar beamed. 'Actually, she is an example of another thing we have in common with Gads Hill; she is my sister-in-law, as dear Georgy is sister to Catherine Dickens.'

The youngest daughter giggled and blushed and was hushed by the sister sitting nearest.

'Excuse Madeleine, Mr Grand,' the eldest, Caroline, said, nudging the girl with her elbow. 'She is at the age when everything seems funny. I think perhaps we will leave you and father to your coffee, and then you may smoke if you wish.'

'I don't wish to smoke, Miss Moptrucket,' Grand said, feeling sorry for the girl who, as the eldest, had to bear the brunt of the name for polite address. 'And as for depriving us of your company, please reconsider. I don't often get to enjoy family meals – I would be so glad if you would stay.' He didn't expect to get much in the way of direct comments from these girls but, if he were careful, he could gain a lot from just watching their reactions. If he had gotten it right, young Madeleine was giggling because there was local rumour about Georgy Hogarth and Dickens, and like all children found it hilarious to consider a parent of hers in the same boat.

Caroline smiled and gave Madeleine a final nudge. 'Then we would be delighted, Mr Grand.'

Gwendoline, the plainest sister, although only plain by comparison with the others, leaned forward. 'I'm afraid you will find our company dull, Mr Grand. We see so few people here in the vicarage.'

'Come, dear,' her father gently admonished. 'I don't think that's quite right, is it? We're not exactly the Brontës, here. I don't think a day goes by without at least one guest.' He extended a hand to Grand. 'For example, look at this wonderful amusement I have brought you today!' All the girls laughed and, for a moment, Grand's hairs stood up on the back of his neck. There was just a hint of the Grimm's Fairy Tales, of the handsome woodcutter taken in by the family and never seen again. He shook it off; this was Kent, for heaven's sake, not Bavaria.

'Papa is joking,' Gwendoline said, having noticed the look

that flew across Grand's face. 'We haven't eaten a guest for . . .' she looked around at her sisters. 'How long has it been?'

Caroline twinkled at Grand. 'Not since lunch,' she said. 'I'm sorry, Papa, I didn't mean to make it sound as if we were recluses. It's just that we all miss our visits to Gads Hill. We can't really call while they are still in mourning.'

Grand's ears pricked up. This was more promising.

'Indeed you can't,' the vicar said firmly. 'I have made my official visit, but I think that we must wait at least until after the funeral until we resume calls.'

'I miss Georgy,' Caroline said to Grand. 'She and I are firm friends, although she is a little older than I am, of course.'

Madeleine could be contained no longer. 'And of course,' she said, 'when Mr Dickens was in residence, she had no time for anyone else. People say—'

The Reverend Moptrucket raised his voice for the first time since Grand had met him. 'Madeleine!' he roared. 'Go to your room!' Then, turning to Grand, 'I apologize for my daughter, Mr Grand. She listens too much to servants' gossip. Caroline, could you go with her, please, and make sure she understands the error of her ways.'

The other two girls, left without the guiding light of Caroline, sat silently from then on, except when Grand was telling them of the pleasures of the London theatre season, of the bustle and hustle he saw every day.

'Papa,' Evangeline, the third of the vicar's daughters com-plained, 'one would think that London was on the moon for all we see of it. You go all the time, but I can't *remember* the last time I was there!'

'It's not all it's cracked up to be,' Grand assured her. 'For instance, although I live in London and have offices just along from Chapman and Hall, the publishers, I have never met Charles Dickens there, though I did once cross the Atlantic on the same ship. Whereas you, living here in the beautiful countryside of Kent county, have met him many times.'

'It wasn't as exciting as you might imagine,' Gwendoline said sulkily. 'He was useless at telling stories, for instance.'

'Gwendoline,' her father grumbled ominously.

'Well, he *was*,' she said. 'Don't you remember when we were there for the Sunday School treat that time? He sat us all down and just recited poems. Not even his poems, either. Some stuff by . . . who was it, Evie?'

'Arnold somebody, wasn't it? It was very peculiar, anyway, and I don't think he got the words right. Not in the right order, anyway.'

The vicar sighed. 'Yes, not a good choice. And I think you mean Matthew Arnold, my dear, not Arnold somebody.' He turned to Grand. 'It was, at least, "The Forsaken Merman", and not one of Professor Arnold's more . . . contentious works. Do you know it?'

Grand shook his head. He was beginning to realize how much he didn't know of the literary world of his adopted homeland, and thought perhaps he should bone up as soon as possible.

'Yes, dear Charles. Not the best memory in the world, dear man.'

'But . . .' Grand was confused. 'I thought he recited long passages of his own works to audiences. Surely, that takes a prodigious memory—'

'Oh, I know all about *that*,' Emmeline broke in. 'He didn't learn it at all. He just told the stories from his books in any words that came into his head.'

The vicar lowered his chin and looked doubtfully at his daughter.

'Don't look at me like that, Papa,' she said. 'Isaac told me. He got it from Bob . . .'

'Bob?' Grand didn't want to seem too nosy, but it paid to know who was who.

'Bob Cratchit, the gardener,' Emmeline told him.

'Who?' Grand had heard that name before. But where?

'Mr Dickens was not above using a real name if it took his fancy,' the vicar chuckled. 'Many folk around here have names that are quite famous now. Or he would change them slightly, but, yes, old Bob . . . I'm not sure how pleased he was when he found out. He had not done it so much of late – I wonder perhaps if one of our more illustrious neighbours took exception.'

Grand couldn't show his ignorance now, so smiled politely.

'Bob *said*,' Gwendoline went on, not anxious to lose the attention of this handsome stranger, 'that Mr Dickens would just go out on stage and tell the story. He was very good, I expect, but I know he didn't learn it.'

The vicar had just realized what his daughter had said. 'I don't think you should be talking with Isaac, my dear,' he said, mildly.

Gwendoline leapt up from her seat. 'You!' she shouted. 'You! You're always criticizing what I do and who I do it with! I hate you!' And she ran out in a flurry of petticoats, with Evangeline in hot pursuit.

The vicar sighed and turned his kind, tired eyes on Grand. 'Daughters, eh?'

Having nothing to add on the subject, Grand spent a little longer with him and then made his excuses. Next stop, Gads Hill.

In the drowsy afternoon, the bees loud in the meadows and the sun burning down on his wideawake, Matthew Grand reached Gads Hill Place. The house was Georgian, red brick and huge, and there was a man in a smock hacking at the foliage with a sickle. Bob Cratchit, if Grand had remembered the Moptruckets' conversation right. He saw the lad Isaac too, carrying boxes again to the back of the house. It seemed to be his lot in life.

Grand rang the bell and listened for the faint, answering ring. There was a black bow on the door and he suddenly felt rather inappropriate in his light grey suit. A crepe armband would have made the point, but he hadn't even got that. The bow fluttered and bounced as the door swung back and an attractive woman stood there. She was perhaps Grand's age, with a pale face, auburn hair tied in a bun, and she was wearing funereal black.

'Miss Hogarth?' Grand tipped his hat and then took it off. He showed her his card. 'Matthew Grand, enquiry agent.'

'Not today,' she said and began to close the door.

Grand was faster and stopped it with his foot. 'I realize this is a bad time, ma'am,' he said, 'but my enquiries very much concern you.'

Georgy Hogarth paused. There was a large American standing in front of her, looking very purposeful. For a moment, she checked on the men in the vicinity. Old Bob was just there *and* he was armed. She could hear Isaac clattering about back in the kitchen, with access to knives without number. Not that anything like that would be necessary, she was sure, but you read such things in the newspapers these days. And there *was* an asylum in Rochester.

'In what way?' she asked.

'Perhaps if I could come in?'

She hesitated again. She had barely had time to sit down since Charles had died. People had been kind. They meant well. Apart from the newspaper people; they didn't mean well at all. But all she really wanted now was a little peace and quiet. And something told her she was not going to get that from this unquiet American.

She showed him into the drawing room where the mantel clock ticked loudly and no breeze wafted in through the net curtains of the open French windows. The front of the house was in deepest mourning, with curtains drawn and sorrow etched. Grand had half expected to see a pair of undertakers' mutes guarding the entranceway, their faces a ghostly white under their weepers and glycerine tears on their cheeks.

'Won't you sit down, Mr Grand?' She offered him the nearest piece of chintz. 'Now,' she sat opposite him, knees together, back ramrod straight, hands in lap. 'What is it you wish to know?'

'Your brother-in-law,' Grand said. 'How did he die?'

'Nobly,' she said, sniffing away a tear. 'Quietly. As you would expect.'

'Yes, of course,' Grand smiled, laying his hat down alongside him on the sofa. 'But what was the *cause* of his passing?'

'It was a stroke,' Georgy said. 'I have it on the best medical authority.'

'Dr Beard,' Grand said.

'Yes. You should talk to him.'

'I have people for that, Miss Hogarth. I was hoping that you could tell me what happened.'

'What is your interest, Mr Grand? I note the address of your offices is near to dear Charles's publishers, but can it be that simple?'

'We have been engaged by a friend of your late brother-in-law,' Grand told her. 'I cannot say more.'

'Trollope?' she asked. 'Wilkie Collins. It'll be one of them. They were always envious of Charles. What writer would not be? They were all blinded by the light of his genius and were positively green with envy.'

'I am not at liberty to say,' Grand said, 'but I assure you, my client has Mr Dickens's best interests at heart.'

Georgy Hogarth chewed her lip. 'Very well,' she said. 'If I must relive the terrible moment again, I will.'

'Could you show me the chalet?' Grand asked.

For a moment, the housekeeping sister-in-law was taken aback. Then she recovered herself and stood up. 'This way,' she said.

The chalet was a summer house, its curtains drawn like those at the front of the house itself. Grand noted that it could be reached from the east and the south. It was visible from only one window of the house itself and its back lay to the dark foliage, rhododendron bushes banked high at the edge of the grounds. Georgy Hogarth hauled up her chatelaine and unlocked the door.

'I've taken to locking it,' she said. 'There are ghouls abroad in Kent, Mr Grand. They are not creatures of the night, as dear Charles believed, but day-crawling monsters. I am sorry if I was a little frosty with you when you arrived, but I was pestered by a fellow countryman of yours only the day before yesterday.'

'You were?'

'Told me his name was Morford.' Georgy swung the door wide. 'Said he was from New York. I, of course, didn't believe a word of it. He wanted to stand, he told me, on the very spot where . . . well, where you are standing now.'

Grand looked down. If this was the scene of a crime, it had been meticulously covered up. The furniture was in place. There was no ruck in the carpet, no stains. Everything was in order; perhaps *too* in order. 'Did you let him in?'

'I did not,' Georgy said. 'I have read of such people in your country, Mr Grand. Snake-oil salesmen, I believe they are called.'

Grand smiled. Had he been anywhere else other than the spot where Charles Dickens died, he would have laughed. 'Indeed they are,' he said. 'So, on the day in question?'

Georgy closed her eyes, willing herself to recount it all again, as she had already, far, far too often. 'It was nearly half past two,' she said. 'Charles had taken an early luncheon and had come in here to work.'

'On *Edwin Drood*?'

'I believe so. Chapter Twenty-One was giving him a little difficulty and he was out of sorts.'

'Unwell?'

'Yes. He barely touched his lunch.'

'Why did you come here?' Grand asked. 'At half past two there was no real reason for you to bother him, was there, especially if – as you say – he was having difficulty with his plot?'

'I was concerned for him. I thought perhaps a little beef tea? A little brandy?'

'Mr Dickens partook?'

'Beef tea, occasionally; brandy, rather too regularly, I'm afraid.'

Grand looked around him. There was a brass-bound tantalus in the corner, with a trio of cut-glass decanters. Alongside it, a box of very expensive Havana cigars. 'You brought the tea from the house?' he asked.

'No. I merely came to ask if he would like some. He was . . . sitting over there, at his desk.'

Grand wandered across the room. The desk was empty. No papers, no scribblings; not even a pen and ink. Georgy read his mind. 'I told you, Mr Grand,' she said. 'Ghouls. Did you know that when hangings were public in this country, people used to pay a small fortune for a portion of the rope used?' She shuddered. 'I couldn't bear the thought of some horror fondling Charles's things, selling his manuscripts, his pens, his inks. That revolting American offered to buy the last collar he wore. Can you imagine?'

Grand could. He had always moved in different circles from a housekeeper in Kent. He was a man of the world.

'Charles looked frightful. I told him to come into the house and lie down.'

'He was still alive?' Grand blinked. This was not how George Sala had told it.

'Of course,' she sniffed. 'Only those repulsive Spiritualists talk to the dead.'

'Did he answer?'

'Yes.' Her eyes filled with tears. 'Yes, he did. And I suppose they were the last words he ever spoke to anyone on this earth. He said, "Yes, on the ground".'

Their eyes instinctively turned to the carpet.

'I called Brunt and we got him on to the sofa, there.'

'Brunt?'

'The gardener.' Grand looked puzzled and she smiled, despite the sorrow she was living with. 'Oh, I can see that you have read somewhere that the gardener's name was Bob Cratchit. Well, we did have a gardener with that name once, and of course, as soon as it became famous, all the gardeners here at Gads Hill were called that, for nostalgia's sake.' She looked around. 'Nostalgia will be our lot, now, for ever, I suppose.'

While she composed herself, Grand looked around. The sofa looked as untouched as the rest of the chalet, as though the whole place was already a museum.

'Isaac went for a doctor, the nearest one, I mean. Steele. But it was too late. We sent for Dr Beard and Dr Steele waited until he arrived. I suppose the two of them compared notes; I don't know. Katie and Mamie arrived later – it must have been midnight by then.'

'Katie and Mamie?'

'Charles's daughters. They insisted on putting hot bricks by his feet, just over there on the sofa.'

Grand noticed that the woman was moving around the room, touching the furniture where her brother-in-law had been. 'His feet were like ice by then, of course. The whole thing was pointless. They were in shock. They weren't behaving rationally.'

She turned to face Grand. 'He died at six o'clock,' she said. 'A single tear ran down his cheek and he just stopped breathing. We put flowers in the dining room where the body was laid out – geraniums red and lobelias blue. Charles always loved them and Brunt was *such* a dear.'

'Who else turned up during the day?' Grand asked.

'Er . . . John Forster, of course, Charles's greatest friend in all the world. Charley, Charles's eldest, the Snodgering Blee. He was distraught, as you'd imagine. Oh, and George Sala turned up. God knows how he got himself involved.'

God and George Sala, Grand thought to himself, but he said nothing. 'And the funeral?'

'Tomorrow, Mr Grand. Close friends and family only. The ghouls, you see. They mustn't be allowed anywhere near.'

'No,' Grand said softly. 'No, of course not.'

*   *   *

There were things about Georgy Hogarth's memories of Dickens's last day that Matthew Grand was unhappy with. The woman had given him the time of day, had answered his questions firmly and with resolve. Perhaps a little *too* firmly; perhaps with rather *too* much resolve. Little things didn't add up. Sala's version was not the same as Georgy's. There were no screams, no hysteria. There had been other women in the house – Catherine the cook and Emma the maid, but there was no mention of them in the housekeeper's account and no sign of them today. There was a groom, George Butler, but he too was invisible on both occasions.

Grand was still pondering all this as he crossed the lawn. The sun was still high and his shadow was sharp on the grass lovingly mown by Cratchit; Grand had no idea who Bob Cratchit might be, but he had labelled the gardener thus in the filing system in his head and preferred this to Brunt, who didn't sound half as pleasant. There was no sound now, only Grand's own footfalls padding on the green. Yet there *were* sounds: the rustle of leaves, the snapping of a twig. Someone or something was trailing Grand through the shrubbery to his left. It wasn't Cratchit, who was sitting alongside a heavy roller with Isaac, the two of them munching on hunks of bread and cheese. If it was the invisible groom, why was he creeping about in the shrubbery and why was he watching Grand? There were ghouls in Kent County; Grand was ready.

The American had promised Inspector Tanner of Scotland Yard that he wouldn't carry his pistol, as it had been known to frighten the ladies. Did Grand realize, the inspector had asked him, that this was England and not the Wild West? Yes, Grand realized that, but the carrying of arms was an American's God-given right; it was enshrined in the Constitution. Inspector Tanner had narrowed his eyes and told Grand, with a wink of one of those eyes, that as far as he was concerned, Constitution was a hill in London. And there the matter had dropped. But Matthew Grand felt naked without his pocket Colt, even here in suburban Kent, and he eased the leather catch on his shoulder-holster, just in case.

He turned slowly alongside the stable block and ducked behind the buttress. A large, brown-suited man, surprisingly light of foot, followed him, and Grand leapt out, the Colt gleaming in his fist, the muzzle cold against the man's forehead.

'Well, you don't see many of those in Higham of a Monday.'

'Who are you and why are you following me?'

The man's hands were instinctively in the air, but he lowered one slowly. 'I'm going to reach inside my coat,' he said, 'That's where I keep my card.'

Grand had not moved. The hammer was back on the pistol and he eased the weapon slightly to accommodate the man's movements. He edged out a white card and passed it to Grand.

'Inspector Charles Field, Chief of Detectives,' Grand read aloud.

'Oh, sorry,' Field smiled. 'That's an old one. Allow me to update you.' He reached again inside his coat and produced a second card.

'Field and Pollaky,' Grand read, 'Thirteen Paddington Green.' He frowned. 'You've crossed Pollaky out. Deceased?'

'Might as well be,' Field said. 'We parted company, Ignatius and I. Investigational differences. Can I put my hands down now and can you put that pea-shooter away?'

Grand eased the hammer forward and slipped the gun into his holster.

'One good turn deserves another,' Field said, letting his hands fall.

It was Grand's turn to produce a card.

'Well, well,' Field said. 'Competition. It's what made Britain great, after all. Are you Grand or Batchelor?'

'Grand,' Grand said.

'From the colonies, by your accent.'

'I can see why you were chief of detectives,' Grand said, straight-faced. 'But none of this explains why you're following me.'

'Charles Dickens and I go way back, Mr Grand. You've read *Bleak House*, of course?'

'Well, I . . .'

'Inspector Bucket in that opus? Well, that's me, that is. Oh, Charles always denied it, of course. I don't suppose you've read any Blackmore?'

'Um . . .'

'R.D. Blackmore? *Lorna Doone* chappie? No, well, he's not

a patch on the master, of course. He's written this load of tosh called *Clara Vaughan*. There's only one decent character in it – Inspector John Cutting. That's me as well.'

'So, you're a fictional detective, Mr Field?'

Grand didn't know what hit him. He felt a slap around his head, his coat was wrenched open and he was suddenly staring down the bore of his own .32.

'I wouldn't underestimate me, Mr Grand, not if I were you. Now, I don't appreciate having a gun pulled on me in the pursuance of my enquiries.' He clicked back the hammer.

'Easy with that,' Grand shouted. 'It's got a hair trigger.'

'No, it hasn't,' Field said. 'It's one of the clumsiest guns Colonel Colt ever churned out. Handy, I concede, to slip into your coat. Short barrel, etcetera. I was confiscating these things when you were still shitting yellow. Now,' he let the hammer go and spun the pistol, handing it butt-first to Grand. 'Now that we're on a more equal footing, so to speak, suppose you tell me what you're doing here.'

The garden of the Olde Oak was empty that evening. Empty except for the two private detectives who sat there, each of them nursing a pint of the landlord's finest. The pub was, in fact, shut, but ex-Inspector Field knew the man of old, had got something on him from the good old days and, when it came to Mr Field, nothing was too much trouble.

'You're a cagey one, Mr Grand.' Field wiped the froth from his thick lips. 'We've sat here now for half an hour and you've told me precisely nothing.'

'Goes with the territory, Mr Field,' Grand said.

'All right,' Field leaned back in his chair, lighting up the clay pipe he produced from his coat. 'I'll put *my* cards down, then, shall I?' For the briefest of moments, his puffy face lit up with the flare of the lucifer and he blew smoke rings to the sky. 'I think that you think that some ill befell old Charles Dickens and you're investigating his murder.'

Grand smiled. 'Now, why would you think that?' he asked.

Field looked around him to make sure the trees did not have ears. Far beyond those trees the setting sun was kissing the mellow stones of Rochester Castle and the Medway was solid with lighters and barges laden with the goods of the empire, glowing in the evening. The old and the new stood side by side in that part of Kent, just as the old and the new detectives sat opposite each other in the Oak's garden. 'Because I think it too.'

'You do?'

'That's why I was at Gads Hill today. Checking on things.'

'Have the family called you in?' Grand asked. 'Miss Hogarth didn't mention you.'

'Catherine,' Field said.

'The cook?'

'The wife. Mrs Dickens.'

'I'd heard they were separated.'

'By a literary mile,' Field said. 'Oh, I never cottoned to Catherine much, but Charles was less than kind to her. Told all and sundry that she hated her children and that the children hated her.'

'Not true?'

'Not a bit of it.'

'Then, why . . .?'

'Why would Dickens make it up?' Field laughed. 'Come on, Mr Grand, the man made his living by doing that.'

'Was there somebody else, in Dickens's life, I mean?'

Field's pipe had gone out and he relit it slowly. 'What have you heard?'

'Miss Hogarth,' he said. 'Rumours . . .'

'Hmm,' Field clicked his fingers to order another round. 'Single, attractive housekeeper seeks lecherous old writer for frolics and fun.'

'Was that how it was?'

'No.' Field roared with laughter. 'God, no. Oh, I daresay if Charles had set his cap at Georgy in the first place, rather than Catherine . . . But all that was years ago. Georgy was just a slip of a thing. And Charles wanted to slip his thing elsewhere . . .'

'You mean . . .?'

'Mr Grand,' Field said, leaning closer and speaking quietly. 'You and I are men of the world. Or at least, I am. I used to be one of Charles's night guides; did you know that?'

'Night guides?'

'When I was in Lambeth, and later, when I joined the Detective

Branch, Charles would go on patrol with me around the streets. Many's the time Sergeant Thornton and I would have to drag him out of places, if you catch my drift.'

'Places?'

'How long have you been in this great country of ours, Mr Grand?' Field asked.

'Five years, why?'

'Well,' Field waited until the host had brought them two more pints and taken away their empties. 'What with that length of time and your professional calling, I'm surprised you haven't noticed the one outstanding thing about Great Britain.'

'I've noticed many things,' Grand said. 'But, in particular. . .?'

'In particular, its outstanding hypocrisy,' Field chuckled. 'I know gentlemen with loving families, who go to church on Sundays and give handsomely to charity. Those same gentlemen can be found of a Friday night in Wapping, or Whitechapel or Westminster, making a selection from a wide range of little girls and boys who should be tucked up safe in their *own* beds. I'm sure I don't have to draw you a picture.'

'You mean, Dickens . . .'

'No, no, no,' Field frowned. 'Nothing like that. He had the odd lady of the night when he was younger, like we all did. Sucker for a pretty face, was Charles. But no, it was the danger he loved, the dark alleys, the rattling kens, the opium parlours . . .'

'Opium?'

'Oh, yes. Deadly stuff, that is. You've never come across it?'

'No,' Grand shrugged. 'Can't say that I have.'

'Read your Dickens, Mr Grand,' Field advised. 'It's all there. Fagin's based on an old Jew we both knew, Ikey Solomon. Bill Sikes – well, he's a mixture of many a villain in my old manor. And as for Nancy . . . well, that would be telling, wouldn't it?' And he patted the side of his nose. 'No, Charles and I go way back. And I'm proud to call him friend. So, when Catherine Dickens, estranged or not, calls me in, I'm bound to do my bit for the old hack, ain't I? And here you are, doing the same thing.'

'Indeed.'

'Just one question, Mr Grand. You know who I'm working for. How about you?'

For a moment, Grand hesitated. Then he threw caution to the winds. 'George Sala,' he said.

'Who?' Field blinked.

Grand smiled. George Sala would be mortified that this doyen of detectives had never heard of him.

Field screwed up his face, thinking. 'What say we pool our resources, so to speak? You'll never interest the Yard in this – since I left, they haven't got a detective force, not really. What say we work together? Trade information? I'm between sidekicks, as you colonials say, at the moment, so time is money and I'm spending too much of mine on shoe leather. You and whatsisname – Batchelor – can be my legs.'

'What?' Grand laughed, clicking his fingers for two more pints. 'And you can be our brain?'

Field laughed softly. 'Something like that,' he said.

FOUR

'Ere, there's a copper . . .' But Mrs Rackstraw got no further than that.

'Chief Inspector Adolphus Williamson, to be more precise.' The large man with the greying beard barged unceremoniously past the housekeeper, his bright eyes focused on James Batchelor.

'An honour, Chief Inspector.' Batchelor stood up and extended a hand, but Williamson did not take it. 'Mrs Rackstraw, some tea for the chief inspector.'

Williamson looked the woman up and down and his first suspicions of her were confirmed. 'No, thank you,' he said, and he plonked himself down on a rather excruciatingly uncomfortable horsehair sofa.

'I'm guessing you're Grand,' the copper said, looking at the tall American as the unwanted housekeeper snorted and left.

'I am Matthew Grand,' Grand said. He had been writing up reports for most of the morning, listening to the sounds of Alsatia drifting in through the window. His coffee had gone cold. 'What can we do for you, Chief Inspector?'

Williamson had acquired the knack of all Scotland Yard detectives over the years, of reading upside down what was written on other people's desks. '"No stone unturned",' he said.

Batchelor looked at him. 'Do you have a stone,' he asked, 'that we can help you with?'

'Oh, I can do that by myself, thank you,' Williamson smiled. 'It'll be a cold day in Hell before the Yard has to resort to amateurs to help them.'

More or less what ex-Chief Inspector Field had said, Grand thought to himself. 'So, this visit . . .?' He was trying to move the conversation along.

'. . . Is by way of a warning,' Williamson said. 'A Dr Beard contacted me.'

'Ah.'

'He says that you, Mr Batchelor, all but accused him of murdering the late Charles Dickens.'

'I did no such thing,' Batchelor retorted, indignant. 'I just don't like brick walls.'

Williamson chuckled and leaned back, trying to come to terms with the horsehair. 'Well, I'm with you there,' he said. 'Tell me, then, as one professional to another, what makes you think Dickens was murdered?'

'Professional?' Batchelor muttered crossly. 'A moment ago we were amateurs.'

'We don't think Dickens was murdered,' Grand lied. 'But our client does.'

'And who would that be?' Williamson wanted to know.

'Aha,' Batchelor wagged a finger at him. 'Sorry, Chief Inspector – client confidentiality. If Beard can clam up about his patients, we can do the same about our clients.'

'Private enquiry agents!' Williamson scowled. 'There'll come a time when you people will need a licence to operate. But until then, there is such a thing as obstructing the police in pursuance of their enquiries.'

'Are you making enquiries, then?' Grand asked. 'About Dickens, I mean.'

Williamson smiled. 'I am now,' he said.

'Well, perhaps you'll get further with Beard than I did,' Batchelor said.

'Count on it.' The chief inspector rose with some difficulty from the glassy embrace of the horsehair and turned to the door. 'I'm not expecting our paths to cross again,' he said, 'but if they do, you won't enjoy the experience.'

'Give our regards to Inspector Tanner,' Grand said.

'Oh, that's right.' Williamson clicked his fingers. 'I knew I'd come across your names somewhere. Dick Tanner used to speak quite highly of you two.'

'Used to?' Batchelor frowned.

'Oh, you haven't heard. Poor old Dick's rheumatism got the better of him and he had to retire. This would be . . . ooh . . . a few months back now. He's keeping a pub in Winchester.' Williamson's pleasant face disappeared and he let his eyes burn into them both. 'So, if you were hoping there was a friendly face at Four Whitehall Place, gentlemen, I'm sorry to be the bearer of bad news. By the way, it's not for me to say, but in the interests of impressing clients, that woman of yours needs work.'

There was a curious hush in the close that day. The precincts of Westminster Abbey were thronged with people, most in respectful black. No one spoke. Even the pigeons seemed to sense the occasion and kept their billing and cooing to a decent minimum. Three carriages rolled up to the west door, but there was not an ostrich plume in sight and all the horses were bay.

'That's Mamie and Katie,' George Sala murmured out of the corner of his mouth. 'Charles's daughters.'

The great journalist stood with Grand and Batchelor on the corner of Great Smith Street, towards the back of the spectators, who all looked as if they had turned up for one of Mr Dickens's famed performances, the ladies fluttering fans under their parasols. The Dickens daughters clung to each other, pale and tearful, but determined not to break down; it was what their papa would have wanted.

'John Forster,' Sala kept up the running commentary, 'the tall one with the eyebrows and dundrearies.'

'Dickens's friend?' Batchelor checked.

'And—' Sala aimed a well-placed spit into the gutter – 'biographer. I understand he was also his go-between with publishers; a man of Dickens's stature wouldn't wrestle with a chimney sweep, if I may borrow a phrase from the late, lamented Mr Peel.'

'I thought *you* were his biographer, Mr Sala,' Grand said, a knowing look on his face.

'I am unofficial, dear boy,' the journalist told him. 'That gives me a certain carte blanche. I also work faster than he does, so *my* version will be on the streets before his.'

'Who's that?' Grand asked. 'The blubbing one.'

'That's George Dolby, Charles's stage manager. Handled all his lecture tours.'

'He seems pretty cut up,' Batchelor said. 'That other chap seems to be holding him up.'

'The other chap is his son, Charley Dickens, apple of Charles's eye. Hopeless writer, of course, but there it is. No, Dolby's an odd one.'

'In what way?' Grand asked.

'Any way you choose.' Sala lit a cigar and tossed the match to the tarmacadam. 'The man has an appalling speech impediment. Given to dancing the hornpipe in railway carriages. Charles found it all very endearing for some reason. I would have had him committed, myself. Very emotional, is George. I doubt you'll get much out of him for a while.'

'He seems to have managed to get himself a very attractive wife, nonetheless,' Batchelor remarked.

'Wife?' Sala almost swallowed his cigar. 'Dolby hasn't got a wife.'

'Well,' Batchelor pointed. 'There's a rather slender and elegant woman walking alongside him. I can't see who she is through that veil, and so I suppose she might well have a face like a rhinoceros, but the rest of her looks comely enough to make that moot.'

Sala peered closer. 'Who *is* that?' he said. He closed his eyes and did some elementary arithmetic, using his fingers. 'I really can't place her. But she obviously is some distant member of the family, someone they couldn't refuse entry.'

'Could it be his wife, sneaking in?'

'Not with a waist that size,' Sala spluttered. 'I wouldn't say Catherine is fat, but she could make two of the mystery lady. No, it'll be a cousin or something. But *certainly* not Mrs Dolby. Perish the thought!'

'So, let me get this straight,' Grand murmured in the rising hum of the crowd. 'You think one of *them* murdered Dickens?'

The three watched as Georgy Hogarth was helped down from the last carriage by Dr Beard. The last man out of the third carriage was Frederic Ouvry, Dickens's solicitor. He looked as all solicitors look at funerals; pale, and mourning a good client gone west. Sala shrugged. 'That's what I'm paying you a goodly sum to find out,' he said. 'The children, no. They all loved their papa and this has come as a genuine blow to them, I'm sure. No, it's those who are *not* here you should be interested in. And possibly Ouvry; I never trust the legal profession. Shakespeare was right when he said let's kill all the lawyers.'

'You've given us *rather* a wide field, Mr Sala,' Grand felt obliged to point out.

'Three carriages,' Sala nodded. 'That's all Charles wanted. He'd always said that – no fuss, no feathers. So, there's no Catherine, for instance. No servants, but you wouldn't expect that. Oh, there'll be plenty at the commemoration, of course. The abbey will be packed.'

'It was only the other day he had breakfast with Mr Gladstone,' Batchelor said.

'And dinner with Mr Disraeli,' Grand chimed in.

'Then there's the Prince of Wales and Leopold of the Belgians,' Batchelor added.

'Not to mention Mr Motley, the American ambassador.' Grand felt he had to fight his country's corner.

'All right, gentlemen,' Sala smiled. 'You've convinced me. You've done your homework and you're earning my over-generous retainer. Now all you have to do is catch me a killer.'

There was a collective sigh from the crowd and the hats came off. The hearse rattled to the west door, pulled by dappled greys, snorting and tossing their heads in the heat. The pallbearers slid down from their perches noiselessly and prepared to manhandle the hearse's contents through the side door.

Something caught Sala's eye and he whipped the cigar out of his mouth before swiping an urchin around the head. 'Get that cap off, you little ruffian. There's a great man in that coffin.'

The boy winced at the pain of the slap and stood, bareheaded and shamefaced, cowering before the gentleman, muttering how sorry he was. Grand and Batchelor, however, were watching something else. As the bearers disappeared into the darkness with their sad load, there was a commotion at the west door. A verger was trying to close it as the mighty organ thundered in the vast cavern of the abbey. He was struggling with a top-hatted man and some of the conversation drifted to Great Smith Street.

'But I'm a close friend,' they heard. 'I've just forgotten my ticket, that's all. I could've gotten in through another door, you know.'

But the verger was insistent and the west door closed. There were boos and hisses from the crowd nearest to the would-be intrusive ghoul.

'Wasn't that . . .?' Batchelor frowned, pointing.

'. . . an American accent,' Grand nodded. 'Yes, it was. Not one of my countrymen's finest moments.'

'No matter,' Batchelor said. 'Looks like he's about to have his collar felt by one of A Division's finest.'

A large policeman in his new Roman helmet was marching resolutely towards the American, who still seemed to be trying to find a way in. The cigar dropped from George Sala's mouth and he began patting his coat feverishly. 'Never mind the bloody American,' he snarled. 'That little ruffian's half-inched my wallet!'

There were three possibilities, and it was an enquiry agent's law that not until the third would James Batchelor strike lucky. He'd left his wallet at home and had kept his eyes peeled all evening. This was Shadwell, where the river, dark and deadly, lapped the stair and the lighters swung at anchor, their lights blurred in the Thames fog.

The heat of the day still clung to the alleyways, their cobbles scummed with grease, and yet more of it blasted out through the open doors of the Brass Monkey. A painted lady jostled Batchelor on the threshold and smiled at him, her teeth black, her breasts threatening to escape from her bodice. She smelled of beer, cheap perfume and unwashed clothing in almost equal measure; the scent of the street. 'You good-natured, dearie?' she purred, insinuating herself against him with practised hips.

'Most of the time,' Batchelor smiled back, 'but not tonight. I'm looking for a man.'

The harlot backed away. 'Bit o' brown, eh? Well, what you do in your own time is up to you, o' course. But believe me,' she peeled her blouse down to reveal her right breast, 'you don't know what you're missing.'

'Oh, I've a pretty good idea,' Batchelor said, and sauntered down the steps to the greasy floor. The Monkey was full that night. There were two ships in from the West Indies and the place was crammed with blacks and mulattos, most of them the worse for drink, stumbling over each other at the bar. Girls glided from lap to lap, tickling ears, licking necks, lifting wallets. Above the row, the reedy screech of a piano accordion and the rattle of bone dice could be heard. There were whispered conversations in cramped corners, deals done in darkness. But there he was, propping up the bar as usual. That waistcoat and that cravat were unmistakeable. And, true to form, there was a girl on each arm.

Batchelor fought his way through a crowd of lascars and stood staring at him.

'Well, of course,' the man at the bar was saying, 'there was absolutely nothing I could do. Science has not yet vouchsafed that particular secret. I remember it vividly. "Barney," he said – and these were the last words he ever spoke – "Barney, I go to my grave knowing that I could not have been in better hands."'

The girl between Barney and Batchelor frowned. ''Ere, I thought he was a German.'

'Who?' Barney took a massive swig of his beer.

'Your patient.' The other one nudged him in the ribs. 'The Prince Consort.'

'Oh, he was, he was,' Barney assured them. 'But all that heel-clicking stuff was just for the public, you know. Now,' he put his arms around both girls, 'that really is enough about me. How are you girls going to make a middle-aged man very happy?'

The smile froze on his face as he caught sight of James Batchelor. He dropped the women, spun on his heel and dashed for the back door, hacking his way through the lascars and treading on somebody's dog in the process. The animal yelped in pain and yelped again as James Batchelor jumped over him.

The night air was warm, but at least the smell of the Monkey had not followed him. The alley was deserted except for a couple thrusting against each other in a doorway. Batchelor tipped his hat to them and crashed around a corner, the squeal of cats and a human scream telling him that Barney had come to grief. Around that corner, where the tenements rose black and forbidding into the night, Matthew Grand was standing with one boot on the neck of a collapsed tippler, who lay face down, groaning.

'Barney, Barney,' Batchelor helped the man up. 'When are you going to learn?'

'Oh, it's you, Mr Batchelor.' Barney tried to grin, but his mouth was full of something from the gutter and he had to spit that out first. 'I didn't recognize you.'

'Liar,' Batchelor said, picking up Barney's hat and handing it to him. 'You've met my friend Mr Grand, I see.'

'Yes,' Barney scowled. 'I have bumped into him from time to time.'

'We'd like a word,' Grand said, and rammed his man up against the wall.

'Look, I'm clean,' Barney assured them. 'Straight up. Ever since that unfortunate business, I haven't practised. I swear.'

Grand rummaged in the man's coat pocket. String. Fluff. Tuppence ha'penny. Then he tried the waistcoat. 'Ah,' he smiled. 'Bonanza.' He peered to read the dog-eared card in the bad light. 'Dr Barnwell Johnson, MD. Ladies' Troubles A Speciality.' He looked at Batchelor. 'You're a literary man, James,' he said. 'What is wrong with that sentence?'

'Well,' Batchelor stroked his chin, wrestling with the problem. 'Let's see . . . I'll assume the name is correct, but the credentials certainly aren't; not since you were struck off the medical register, eh, Barney, for conduct unbecoming. But it's the last bit that bothers me, Matthew.'

'Me too,' Grand nodded, frowning solemnly.

'You see, abortion – and there's no nice way of putting that – is illegal in this great country of ours.'

'And ours,' Grand nodded, not wishing to be outdone.

'That's on account of people like you preying on unfortunates and quite possibly killing them into the bargain.' Batchelor wasn't smiling now.

'All right,' Barney sighed, his shoulders slumped in defeat. He rummaged in his trouser pocket. 'I haven't got much.'

'We don't want your money,' Grand told him. 'What would an enquiry agent do with money, when all's said and done?'

'What we want,' Batchelor tapped Barney's temple and made him flinch, 'is what's inside there, before the gin washes it all away.'

'How do you mean?'

Batchelor checked that the alleyway was empty before he carried on. 'You may have been struck off, Barney, but I happen to know that before that catastrophic occasion, you knew your stuff.'

'You flatter me.' Barney half bowed. 'But, yes, as a matter of fact, I do.'

'Let's suppose,' Grand said, 'that we have a dead man.'

Barney looked at him in surprise. He didn't like the direction this conversation was travelling.

'A man,' Batchelor joined in, 'who to all intents and purposes has died of a stroke.'

'How old is this man?' Barney asked.

'Fifty-eight,' Batchelor said, perhaps a little too quickly. 'Give or take.'

'To all intents and purposes?' Barney queried.

'Could there be another cause?' Grand came right out with it.

Barney thought for a moment. 'There *could* be,' he mused. 'Who's the doctor?'

Grand chuckled. 'Come on, Barney,' he said. 'You know better than that.'

'No, it's just that . . . well, there are, or so I'm given to believe, some rather unscrupulous people in my profession. If your doctor is bent, he could say what he liked, couldn't he? And who would be the wiser?'

'Yes, we've considered that,' Batchelor said. 'Are still considering it, in fact. But we want to get behind the medical mumbo-jumbo. For a bent doctor to get away with a wrong diagnosis like that, he'd have to have *some* science on his side. In case somebody asked some awkward questions, that is.'

'Somebody like us,' Grand underlined the point.

'Hm,' Barney was lost in thought. 'I'm not sure I can help.'

Grand sighed, holding up the ex-doctor's card. 'I wonder who's on duty at the Yard, tonight, James; that nice Chief Inspector Williamson?'

'Laudanum,' Barney blurted out. 'That'd be my best guess.'

'Laudanum?' the detectives chorused.

'Doesn't Mrs Rackstraw take that for her gout?' Grand asked.

'I used to have it when I was a toddler,' Batchelor remembered. 'Mama swore by it.'

'Yes,' said Barney, 'but your mama was trying to get you to go to sleep, I assume, not kill you. Although . . .'

'Oh, ha,' Batchelor snorted.

'Better let us do the jokes, Barney,' Grand advised. 'I'm still holding all the cards,' and he waved one in the air. 'Laudanum's a poison, right?'

'It isn't a poison as such.' Barney struck a pose, his chin in the air, his thumbs in his waistcoat sleeves. 'But, like so many things in our pharmacopeia . . .' all three men looked at each other, impressed that he could get the word out both accurately and first time, 'given in the wrong quantities, it's as sure as a bullet. Surer, in fact. A bullet can miss. An opiate will get you every time, enough of it.' He became confidential. 'What you'll have to do is find out what your corpse had to eat in the days leading to his death. And what the symptoms were beforehand.'

'What should they have been?' Batchelor asked. 'In laudanum poisoning, that is.'

'Well,' Barney ruminated, enjoying himself now, as if he were back in his old surgery again, before . . .

'In about half an hour after ingesting the dose, headache and weariness. Lethargy, followed by sleep. The patient may appear a little flushed, the breathing would be slow. The pupils would be contracted and the skin warm and moist . . .'

'Which it would be anyway.' Grand was thinking aloud. 'He was in a stuffy room on a hot day.'

'Eventually, the face becomes pallid, the breathing difficult to detect. The actual cause of death is slow asphyxiation and heart failure.' He looked from one detective to the other, both of them locked into their thoughts. When neither of them said anything, Barney went on. 'Of course, there's a snag.'

'There is?' Grand asked.

'The smell and the taste. Both absolutely revolting.'

'How revolting?' Batchelor queried. 'Would everyone find it so?'

'Well, not so much the smell, perhaps, which is poppies, but the taste is horrible.'

'I remember,' Batchelor grimaced. 'Mama always used to give me a spoonful of jam afterwards, to take away the taste.'

'It's quite common in suicide,' Barney told them, 'but I've never met it in murder.' He chuckled. 'And if I know you boys, that's what we're talking about, I assume.'

Grand smiled, patting the man on the cheek. 'You don't know us, Barney,' he said, 'not like we know you.' He evaded the former physician's attempt to get his card back. 'No,' Grand said, 'I think I'll hang on to this. You never know when a good doctor is going to come in handy.'

*   *   *

They took a cab back to Alsatia, one of the few still running at that time of night, its lights bobbing over the cobbles of the dark streets.

'We know Dickens ate with Gladstone and Disraeli in the days before he died.'

'Hedging his political bets, I'd say,' Grand commented. 'And with the Prince of Wales and the King of Belgium.'

'King of the Belgians,' Batchelor corrected him.

'Whatever,' Grand brushed the nicety aside. 'I'm assuming *they're* all right; no poisoning symptoms, I mean.'

'I think we might have heard about it by now,' Batchelor said, 'considering the status of those gentlemen. And besides, *if* Barney is right and *if* it is laudanum, the timing is all wrong. It takes a matter of hours – or less, if I understood him right. So it can't have been in any of those dinners. He would have died on the way home, or at the most shortly after he got back.'

'So,' Grand leaned back as the hansom rattled under Temple Bar. 'One of us is going to have to go back to Georgy Hogarth.'

'The housekeeper.'

Grand nodded. 'She's the only one likely to have a working knowledge of what Dickens ate in the run-up to his death. And the cook, I guess.'

'Well, that has to be you,' Batchelor shrugged.

'Why me?' Grand asked.

'Well, from what you told me, Georgy took quite a shine to you. Tall, dark, American – that sort of thing. And it'll give me a chance to talk to the staff.'

'Ah,' Grand nodded. 'The missing menials. Now we're getting somewhere.'

As the train rattled south from Charing Cross, Grand retracing his steps, Batchelor looking about him at every new, passing mile, they were quiet. They both had their jobs to do and experience had taught them that planning was futile. Whenever questioning anyone, they had found, open minds were the only kind to take into the room. Prejudging never did anyone any good, but especially not an enquiry agent with a reputation still to make. The train remained mercifully Moptrucket-free, although Grand was still miffed that Batchelor refused to believe the name, saying that it couldn't possibly exist outside of one of Dickens's own tales. But soon they were at the station and, with no brougham to take them there this time, strolling off in the direction of Gads Hill Place.

Having seen the house before, Grand watched for Batchelor's look of delight when the building emerged at the end of its short carriage drive. It was symmetrical almost to the point of obsession; every window, every roof tile placed just in exactly the right place to please the eyes. While Grand bounded up the steps to ring the bell, Batchelor made his way around the building, looking for the missing menials.

Grand pulled the bell and heard it jangle deep in the house. After just a few seconds, he heard the tap of a woman's heel on tile and Georgy Hogarth opened the door. Her housekeeper's welcoming smile was just a little slow in coming but, when it was in place, Grand took his chance.

'It's good of you to see me again, Miss Hogarth,' he swept off his hat and waited. It had been five days since the funeral and there was to be a commemoration service – two, in fact: one at the abbey and one at the cathedral in Rochester. If someone *had* murdered Charles Dickens, would his murderer turn up in either place, like a bad penny? Ghouls, Georgy Hogarth had said the last time she and Grand had met; there would be ghouls aplenty in those cloisters, rubbing shoulders with the great and the good, numbered with either the quick or the dead.

'Do I understand,' Grand asked her, 'that the commemoration services are open to all?'

'They are, Mr Grand.' She stepped aside and ushered him in, closing the door gently behind him. The hall was beautifully cool and dim after the heat and glare of the sun outside. 'Charles was universally loved, you see.' She showed him into the drawing room again and sat him down, taking her seat by the empty fireplace. 'Will you take some tea with me? I'll ring and Catherine can send something up.'

'No,' Grand said, perhaps a little too quickly. He knew that Batchelor would probably be already in the house, talking to the domestics, and the last thing he wanted to do was to interrupt that. More importantly, he didn't want some chatty tweeny to bring news of a visitor in the kitchen; he didn't know Georgy

Hogarth well, but she didn't look the sort of housekeeper to leave that kind of thing uninvestigated. 'No. I'm really fine at the moment, thank you.'

'Well, then,' she said, clasping her hands in her lap. 'The purpose of your visit?'

'Tell me, Miss Hogarth, and I apologize for this question in advance: was Mr Dickens in the habit of taking anything for his health? A tonic of some kind; say . . . laudanum?'

Georgy blinked. 'I believe he took a little elixir for his head-aches. I understand a lot of men do.'

Grand understood that too.

'You must understand, Mr Grand,' she went on, using the same word again, trying to control the conversation, 'that dear Charles had bouts of illness on and off throughout his life. A sensitive man like him, a writer . . . Catherine used to say . . .'

'Catherine, the cook?'

Georgy Hogarth looked a little nonplussed for a moment, and then realized that she had already mentioned the cook's name. This man missed nothing; she would have to remember that. 'No. Catherine, my sister; Charles's wife.'

'Ah, yes.' Grand played dumb. 'I meant to ask: how has she taken all this?'

'With resolution,' Georgy said, 'as we all must. You know, of course, that they are separated?'

'Yes,' Grand said. 'And yet you stayed with him.'

Georgy straightened, ice in her veins for the first time. 'What are you implying?' she asked.

'Implying?' Grand was innocence itself.

Georgy swept to her feet in a soft rustle of black satin. 'Come, come, Mr Grand, I am aware of the common gossip; what people said of us. They implied a revolting – nay, almost incestuous – relationship between Charles and myself. People are so cruel.' She paused in front of the huge window and turned back to him. 'And so wrong.'

Grand saw his chance and took it. 'Was there someone else in his life?'

Georgy Hogarth looked at him, stricken. Her eyes were wide and her mouth trembled a little. 'Mr Grand,' she said, 'I really must offer you some refreshment.' She pulled the bell. She turned to the mantelpiece and looked down into the empty fireplace. He could tell that she was trying to come to a decision and that alone gave him the answer he needed.

The door opened and a pretty little maid in a white cap and apron bobbed a brief curtsy. 'Yes'm?' she said.

'Ah, Emma. Umm . . . Mr Grand would like . . .?' She turned to him.

Grand flashed his most winning smile at the girl. 'Why, nothing, thank you,' he said, laying the accent on thick. It worked with most women, but most of all with domestics, he had found. Although he would never have Batchelor's natural skill with a tweeny.

'You're sure?' Georgy asked, and he nodded. 'I'm sorry to have bothered you, then, Emma,' she said. 'We won't be requiring tea. Tell Mrs Brownlow I will be down shortly to discuss the menus for the week.'

With another bob, the girl was gone, closing the door carefully behind her. Grand looked at her with avid eyes – Mrs Rackstraw would have had it off its hinges.

Grand was a man on a mission, so he asked his question again.

For a long moment, she looked at him, but this time, replied. 'There was,' she said, 'I cannot tell a lie.'

'Who?'

'I cannot tell a lie, Mr Grand, but I am under no compunction to tell you anything. I have no doubt that the more salacious newspapers are digging around as we speak. Charles will be branded an alcoholic, when all he drank was a little homeopathic cocoa. He will be called a womanizer because he found beautiful women attractive. And because he had so many men friends, he will be touted as a . . . I'm sorry,' she shuddered, 'I do not have the vocabulary for that.'

'Homeopathic cocoa?' Grand was a superb picker-up of unconsidered trifles. He also wanted to help her over the molehill of potential homosexual peccadilloes.

'Yes, I brewed it for him myself. Every day. Poor Charles had gone off tea and coffee. He said it clogged his clarity of mind. And of course,' she lowered her voice, 'sometimes Catherine's cooking does miss its mark somewhat.'

'Was your brother-in-law a hypochondriac?'

'No, Mr Grand. He was a genius. Was there anything else?'

Grand knew the rogue's march when he heard it and he saw himself out. He just hoped that she wouldn't go down to the kitchen to discuss the menus as quickly as she had promised and catch Batchelor there still quizzing the staff. The thought of an already irate Georgy Hogarth crashing into the kitchen to find Grand's confederate working on her people made his blood run a little cold.

He walked off down the lawn, sloping away to the road, to the appointed place where he and Batchelor had agreed to meet. They had set their timepieces, allowing an hour to interview their respective quarries; probably not long enough for James Batchelor, but far too long, as it had turned out, for Matthew Grand. On his way, the rhododendrons shivered again.

'Mr Field,' Grand stopped in his tracks. 'We can't go on meeting like this. Why don't you come out if you want to talk to me?'

There was a long pause, then a rustle of leaves and a spotty youth with red hair shambled into Grand's presence.

'Ah.' Grand folded his arms. 'My apologies. I mistook you for an ex-policeman.'

'Peeler? Me?' The boy grimaced. 'No fear.'

'You're Isaac, aren't you?' Grand asked, 'The house boy.'

'Yessir.'

'Do you have a last name, Isaac?'

'Armitage, sir.'

Grand closed to him. 'I'm Matthew Grand, Isaac,' he said. 'I saw you the other day . . .'

'You were wi' the vicar,' Isaac said.

'That's right,' Grand agreed. 'Lovely man, the vicar. And I was a friend of Mr Dickens, back in the day. Sad loss, huh?'

'You're not from round here, are you?' Isaac's eyes narrowed. He was not naturally suspicious of strangers, being a simple, friendly soul, but he was suspicious of this one. The man was so big, his hat so wide and his clothes so . . . foreign.

'No, I'm from Boston, originally, although I lived in Washington when I was your age. You liked Mr Dickens?'

'Oh, yes.' Isaac's face broadened to a grin. 'He was the best. He used to give me ear money.'

'Ear money?' Grand had only been in England for five years; there was much that was still alien to him.

'Yeah, you know. Er . . . got a penny, guv?'

Grand ferreted in his pocket and passed the coin to the lad. Isaac slipped it between his fingers and, hesitantly, reached up to produce the penny from behind Grand's ear. 'Ear money,' Isaac said triumphantly, and was about to pocket the coin except that Grand was already holding his hand out. 'He did that to all the young 'uns, did Mr Dickens.'

'Er . . . he did *know* you were thirteen, Isaac?' Grand felt obliged to ask.

'Fourteen, sir, if you don't mind – that's how come Mr D used to give me the odd nip of his brandy, too. I had a cigar last Christmas – only I threw up. No, Mr D, he was a big kid himself. I'm gunna miss him.'

'I'm sure you are,' Grand nodded. He put an arm around the lad's shoulders and led him down the lawn away from the house. 'Tell me, Isaac, did anybody come calling here at Gads Hill, in the days before Mr Dickens died, I mean?'

'There was always people calling,' Isaac told him. 'He was that famous, was Mr D; everybody wanted to see him.'

'Yes, of course, but anyone in particular. Anyone you remember.'

'Well, there *was* that American bloke. 'Ere, I bet you know him. He was surprised when I didn't, anyway.'

'He was?'

'Yes, he said . . .' and Isaac launched into what Grand realized was meant to be an American accent, '. . . he said, "Henry Morford, at your service. No doubt you've heard of me." Well, I hadn't. And I told him.'

'He wasn't pleased?'

'No,' Isaac remembered. 'Came over all unnecessary, he did. Anyhow, he wanted to see Mr D, but he wasn't in.'

'Did he leave his card?'

'I dunno. You'd have to ask Georgy . . . er . . . Miss Hogarth.'

'Anybody else?'

'Well, just the usuals. That Mr Forster. Mr Trollope. Mr Ouvry. They're always round here. Oh, there was that woman.'

'What woman?'

'Stella.'

'Stella?'

'Well, that's what she said her name was.'

'When did she call?'

'Ooh, it would have been a couple of times. Three, maybe.'

'Do you remember when this was, Isaac?'

'Nah. One day's very much like another at Gads Hill, Mr Grand. There's always people here; tripping over each other, they are.'

'Why do you remember Stella in particular?'

'Well, I didn't like her to be honest. 'Course, it's not my place to say . . .'

'You're among friends,' Grand assured him. 'What was it about her you didn't like?'

'Well, she was a bit . . . familiar, you know. Patted my cheek and said what a nice growed-up boy I was. And she, sort of, looked me up and down, you know. Fair made the hairs on the back of my neck stand on end, she did.'

'Did Stella stay for lunch or supper?' Grand asked.

'Neither as far as I know. She only ever went to the chalet, not to the big house.'

'Tell me, Isaac. Did Miss Hogarth like Stella?'

The boy shrugged. 'I don't know that Miss Hogarth ever saw her,' he said. 'That was another peculiar thing. She only ever turned up when Miss Hogarth was out.'

FIVE

James Batchelor was good with staff. Anyone watching him trying to deal with Mrs Rackstraw would probably disagree, but with other people's staff, he was a master of his craft. He never actually said that he was one of them, but he managed to give the impression that Below Stairs was his natural habitat. He went round the corner of the building while Grand was ringing at the front door and kept on turning left until he found the way into the kitchen.

He didn't even have to knock. As he turned his final corner, he walked into a cloud of fluff and grit as the maid shook a mat right into his face. Coughing, he emerged from the ghibli she had created to see her standing there, rug hanging limp in one hand, the other hand pressed to her mouth. Her eyes were dancing and her laugh escaped from behind her fingers.

'Oh, sir,' she said, suppressing her giggles with difficulty. 'I'm ever so sorry. I didn't hear you coming through the yard.'

'No, really, it's nothing.' James Batchelor wasn't as striking to look at as Matthew Grand, but his innate vulnerability got him places where Grand's looks would only intimidate. But with a feather on a lapel and a large puff of fluff in his hair, no maid could resist him.

'Come in, come in,' the girl said, pulling at his sleeve. 'Let me brush you down.' She took him down a dark passageway and into a kitchen which, on a day already hot and humid, was like a circle of Hell. The range was burning brightly and Batchelor could feel the blast of heat coming off it right across the room. Laundry was hanging overhead on racks pulled up to the high ceiling, making the room seem low and dark. Under the sheets, at a huge, scrubbed table, a cook was rolling pastry, every now and then pausing to push an errant lock of hair off her sweating forehead.

When she saw the girl and the dust-trap she was towing behind her, she screamed and gestured with floury hands. 'Get him away;

I don't want fluff and filth in my pastry. Get away!' She flapped her apron at Batchelor as if he were some vermin she had found in the flour bin.

Batchelor flinched as the flecks of damp, uncooked pastry flew in his direction. He certainly didn't need to be covered in any more random Dickensian detritus.

'Ooh, Mrs Brownlow,' the maid said, standing between Batchelor and the airborne pastry, 'it's all my fault he's fluffy. I shook the mat over him.'

'Stupid girl,' the cook snapped. 'Take him outside and brush him down. Make sure you stand downwind. That'll be the fourth cap and apron this week, otherwise.'

Batchelor and the maid made their escape back down the corridor and into the yard outside. They could see through the window that the cook had returned to her pastry, dimly lit by the roar of the fire.

'She never goes out, you know,' the maid observed, as she brushed Batchelor down vigorously. 'She doesn't know there hasn't been a breath of wind in weeks. She slaves in that hell-hole day and night, and can't see that her pastry is like lead because the room is so hot. We've got a still-room and all, but she says it's too cold in there. She's a martyr to her tubes, she says.'

Batchelor squirmed as her brushing became a little intimate and pushed her hand away. 'I'm not sure any fluff actually got there,' he said.

'Sorry,' and again the girl was suffused in giggles. 'Here, turn round, let me do your back.' She brushed him efficiently from the shoulders down, and then, with a final flourish, whipped the brush down the back of each leg. 'There, you'll do.' She spun him round again. 'If you'll just let me . . .' and she reached up and plucked the fluff from his hair. 'There. Spick and span.' She stepped back and looked him up and down. 'Now, what was it you were wanting?'

'Pardon?' Batchelor was a little discombobulated, as Grand would have said had he been there. It seemed to him that one minute he had been the efficient if rather undercover enquiry agent and the next a figure of fun. He hitched his jacket into a more comfortable position and began as he had meant to go on. 'I am a . . . journalist,' he said. He held his hand up as the maid took a step towards him, clothes brush raised. 'I am here to write an article about the staff who worked so tirelessly to ensure that our greatest writer could live so comfortably and not have to worry about a thing. It's because of you that we have so many masterpieces from his pen.' Even as he spoke, it sounded hopelessly unconvincing, but then he watched as she swallowed it, hook, line and sinker.

Even so, she had had her orders. 'We're not supposed to talk to your sort,' she said, but didn't sound very sure.

'Oh, but I'm not my sort,' he said. 'I write for *The Servants' Magazine.*' He had spotted a very thumbed copy on a shelf in the kitchen.

Her eyes lit up. 'Really? And they want you to write about us?'

'It will be a freelance article, but they have expressed an interest, yes.' Even after five years in the enquiry agent business, and being a journalist before that, Batchelor still had trouble with outright lies.

The maid tugged at his sleeve. 'Let's go back inside,' she said. 'Mrs Brownlow will want the kettle on soon and I'll have to make the tea for Miss Georgy. I heard the bell go, so she might have company. Come on,' she tugged again and, much against his will, Batchelor allowed himself to be taken back to the kitchen. He began to sweat almost before they reached the door and the girl turned to him, seeming to read his mind. 'Mrs Brownlow doesn't mind if gentlemen take off their jackets,' she said. 'She knows she keeps it a bit warm. 'Ere, haven't got a camera, have you? Only if you have, I need to tidy meself a bit.'

Batchelor apologized that he had not and, when stripped down to his shirtsleeves, the room became merely unbearable. The pastry was now draped limply over some pie dishes, and some pigeons lay, divested of feathers but still with their heads and feet, waiting to be packed inside. Batchelor liked his food as well as the next man, but had always had a slight antipathy to the mechanics of how it had reached his plate. The pigeons still looked as if, with a little effort, they could hop down from the table and fly away. He turned slightly, so they were no longer in his eyeline.

The cook looked at Batchelor suspiciously and then at the

maid. 'You know Miss Georgy don't allow followers, young Emma,' she said.

'No, Mrs Brownlow,' Emma breathed, excitedly. 'He's come to write a story about us, about how we looked after Mr Dickens so's he could write all his stories.'

Mrs Brownlow, who had seen more life than Emma, looked at Batchelor even more suspiciously but, to his relief, something of the pressman clearly still clung to him and she nodded. 'Well,' she said, 'I'm still not sure. But Miss Georgy's got enough on her plate.' She smiled at Batchelor. 'Would you like a slice of my parkin, Mr . . .?'

'Batchelor. I'm sure it would be delicious. Thank you.'

'Emma,' snapped the cook. 'Put the kettle over the heat and slice a piece of parkin for Mr Batchelor. It's time the outdoor men were in for their bever anyway. And Miss Georgy's got a visitor. They'll be a-wanting something.' As she spoke, a bell rang over her head. 'There you are, young Emma. That's the bell for tea. Put your cap straight and go and see what she wants.'

Batchelor pulled out a notebook from his pocket and licked his stub of pencil. 'Can I start with you, Mrs Brownlow, while we wait for the others?'

The cook dimpled at him and tucked the lock of hair away for the umpteenth time. 'Mr Dickens, he loved my cooking,' she said. 'He had to watch his digestion; oftentimes things would upset his stomach and he swore by my beef tea then.'

Batchelor leaned so hard on his pencil the tip broke off, and the rest of his notes, when he looked at them later, proved to be all but illegible.

She leaned forward more, leaning her substantial bosom on the table. 'If he was took really bad, I'd put a drop of my medicine in it for him. I suffer with my tubes something dreadful, you know. A few drops of McMunn's Elixir soon had him right as rain.'

'McMunn's . . .?'

'Elixir, yes. A drop of laudanum soothes the stomach, I always say. A good, healthy medicine. I swear by it.' Her rather piggy eyes suddenly sparkled. 'Perhaps if you put that in your article, Mr Batchelor, McMunn's might give me something, do you think? For the advertising?'

'Who knows?' Batchelor said, with a thin smile. 'So, your beef tea; a favourite of his, you say?'

'Oh, yes. Whenever he was feeling peaky.'

'And had he been feeling peaky lately?' Batchelor tried to sound calm.

'He'd gone off his tea and coffee,' Mrs Brownlow mused. 'And he hadn't eaten anything like his usual amount of eggs and anchovies, nor his Stilton; said it tasted funny.' She wrinkled her nose. 'But I says to Emma, I says. Stilton *always* tastes funny to me, so how can he tell?' She leaned back and slapped her knee with the joke.

'I can't help noticing that you share a name with one of his characters, Mrs Brownlow.' Batchelor decided to change the subject.

'Do I?' The cook was a little nonplussed. 'Oh, I see what you mean. No, my *real* name isn't Brownlow. All the cooks here are called Brownlow, just like the gardeners is all called Cratchit. No, my name's not Brownlow.'

There was a pause which began to grow awkward. Finally, Batchelor couldn't stand it any longer. 'And what *is* your name, then, Mrs . . .?'

'Oh, you can still *call* me Mrs Brownlow,' the cook said, smiling comfortably. 'I'm used to it by now. But my real name, my *given* name, you might say is Gamp. Catherine Gamp.'

Batchelor couldn't really think of anything to say after that, so busied himself writing in his notebook.

They both looked up in alarm as Emma burst in, eyes wide and sparkling. 'Oh, my word,' she breathed. 'Miss Georgy has a visitor, a most handsome and amusing American man. Do you think he is here courting, Mrs B, now that Mr Dickens is gone?'

'Emma!' The cook looked sharply at Batchelor. 'Not in front of guests. Does she want tea?'

'No. She did offer it to Mr Grand,' she smirked to say the name of the gorgeous stranger, 'but he said no, he wouldn't trouble me, thank you.' She sat down with a bump on one of the kitchen chairs. 'Ooh, he's ever so handsome.'

Batchelor couldn't see it, himself, but he had noticed that his partner had this effect on women. He kept his counsel; after all, he wasn't supposed to know the man.

There was a tramp of hobnailed boots in the yard and men's voices raised in greeting. Emma jumped up to set the kettle back on the boil and for a moment or two all was bustle. Two men came in, in their shirtsleeves already; it was clear they knew Mrs Brownlow's domain of old. They both cast sideways looks at Batchelor.

'This is Mr Batchelor,' Emma said, putting the enormous brown teapot down in front of the cook. 'He's a writer.'

'Oh, ar.' The larger of the two men, the gardener by his finger-nails, pulled his cup towards him and poured some of the contents into the saucer. He blew furiously on the surface and slurped it down in one. 'What sort of thing d'you write about, then? Stories, like the master?'

'No one writes quite like your master,' Batchelor gushed. 'I write stories for magazines.'

'Ar, like I say,' the gardener said. 'Stories for magazines.'

'What's your name?' Batchelor asked. 'I'd like to put you in the story I'm writing.'

The gardener snorted and sucked down another saucerful of tea. 'There's a question. The name's Brunt, and I'd be glad if you could call me by that, seeing as it's an old name, well known around these parts. Bob Cratchit, he was gardener here one afore last and Mr Dickens, he was tickled to call us all by that ever since. But Brunt's the name and I'd be obliged.'

'Of course, Mr Brunt,' Batchelor said, jotting it down. 'Do you like working here, at Gads Hill?'

'It's too much work for one,' the man muttered, round a mouthful of leaden parkin. 'But it serves. Got a nice little cottage in the grounds. Wife likes it. Good for the little 'uns.'

'Oh, you have children, Mr Brunt?' Batchelor was a little surprised. Brunt looked rather old to have a young family.

'Six, and another 'un on the way,' the gardener said and shut his mouth like a steel trap. Slurping the rest of his tea, he pushed his chair back and stood to leave. 'Can't stop. There's some more funny business going on in the shrubbery, branches broke and beds trampled. I'll flush the beggars out, you see if I don't.' And with that, he left, his hobnails crunching on the tile floor of the corridor.

In the silence that followed, the groom spoke for the first time.

He was a much smaller man than the gardener and rather dapperly dressed. 'You'll have to excuse Bob,' he said. 'The family is rather a touchy subject.'

'Yes,' Emma said, leaning forward and coincidentally putting her hand on the groom's knee. 'Mrs Cr . . . Brunt is a lot younger than he is and is . . .'

'Like a rabbit,' the cook said, shutting her mouth firmly and looking at Batchelor down her nose. 'No sooner pops out one than another's on the way. It's disgusting, the way she goes on.'

'But, surely,' Batchelor was anxious to spread the blame. 'Mr Brunt must have something to do with it?'

The groom looked sly and smiled at the maid. 'Not really that much, Mr Batchelor. His wife was maid here before Emma, wasn't she, Em?' The maid nodded. 'She got herself into a bit o' trouble and master persuaded old Bob to marry her. Got him a nice cottage out of it, so he didn't mind. Then, o' course, nothing changed. She kept on getting herself in family way.' He laughed coarsely and slapped Batchelor on the shoulder. 'None of 'em looks like old Bob, that's for sure.'

Batchelor looked around the table. He couldn't speak for the moment, because he had taken an unwise mouthful of parkin and it had glued his mouth shut. In the silence, the cook came to his rescue.

'Well, Mr Batchelor, George is right, although I would thank you to keep such talk out of my kitchen, Mr Butler, if you please! They all have a look of . . . well, let's say they all have the same father, even if it isn't old Bob.' She looked at the others, who nodded. 'And he *did* get a cottage out of it.' More nods.

Emma got up and picked up the teapot. It was clearly a sign that the bever – which Batchelor had realized to his relief was simply a local term for the mid-morning break – was over. The groom blew some glutinous crumbs from his moustache and left, turning to wink at Batchelor and give the slightest inclination of his head. The cook rose out of her seat, like Leviathan from the Deep, and bustled off into the pantry. The maid loaded her arms with plates and cups, leaving herself rather at the mercy of the groom, who pinched her cheek and patted her behind in one perfectly judged manoeuvre.

Batchelor struggled into his coat and said thank you and

goodbye to the maid, then trotted off down the corridor in hot pursuit of the groom.

The man was waiting around the corner leading to the stables, leaning on a wall and rolling what was possibly the thinnest cigarette Batchelor had ever seen. Striking a match on the wall and lighting up, Butler looked at Batchelor under his lashes.

'So, you want to know about old Charlie and his shenanigans, do you?' he said, picking a piece of tobacco off his tongue.

'Heavens, no,' Batchelor protested. 'I'm just here to write an article . . .'

'Don't give me that,' the groom said. 'I reckon . . .' He looked up at the sky as though doing a complex equation. 'I reckon you're a private snoop, here to look into old Charlie's death.' He looked Batchelor straight in the face. 'That's what I think.'

Batchelor toyed with continuing to deny it, but although the man was small, he was wiry, and Batchelor wasn't at all sure who would come out best if it was reduced to fisticuffs. 'How do you know?' he said. If it was something really obvious, he would take pains to avoid it in the future.

'Don't worry,' the groom said, laughing. 'I saw your card on his desk one time and I heard young Miss Georgy call your friend Mr Grand when she let him in at the front door. Grand and Batchelor, enquiry agents. It sticks in the mind, that does. So, you're here because old Charlie boy was murdered, you reckon?'

Batchelor tried to regain the control of the conversation. 'Not definitely. We are just exploring all avenues.' He knew it sounded pompous, but it was out now.

The groom ground out the soggy end of his cigarette on the bricks. 'Well, I could tell you a thing or two, that's for sure. Such as, where did he go, the old hellion, when he wasn't in the challey working. Or . . .' and he gave vent to an evil chuckle, 'whatever else he used it for.' He looked at Batchelor again and laughed. 'Yes, I could tell you a thing or two.'

Batchelor could hardly believe it. The answer could be as close as this; one word from the man and the case could be closed. But he would have to be careful. 'Such as what?' he said, trying to sound devil-may-care. 'We have already found out a great deal, you know.'

'You don't know about this,' the groom said, turning to go.

'You don't know about Miss No-Better-Than-She-Should-Be in Nunhead, I'll lay.'

'Miss Who?'

'Wouldn't you like to know,' Butler said, disappearing into a tack room and closing the door. Batchelor turned to go and, as he was crossing the yard, the top half of the door flew open. 'And you don't know about this, neither,' the exasperating little man said, blowing through his moustache. 'You don't know where he was nor what he did on the day he died. Now, then.' And with that, he slammed shut the door and Batchelor heard the bolts shoot home. It was something. Maybe, with what Grand had discovered, it might be enough.

Isaac had gone by the time Batchelor came trotting over the grass. He had swept off his jacket again and had slung it over his shoulder.

'Have I got news for you!' he muttered under his breath as he reached the road. Brunt had said that there were goings-on in the shrubbery – you couldn't be too careful.

'Not as impressive, I'll wager, as the news I've got for you,' Grand countered.

Batchelor held up his hand. 'Not here, Matthew. Rhododendrons have ears.'

And that came as news in itself to Matthew Grand.

One by one, Grand and Batchelor interviewed as many of the late Charles Dickens's children as they could find. They focused on those who had attended the funeral and found them exactly as George Sala had told them they would. They had all loved their father, especially the Snodgering Blee, who sobbed throughout the entire interview and told them that the world was an emptier place without him.

They drew straws for the close friends; it was Batchelor who got Ouvry, the solicitor. An articled clerk showed him into a palatial waiting room, the wall heavy with framed credentials. Frederic Ouvry, Batchelor guessed, was in his late fifties, more or less the late Dickens's age, and his offices at 66 Lincoln's Inn Fields were a revelation. He was not there when Batchelor was shown in and was told to wait, so the ex-journalist took the opportunity to drool over his leather-bound volumes. They were wall-to-wall and extended to the ceiling.

'No,' a voice made Batchelor jump. 'I know I shouldn't keep my first folios at fingering level. They'd be safer higher up. But, like you, I can't resist a fondle every now and then.'

Batchelor was embarrassed. He glanced back at the Shakespeare editions to make sure he had left no marks on the binding. 'I'm sorry,' he mumbled.

'Don't be, don't be. Had they been original Marlowes, now, I might have recourse to take umbrage. Frederic Ouvry.' The solicitor held out his hand. 'And you are . . .?'

'Sorry,' Batchelor said, for the second time in as many minutes. 'My card.' He whipped it out.

'"No stone unturned",' Ouvry read. 'Intriguing, Mr Grand.'

'Er . . . Batchelor,' Batchelor said.

'I see.' Ouvry ushered his visitor to an uncompromising Chesterfield, polished by the crinolines of clients without number. 'But I'm afraid we already have people for our enquiry work.'

'You do?'

'Why, yes.' Ouvry sat behind his desk and spent a little while arranging his pens just *so* on a ghastly inkstand which from Batchelor's angle appeared to be covered in lizards and snails; clearly, a trick of the light. 'You probably know him – a Mr Polliak.'

'Paddington Pollaky?'

Ouvry chuckled. 'That is the . . . umm . . . monicker he uses, yes.'

'Well, I haven't met him, but a friend of mine has met a friend of his.'

Ouvry looked confused.

'Er . . . ex-Chief Inspector Field?'

Ouvry snorted. 'Charlie Field!' He disappeared below his desk and emerged seconds later with a decanter and two glasses. 'Port, Mr Batchelor?'

'Thank you, that's very kind.'

'No, forgive me for that outburst just then; but Charlie Field . . . We used to employ them both, Pollaky and Field, when they were still partners. The trouble with Field is that he couldn't let the job go. Still referring to himself as chief inspector years after

he'd hung up his truncheon. Here's lead in your probate!' and
he passed Batchelor a tincture of the ruby.

'Cheers.' Batchelor sipped. Good. Expensive. Clearly Ouvry's
side of the law was the place to be. Enquiry agents, perhaps not
so much.

'So, you see,' Ouvry savoured the burgundy elixir, 'if it's work
you want, I'm afraid . . .'

'No,' Batchelor corrected him. 'It's about Charles Dickens.'

'Charles?' Ouvry frowned. 'What about him?'

'My colleague and I are of the opinion that he was murdered.'

Ouvry paused in mid-swig, then finished the port and put the
glass down, heavily. 'Are you insane?' His voice was barely
audible.

'No, sir. I assure you . . .'

'Haemorrhage of the brain, sir,' Ouvry said. 'A stroke, in
layman's terms. Talk to Dr Beard.'

'I have.'

'Well, then.'

'He expressed some doubts,' Batchelor lied. He hated doing
it, but in for a penny, he thought, and solicitor Ouvry was showing
all the signs of most of the rest of Dickens's ménage by clam-
ming up when anything suspect was raised.

'Did he?' Ouvry blinked. 'Well, let's see.' He was pouring
himself another port and upset his stack of pens as he did so.
'Bugger! Let me see, in the years I knew him, Charles had
rheumatism, swollen feet – he denied gout flat out – piles, of
course (but then, who doesn't?) . . . oh, there was that unfortunate
small malady . . .'

'Small malady?'

Ouvry took another swig. 'We are all men of the world,
Batchelor; surely I don't have to be *too* specific. Bathing at
Broadstairs wouldn't do the trick. As Charles himself put it to
me, when I hadn't been in his service long, "I suppose there is
no nitrate of silver in the ocean".'

Batchelor still looked blank.

'The pox, man. Cupid's measles. I thought you were an enquiry
agent.'

'But none of this was likely to kill him, surely?' Batchelor
was thinking aloud.

'No. No, I told you. It was a stroke.'

'*Cui bono*, Mr Ouvry?' Batchelor asked.

The solicitor's face darkened. 'You sit there, sir,' he said, 'quoting Cicero to *me*? You have the bare-faced cheek? It's none of your business who benefits from Charles Dickens's death, Mr Batchelor; none whatever. He was a rich man, as you would expect from the country's most prolific writer. How he crammed such an output into one day, I will never know. So, yes, he was wealthy. Yes, he had various properties hither and yon. Yes, the man was a friend of mine and therefore, no, I have no intention of telling you anything else. That wooden thing over there, sir, is the door. Please take yourself through it. And think yourself lucky I have not charged you for my time.'

The lights burned blue in Alsatia that night, and Grand and Batchelor were sitting alongside each other in their respective armchairs, looking at a blank wall. Blank, that is, except for pieces of paper pinned to the plaster with tacks.

'Right, James.' Grand blew cigar smoke to the ceiling. 'You first.'

Batchelor winced as the brandy hit his tonsils. If truth were told, he didn't really like the stuff, but George Sala was paying, so what the hey? 'Basics,' he said. 'Let's start at the beginning. Charles Dickens.'

'Great writer,' Grand ruminated. Perhaps that was a little *too* basic, but it was a beginning.

'Prolific,' Batchelor agreed. 'Caught the conscience of the nation.'

'Actor of sorts,' Grand added. 'Wowed them at every point of the compass from Basingstoke to Milwaukee.'

'His Little Nell got them weeping,' Batchelor nodded, lighting up his own cigar. 'His murder of Nancy had them terrified.'

'What's the common denominator there, James?' Grand was letting his eyes wander over the random jottings on the wall. He was wondering how much longer he could go before someone realized that he had never read a word that Dickens wrote.

'Death,' Batchelor said.

'Which brings us to Dickens's dark side. You've read more of his stuff than I have,' Grand said, without a word of a lie. 'Is there anything specific in his writing that could account for his murder?'

Batchelor sighed. 'Well, it's difficult,' he said. 'The man wrote so much. Still, if you'd shown me, say, *The Pickwick Papers* and *Edwin Drood*, I'd have said they were written by two different people.'

'What do they call that?' Grand asked.

'Genius?'

'*Nearly* everybody we've met would say so.'

'Ah,' Batchelor wagged a finger at him. 'Now we're getting somewhere. Of those we've seen so far, the family, still in mourning, sees him as a saint.'

'The professionals,' Grand moved on. 'You saw two of them – Beard and Ouvry.'

'Like all doctors,' Batchelor said, 'Beard's watching his back, sitting there like a giant clam.'

'There'd be a lawsuit against the man in the States,' was Grand's opinion.

'Why? Because he wouldn't tell me anything?'

'Because you learnt more about Dickens's health from the cuss's solicitor. I wouldn't mind if Beard had filled us in on Dickens's financial situation.'

'But dear old Barney was helpful,' Batchelor reminded him.

'He was,' Grand nodded. 'Which just underlines precisely how unhelpful Beard was.'

'All right,' Batchelor said, after a pause. His cigar had gone out and he had to wrestle with it. 'Let's stick with the medical thing. Everybody at Gads Hill seems to be falling over themselves giving the late lamented pick-me-ups. There's Mrs Brownlow/ Gamp's McMunn's Elixir . . .'

'Georgy Hogarth's homeopathic cocoa . . .' Grand threw in.

'Everybody's beef tea,' they chorused.

'So,' Grand was piecing it together, 'if Dickens *was* poisoned, the *how* isn't too difficult. It's the why that's bothering me.'

Batchelor nodded. 'And the why will give us the who.'

Another pause. Another silence. Through the open window, the Alsatia night had at last fallen silent too. The rattling hansoms had gone home, taking the theatre boulevardiers with them. Now only the staccato tap of E Division's boots on the pavement beat the London refrain at the dead of night.

'Georgy Hogarth.' Grand put his accusatory toe in the water.

'Say on.' Batchelor was all ears.

'She's what? Mid-forties, I'd say.'

'Funny age?' Batchelor queried.

'The funniest, in my experience,' Grand nodded. 'Spinster housekeeper. It's a definite type. But . . .'

'But, in love with her ex-employer, would you say?'

'That would be my guess, yes. But it was unrequited.'

'Because . . .?'

'Because she was his sister-in-law. She's a respectable woman. There was somebody else.'

'Precisely.' Batchelor was finally puffing away again. 'The tale of the gossiping groom.'

'Remind me,' Grand said. 'The way you told it, the man seemed kinda keen to dish the dirt on his old master.'

'He did,' Batchelor agreed. 'Stick around, Matthew my boy. Butler's the Jack's-as-good-as-his-master type. I always said it was a mistake on Mr Disraeli's part to extend the vote.'

'Now, James,' Grand scolded. 'No politics in the Mess. It's Dickens's mess we're concerned with now.'

'Right.' Batchelor was remembering his conversation with the groom. '"Miss No-Better-Than-She-Should-Be in Nunhead",' he said.

'I can't keep up with you literary types,' Grand chuckled. 'I thought that was a character in *The Water Babies*.'

Batchelor laughed. 'We've got problems enough with Dickens,' he said, 'without bringing Charles Kingsley into this. I think we can assume that Dickens was having an affair.'

'Georgy Hogarth admitted as much,' Grand remembered. 'But what's the big deal? Dickens was divorced or separated, or however his domestic land lay. No reason why a man shouldn't take up with a lady friend in that situation.'

'Matthew, Matthew,' Batchelor patronized. 'This is London, dear boy, or at least the fringes of it. No one's seen the Queen for nine years and most married men have never seen their wives naked.'

A vision of the naked Victoria swam briefly before the eyes

of both men; then they shook themselves free of it and moved on.

'Think Washington society at its most puritanical,' Batchelor said. 'Then add on the snobbishness of the Old Country. Dickens was a national treasure. We all need our plaster saints. He'd have to keep any hanky-panky *very* close to his chest.'

'So,' Grand was going further, 'in the cause of *cherchez*-ing *la femme*, we're looking for some woman Isaac didn't like; we're looking for Stella.'

'We may well be,' Batchelor said. 'And I've heard the name somewhere – and not at Gads Hill.'

'She, I take it, was the mystery woman we saw at the funeral, the one with Dolby.'

'I thought she was his wife.' Batchelor was confused.

'Sala said that Dolby wasn't married. Perhaps *he's* having an affair – Dolby, that is. No. wait, though,' Grand was thinking it through logically. 'I wouldn't imagine he would take his fancy bit to a private funeral.'

'No, stands to reason,' Batchelor said. 'We'll need to talk to him next, sort that out.'

'What about the wife?' Grand saw the perplexed expression on Batchelor's face and read his mind. 'Not *Dolby*'s wife, if he has one. No, Dickens's wife.' He flicked through the pages of the notebook on his lap. 'Er . . . Catherine.'

'Yes, we must talk to her, too. But as for a motive there, I don't see it. She and Dickens had been separated for years. Oh, I can believe she had it in for Georgy; after all, the woman is her sister and she ran away with her old man, to all intents and purposes. But the fact that Dickens was getting his leg over somebody else after all this time . . . No, it doesn't make any sense. *And* she's employed Charlie Field to investigate. Would she do that if she was behind it all?'

'Helluva determined suicide,' Grand said. 'What else did the groom tell you? And, by the way, is it just me, or is having a groom called Butler just a *tad* convoluted?'

'Mrs Brownlow,' Batchelor shrugged, 'Bob Cratchit, the Snodgering Blee. *Nobody's* what they seem in the world of Charles Dickens. So, come on, Gradgrind, what are you thinking?'

'Didn't Butler say, "You don't know where Dickens was nor what he did on the day he died"?'

'Yes, he did,' Batchelor agreed. 'But we know where he died, in the chalet, according to . . .'

'According to Georgy Hogarth, yes. But I was there,' Grand reminded him, 'not two days after the unhappy event. I've never seen a room so spotless.'

'Emma will have cleaned up,' Batchelor said.

'I suppose that's it,' Grand muttered. But neither of them was happy. 'It's not much to give Sala, is it?' he said.

'No,' Batchelor agreed. 'Call it.' He tossed a coin in the air.

'Heads,' said Grand.

'The Queen it is, God bless her,' Batchelor said. 'Who do you want, Dolby or Sala?'

'Dolby every time,' Grand said. 'George Sala brings me out in spots. Oh, and James,' he leaned towards him. 'You might point out that a retainer is not set in tablets of stone. There *are* such things as expenses.'

SIX

G rand wasn't quite sure what he was expecting from the offices of Dickens's tour manager. Totting it up quickly in his head, even at ten per cent – and he knew that there would be other emoluments on the side – the man should be living in a gold-plated mansion. So the little room at the very top of a winding and rickety stair in Denmark Street rather took him by surprise. The door bore someone else's name painted on the glass, half-heartedly rubbed out with something sharp, and 'Dolby' was written in pencil on a piece of paper gummed in the middle of the pane. Grand knocked and heard sounds from inside the room but no one answered. He tried the handle and the door was open, so he peered in.

A thin man, with receding hair and thick glasses, was sitting behind an enormous desk. The desk itself was covered with what looked like reams of paper, and tottering piles of envelopes were precariously balanced in a series of labelled wire trays. It looked like chaos, but Grand guessed, quite rightly, that Dolby could put his hand on anything, within seconds, as long as no one moved so much as one piece.

'Mr Dolby?' Grand asked, still peering round the door.

'Yes, yes, do come in and shut the door. Draughts are an-an-anathema to my filing system. Um . . . you don't have a cold or anything, do you?'

In the hottest June anyone was able to remember for many a long year, this seemed to Grand to be unlikely, but he was a polite man and answered sensibly, 'No, no cold.'

'You don't suffer from sneezing fits at all?' Dolby looked anxious.

'No, no. Ah . . . I see. Sneezing would also mess up your filing system.'

Dolby smiled and rubbed his hands together. 'You understand,' he said. 'Good man. Not everyone does, you know. Some people,' and he became confidential, 'some people try to tidy my desk.'

'Shocking!' Grand was suitably outraged and also seized his opportunity. 'Wives, for instance. Shocking for that, or so I'm told.'

'Oh, no,' Dolby said. 'I don't have one of those to trouble me. Charles left me no time for things such as wives, dear me, no. Look here, Mr . . .?'

'Grand. Matthew Grand.'

'Mr Grand. Hello. How'd'ye do? Would you mind, Mr Grand, if we went elsewhere? Charles's untimely . . . umm, well, you know . . . has left me with rather a lot of work. Cancelling here, adjusting there. You understand, I'm sure.'

'Adjusting?' Grand was confused. 'Surely, cancellation is the only option?'

'Well, no,' Dolby admitted, as he ushered Grand out and shut the door with infinite care. He listened for a moment at the door, but there was no sound of slithering correspondence, so he led the way down the stairs. 'There were some venues that, believe it or not, were happy to have an actor reading Charles's immortal lines. Cheaper. Much cheaper, of course. And we could leave those bookings intact. But I felt it only . . .'

'Respectful?'

'Respectful, yes, thank you. Respectful. I felt it only respectful that we had a few . . .'

'Break?' Grand was beginning to enjoy this game. If only they had had a bottle handy, to spin, it would have been a lot of fun.

'Respite,' continued Dolby. 'It wouldn't have been proper to just go ahead as though nothing had happened. I believe, though, that the business will be able to continue, without dear Charles.'

'It must be a lot of work for an actor, though,' Grand said. 'Having to learn all of Mr Dickens's new works all the time?'

'No, not really,' Dolby said, pushing open the door of a coffee shop in the Charing Cross Road and taking a seat just inside the door. 'Excuse me sitting here,' he said suddenly. 'But the pro . . .'

'Proprietor?'

'Yes, him. He doesn't really like me much.'

'Any particular reason? We could always go elsewhere.' After all, the Tivoli Restaurant was just down the road, and George Sala was still paying. Grand was beginning to find this little man rather fun to be with, in a twitchy sort of way. He took a lot of keeping up with, that was for sure.

'Well, last time I was in here, I put a rubber snake in a coffee urn. Gave him quite a turn.' He gave a reminiscent chuckle. 'Brought the house down. He didn't like it, though. He had a heart attack.'

'It would give anyone a bit of a turn,' Grand observed.

'No,' Dolby said. 'It really did give him a heart attack. Nothing serious, as it happened. In my opinion he should be grateful to me; he had no idea he had a dicky ticker until then. He could have dropped dead any moment.' He took off his glasses and wiped his eyes, which had watered with the memory of bringing the house down. 'Where were we?'

By some miracle, Grand had kept up. 'You were telling me how it isn't really difficult for actors to learn Mr Dickens's new work.'

'Ah, yes. My word, you have quite a marvellous memory yourself, there, Mr . . . umm . . .'

'Grand.'

'Yes. You'll have to forgive me. I have an atrocious memory. Now, where were we?'

'Actors. Memory. Dickens.' Grand was suddenly finding his companion rather less droll.

'Yes, well, the audiences all want the usual, of course. Little Nell. Nancy. Barkis is willing. All the old chestnuts. Pickwick. Squeers. That always goes down well. So the actors only need to have a knowledge of those. And Charles of course, bless his heart, he didn't learn it either.'

'He read it?' Grand had heard of Dickens's bravura performances, and somehow it didn't sound like a man reading from a book.

'No, no. Charles would just tell the story. I suppose, in time, the words did become a little . . . samey. But he would put new bits in every now and then. Sometimes he would use any good phrases he came out with in other works. He would steal names as well, of course. Shameless for that, he was.'

'I'm surprised he didn't use yours, Mr Dolby.'

The little man simpered. 'He did ask, but my dear old mother was still alive then and, well . . .' he lifted the glasses again and wiped away a tear, 'she was very protective of the name and didn't really want it on the front of *Household Words*. So he called his character Dombey, instead. It wasn't the same, but *I* knew, and that was the main thing.'

'I had heard that he had a habit of using names he came across.'

'Oh, I can see you've met the Reverend Moptrucket. Dear, dear man, he tells that story every time.' The handkerchief was brandished again, this time so that the little agent could trumpet into it, to clear away his backlog of unshed tears.

Two cups of coffee had arrived, carried by a buxom girl of about nineteen. 'Father says,' she hissed, 'to drink up and git out. If you wasn't with company, he'd have Jem kick you out bag and baggage.' Then she turned to Grand. 'Sir.' And with a little bob and a flounce, she was gone.

'You really do tend to annoy people, don't you, Mr Dolby?' Grand remarked.

'Yes,' he said, with a sigh. 'I just can't help the joking, though. I do so love a practical joke. Charles and I would have such larks. There was one time, one time . . . I can't remember exactly where it was . . . America, certainly.' He looked up sharply. 'Do I detect a slight twang in *your* voice, young Mr . . . Mr . . .'

'Grand,' Grand said. It was nothing he had not heard before. 'Boston, by way of Washington.'

'How fascinating. Did you ever see Charles perform? He packed houses all over your home country.'

'No, I never had the pleasure.' Grand thought it was time to move on to the crux of the matter, but Dolby wouldn't be diverted.

'Anyway, this one time,' he said, dissolving into giggles, 'Charles and I put a raspberry cushion on every seat in the house. Cost us a fortune, mind you, but everyone who sat down made a noise, like a . . .'

'Raspberry.'

'Quite. It was hilarious.' He took a sip of his coffee, grimaced and then sipped again. He held the cup out to Grand. 'Does this taste all right to you?'

Grand took it and was about to take a sip when the waitress snatched it out of his hand.

'No, sir,' she said. 'That's not for *you*. Papa has . . . added a

little something. Since Mr Dolby is so fond of practical jokes!'
She took Grand's cup as well and made for the swing door into
the kitchen. 'On the house,' she said, before plunging into the
steamy rear of the kitchen.

Dolby was wiping his tongue on his ever-present handkerchief.
'What do you think . . .'

'Probably . . . soap,' Grand guessed, although he had a good
idea it was nothing of the kind. 'Mr Dolby, I know you're busy.
What I wanted to ask you was, do you think Charles Dickens
had any enemies?' Somehow he knew instinctively that asking
this odd little man about mistresses and strange women in the
shrubbery and under veils at funerals was not going to get him
very far.

'Enemies?' Dolby's eyes filled with tears. 'Charles? Oh, no.
Everybody loved Charles.' And, while he was wiping his eyes
and blowing his nose once more, Grand tipped his hat and left,
before another anecdote lost him another ten minutes of his life.

'There's a nob downstairs,' Mrs Rackstraw announced. Her hands
were covered in suds and there was a teacloth slung over her
shoulder. She handed him a rather soggy piece of pasteboard.
''E give me this.'

'A nob, Mrs Rackstraw?' James Batchelor couldn't believe his
ears. 'I really must ask you to . . . oh, my God.' He was on
his feet. 'This is Lord Arthur Clinton, son of the Duke of
Newcastle. Oh, my God. Show him up. Show him . . . no, on
second thoughts, you go back to your washing. I'll see to His
Lordship.'

This was a moment of realization for James Batchelor. Yes,
Mr Disraeli had extended the electorate – doubled it, in fact – but
that leap in the dark had not included an impecunious enquiry
agent whose income was, to say the least, hit and miss. Even if
Mr Disraeli had been allowed his Fancy Franchises, giving the
vote to graduates. James Batchelor still didn't qualify. So, here
he was, that Monday morning, flying down the stairs through
Mrs Rackstraw's washing-day steam, a voteless man facing the
son of a peer of the realm. Some, he kept thinking to himself on
every stair, have greatness thrust upon them.

'My lord,' he bowed as he caught sight of the man.

'Are you Grand or Batchelor?' the man asked.

'Batchelor, sir,' Batchelor gushed. 'May I say, what an honour . . .'

'Yes, yes. I'm here at George Sala's suggestion. He didn't tell me you were a crawling toady.'

'Toady?' James Batchelor had read *The Communist Manifesto* – well, the bits he could understand with the aid of a dictionary – and he suddenly found himself in the camp of George Butler. Jack was indeed as good as his master; Karl Marx and Dickens's groom were right – brothers under the skin.

The man looked him up and down. 'A little harsh, perhaps,' he said. 'I apologize. Life is a little trying at present. Do you have somewhere private? You will have gathered from my card that I am Arthur Clinton. I have come on a delicate matter.'

Arthur Clinton was Grand's age; shorter, slimmer, with a small waxed moustache and languid, heavy-lidded eyes. His frock coat was immaculate and the gold Albert in his waistcoat pocket could have bought number 41 The Strand, Batchelor guessed, several times over.

'Up here, Lord Arthur,' he said. 'We can talk in the drawing room; unless you would like to accompany me to our offices; they're just a few doors down?'

Clinton had that unfortunate appearance of having a permanent smell under his nose. He had taken the trouble to seek Batchelor and Grand out here, rather than at their offices, he seemed to imply without speaking a word, and now he was being asked to go elsewhere. It was, really, all too much. 'The drawing room will be adequate,' he said, 'as long as we will not be overheard. Staff, you know. One can't be too careful.'

'We just have Mrs Rackstraw,' Batchelor explained, and didn't notice the Honourable Arthur flinch. He led the way up the stairs and opened the door into the drawing room, work room, consulting room – it fulfilled every purpose that was asked of it.

Clinton walked in and took in all that he saw. The cluttered desks, two of them; books along two walls. There were pieces of paper at odd angles on the third wall: names, jottings. He missed nothing. 'Where is Grand?' he asked.

'Visiting a client, sir,' Batchelor said, gesturing to the most comfortable chair they had.

'You will have to relay to him what I am about to impart

yourself,' Clinton said, flicking the furniture with his coat-tail.
'I have no intention of saying any of this more than once.'

'Very well,' Batchelor said. He sat and waited.

'The window, if you please.' Clinton pointed to it.

Batchelor shrugged. It was hot as Hell as June flamed outside,
but he slid the sash down and felt the sweat crawling down
his back. 'Er . . . could I offer you some refreshment, Lord
Arthur?'

'Thank you, no. I shall be lunching at my club later and
breakfast was rather gargantuan this morning. I'll come to the
point. What can you tell me about "Dolly" Williamson?'

'Chief Inspector Williamson, Scotland Yard?'

'That's the chappie. Why's he called Dolly?'

'I believe his name is Adolphus, sir,' Batchelor said.

'Oh.' Clinton looked a little crestfallen. 'Oh, I see. You've
worked with him, professionally, I mean?'

Batchelor chuckled. 'I wouldn't say *with* exactly,' he said.
'Mr Williamson has, shall we say, certain views about enquiry
agents.'

'Yes, I'm sure he has. Is he bent? By which I mean, can he
be bribed?'

Batchelor looked horrified. 'I really don't know, Lord Arthur.
I've never needed to raise the issue. Not that I could afford him,
of course.'

'Hm,' Clinton snorted. 'Well, every man has his price, Batchelor.
What's yours?'

'Sir?'

'How much do you charge?'

'That depends on the service,' Batchelor said.

The flicker of a smile flitted across Clinton's face. 'You naughty
boy,' he said. 'I want something hushed up.'

'Oh.' Alarm bells were ringing in Batchelor's head. 'What?'

'I don't need to tell you, Batchelor, that if all goes according
to plan, I shall, one day, be a peer of the realm.'

'Congratulations, my lord,' Batchelor beamed.

Arthur Clinton wasn't good at sarcasm, at least other people's,
and he let it go. 'And I won't pretend that my family is lily white,
either. My brother, Albert, was cashiered from the Navy: he had
his hand in the till, so to speak. My sister Susan was, until his

tastes wandered, a close friend – I find the term "mistress" so coarse, don't you? – of the Prince of Wales. And don't get me started on my father.'

'Do I take it you're the white sheep, my lord?' Batchelor asked.

Clinton's scowl changed slowly to a smirk and he wagged a finger at the man. 'You're very droll, Batchelor,' he said. 'Droll and perceptive. I like that in a man. I can see why George Sala recommended you.'

'I'm very flattered, sir, of course,' Batchelor said, 'but I don't see—'

'Picture the scene,' Clinton interrupted, waving his hand as if to create a *pose plastique* in Batchelor's consulting room. 'I went to the theatre the other night, not far from here, in fact, at the Strand.'

'Go on.'

'I went with two friends, dear boys called Ernest and Frederick.'

'When was this, exactly?' Batchelor was reaching for his pen.

'No,' Clinton said sharply. 'Nothing written down, if you please, Batchelor. Least written, soonest glossed over, if you catch my drift.'

'So be it.' Batchelor put the pen down.

'It was the twenty-eighth of April, a Thursday.'

'And what was the show?'

'What?'

'The play at the Strand, what was it?'

'My dear fellow, I have absolutely no idea. Seen one piece of music-hall drivel, seen them all. We went, naturally, into my private box.'

'You and Ernest and Frederick?'

'And Hugh and John.'

'That must have been rather a squeeze,' Batchelor commented. 'Five of you in a private box.'

Clinton bridled. 'My father *is* the Duke of Newcastle,' he said. 'I have a very large box.'

Batchelor committed that to memory. 'Was there an incident?' he asked.

'There certainly was,' Clinton recounted, 'on the part of the

police. Unbeknownst to us, we were followed all the way from
Wakefield Street.'

'Wakefield Street?'

'Number Thirteen, to be precise. Ernest and Frederick have
their lodgings there. Perfect bitch of a landlady.'

'You were followed by the police?' Batchelor wanted to be
sure. 'Why?'

'Why is grass green, Batchelor?' Clinton countered. 'I have
noticed in my thirty years on this earth that there is a certain
kind of lout who has it in for men of my class. Trust me, when
that traitor to the Conservative Party, Robert Peel, set up the
Metropolitan Police, he did more harm than he knew. Not a
gentleman among them.'

'What happened at the theatre?'

'Nothing,' Clinton insisted, 'until we left. The national anthem
had just finished – they play it before and after the turns at the
Strand, for some reason – and we all, to use the revolting
vernacular of the street, had our collars felt.'

'By the copper who'd been following you?'

'Oh, dear me, no. By two sergeants and a chief inspector, no
less – Williamson.'

'I see.'

'The blighters had been hiding in the theatre, dressed in mufti,
as though they were human beings.'

'Disgraceful.' Batchelor shook his head and tutted. As usual,
it all sailed over Arthur Clinton's head. 'What was the charge,
exactly?'

'Yes,' Clinton growled. 'I thought you'd ask that. And here
we come to the crux of the matter. I was, as were the others,
accused of – and I quote – "conspiring and inciting persons to
commit an unnatural offence".'

'In the large private box?'

'Probably,' Clinton shrugged, 'although I assure you no such
event took place.'

'Not in the theatre.'

'Not anywhere!' Clinton exploded. 'I *am* William Gladstone's
godson.'

'Of course you are.'

'That very night,' Clinton could barely speak for fury, 'that very night, I suffered such an indignity to my person . . . so did poor Ernest and Frederick.'

'Really?'

'The police surgeon, at Williamson's insistence, carried out an intimate examination, in order to determine whether any of us had . . . and I won't beat about the bush . . . had anal connection.'

'I see.'

'The beak at Bow Street was less than sympathetic.'

'Who was that, sir?'

'Er . . . Frederick Flowers, I believe. Reptile of a man. We didn't hit it off.'

'And you all appeared?'

'No, no. Hugh got the Hell out, as John said he would.'

'The Hell out?' Batchelor had only heard that phrase on the other side of the Atlantic.

'Abroad,' Clinton said. 'France or somewhere. Oh, I see, you mean the phrase? Picturesque, isn't it? John is colonial, you see. From America.'

'John . . . er . . .?'

'Fiske. He's the American consul in Edinburgh. That, of course, gives him diplomatic immunity. Which rather left Ernest, Frederick and me holding the baby.'

'Forgive me, Lord Arthur, but I don't see how my colleague and I can help.'

'I got this yesterday.' Clinton whipped an envelope from inside his coat. 'A subpoena. I presume Ernest and Frederick have theirs.'

Batchelor checked it. All legal and above board, signed and sealed with the full majesty of the law.

'I still don't—' he began.

'I want this to go away, Batchelor,' Clinton said, 'which is why I asked you about Williamson. I don't know what, if anything, that nasty little doctor chappie with his grubby fingers can prove. But I know how courts of law work. I wasn't Liberal MP for Newark for nothing. If we can't bribe these people, we can, I believe, smear them. I want you and your confederate to dig up all the dirt you can – on Williamson, the doctor; anybody else who'll be a witness for the prosecution. I will not have the name of Pelham-Clinton dragged through the mud any more than it has been already.'

'Lord Arthur,' Batchelor said, 'I think Mr Sala may have been a little optimistic in recommending us. This subpoena is in order. The crime of which you stand accused is indeed an offence – its unnaturalness will depend on the eye of the beholders in the jury, I suppose – but what you are suggesting is, at the very least, underhand.'

'Underhand, sir?' Clinton snapped. 'Underhand? The conspiracy against me, against me and my family and my social class, *that's* what's underhand.' He paused, calming himself until his face had stopped flushing purple. 'If it's a matter of money . . .' he began.

'No, I . . .' but Batchelor hadn't finished when Clinton whipped out his gold hunter and threw it and the Albert on to the desk. The metal flashed in the sunlight; more gold than James Batchelor had ever seen in one place in his life.

'Talk it over with your friend Grand,' Clinton said. 'And call on me at my club tomorrow. Ten sharp. Dinner will be over by then and we can talk in private.'

'Well, I—'

'Ten sharp, Batchelor.' Clinton was on his feet. 'The Rag, Pall Mall.'

SEVEN

'The Rag?' Grand repeated. It still didn't sound right.

'Army and Navy Club to you and me, Matthew. I've never been across its portals. I *nearly* did, when I was with the *Telegraph*, but the members don't cotton to the Press much. That's why I think your *other* card would look better tonight.'

The cab lurched to a halt at the corner of the Mall and St James's Square. The place was buzzing, people everywhere, laughing and joking away the warm, glowing night. The lights burned late at the Horse Guards and, far away through the trees, Buckingham Palace had never looked so radiant. All London knew the Queen was not there. The widow was skulking at Windsor, the gossip ran, her heart forever broken over her beloved Albert. At the palace, it must have been the Prince of Wales holding a soirée.

Grand was impressed with the opulence of the Rag, its brass gleaming in the firelight, its windows with a promise of good food, good wine and good company. The flunkey on the door tipped his hat to them, although he was a *little* surprised that they were not in evening dress. Gentlemen in infantry scarlet and cavalry blue sauntered in the foyer, interspersed with white cravats and black tails and the obligatory full sets of the Navy.

The visitors' dress might not have been right but the card did the trick. 'Captain Grand,' the man on the desk beamed. 'Third Cavalry of the Potomac. Welcome, sir. It's not often we have an officer from the colonies. Er . . . former colonies. May I enquire who you wish to see?'

'We have an appointment,' Grand said, 'with Lord Arthur Clinton.'

The man's face darkened. 'Ah, could you bear with me for a moment, sir?' and he slipped into an anteroom.

'This could go one of two ways,' Batchelor murmured out of the corner of his mouth. 'Since His Lordship called yesterday, I did some digging. Not only is he not an MP any more, he's not in the Navy, either. Resigned in April, apparently. Oh – and the bad news? He's seriously in hock. He was declared bankrupt two years ago.'

'Well,' Grand said, retaining the smile for the benefit of passing members, 'you *have* been a busy little enquiry agent, haven't you? And when were you planning to fill *me* in on these little details?'

'About now,' Batchelor winked at him. 'Look, Matthew, I know we don't have time for this, what with the Dickens case. And I don't know that there's much we can do. But at least I've got across this threshold – one of my little ambitions: humour me.'

'Gentlemen,' the desk man was back, looking grim. 'Could you follow me, please?'

They did, into the bowels of the building, through twisting passageways without number, until they came to a dark door. The flunkey knocked.

'Enter,' they all heard and the flunkey opened it.

A large man sat behind a leather-topped desk. He wore naval mess dress and had a large glass of rum on the table beside him. 'Thank you, Thompson,' he said, and the flunkey left.

'I'd get up, gentlemen,' the naval gent said, 'but I'm afraid my gout has the better of me tonight. That's why,' he waggled the glass at them, 'I'm dining down here, alone.'

'We have an appointment,' Batchelor said. 'With Lord Arthur Clinton.'

'One he won't be keeping, I fear.'

Grand and Batchelor looked at each other.

'Brace yourselves, gentlemen,' the man said. 'Lord Arthur is dead.'

They looked at each other again.

'Suicide?' Batchelor asked.

'Scarlet fever,' the man said. 'Oh, forgive me. This has all come as something of a shock. I am Anthony Rivers, Commodore. I served with Arthur when he was a midshipman in the Crimea. Dear boy, dear boy. You are . . .?'

'Grand and Batchelor,' Grand said. 'Enquiry agents.'

'Really?' Rivers raised an eyebrow.

'Lord Arthur consulted us,' Batchelor said, 'on a matter of some delicacy. Yesterday.'

'Yes, well, there it is,' Rivers sighed. 'That's the very devil about scarlet fever, isn't it? Right as rain one day, in God's jollyboat the next. Tell me, this "matter of some delicacy" – may I enquire as to its nature?'

'No, sir,' Grand said. 'I am afraid you may not. It is, as we have all agreed, a matter of some delicacy and you are not, I believe, a blood relative of the deceased.'

'Oh, no, dear me, no.' Rivers sipped at his grog. 'Merely a ship that passed him in the night.'

They made their excuses and left and it was not until they were in a cab again, jingling back to the Strand, that Batchelor said, 'I didn't know that about scarlet fever, Matthew, that it kills so quickly.'

'It doesn't,' Grand said. 'Leastways, not in the States. Maybe you've got a different brand over here.'

The offices of Chapman and Hall were still in sombre mood that Friday morning when Frederic Chapman arrived. The black bow still graced the front door. Miss Emmeline Jones was at her desk, ledger open in front of her, checking the stamp petty cash against letters sent. Sometimes, she could curse – in only the most lady-like way, of course – Anthony Trollope and all his works up in a heap; and that didn't even include his dratted son, the young idiot, who drove her beloved Frederic to such apoplexy. This morning, she cast all Trollopes from her thoughts and smiled up at Chapman as he entered in a waft of Thames miasma, a sight to chill the blood of the strongest man.

Frederic Chapman was in no mood for niceties. He swept through the outer office and disappeared into his own inner sanctum; he needed to have a serious think. *Edwin Drood* was preying on his mind. It was sad, of course, very sad, that Dickens had dropped off his very lucrative twig at all, but to do it at a pivotal point of one of the few books he had ever written that could be said to be brimful of suspense – that was just downright perverse. He was already muttering to himself as he divested himself of his coat and pushed back his shirtsleeves, ready to make what notes he could, to try and bring this wretched business to a conclusion. As far as he could see, it had to be Uncle Jasper – but surely a writer of Dickens's calibre couldn't be *that* obvious. He shrugged to himself; all things being equal, Dickens had never been what you could call subtle.

'Hello.' The voice, issuing as it did from the depths of the armchair pulled up to the empty grate made him yelp with surprise.

'Verdon! How did you get in here?' Chapman was holding his chest and leaning heavily on the corner of his desk. 'You could have killed me, man.'

'It isn't hard to get in here, Frederic,' Verdon said. 'All you need to do is to get in before Em . . . I'm sorry, Miss Jones, gets here and you can walk into any of the offices you like. She is like Cerberus's dog, but even she has to sleep.'

Chapman grunted and sat behind his desk. 'I was always of the opinion that Miss Jones spent all her life sitting at that desk,' he said. 'I don't think it has ever occurred to me that she left her post.' He bestowed a wintry smile on the editor, despite the stickiness of the season, to show that he was joking. 'Please, don't do it again. And . . . excuse me a moment.' He reached over and took a brass speaking tube from its hook on the wall, removed the stopper and blew down it sharply. Both men heard Miss Jones's shriek of surprise through the door. After a moment, her voice came, uncannily, both from the outer office and through the tube, in spectral echo.

'Yes, Mr Frederic, sir?'

'Miss Jones. Do these offices lock?'

'Beg pardon, sir. I don't quite . . .'

'Hell's teeth, woman. I couldn't be much clearer. These offices. Are there keys?'

'There are keys to the street door, sir.'

'But nowhere else.'

'I believe in your uncle's day, sir. But not any longer.' There was a pause. She did *so* like to be helpful. 'There are keyholes.'

'God give me strength. They are not much help without keys, woman. Kindly engage a locksmith. I want all of these rooms lockable by nightfall. Do you understand me?'

'Yes, sir.'

'Good. Now don't sit there counting your stamp collection or whatever it is you're doing. Get that locksmith here. At once.' He slammed the speaking tube back in its holder; Miss Jones

– who was still cradling her end at her ear, hoping for more words from the golden lips of her beloved – was half deafened. She rang her bell for the office boy and sent him in search of a locksmith. Some things, she thought, as she tried to recall how far she had got in her stamp counting, really were beneath her dignity. Cradling her ear with one hand, she began again from one.

In his office, Chapman was giving Verdon short shrift. 'I am happy to know, Gabriel, that I shall not be finding you in here uninvited again. We may have known each other for years, but there are standards! However, since you are here, may I ask why?'

'I was just . . .' Verdon was suddenly tongue-tied. 'With the sad demise . . .'

'Yes, yes, yes. I suppose you're here like all the rest. You have written a novel, blah, blah, blah. In deference to the great man, *Drood* should remain unfinished, blah. To fill the pages, you have a tale that will wring withers, freeze blood and make a maiden blush; pick any two per episode. Am I right?'

'Not quite,' Verdon began.

'Near enough, though, I'll warrant,' Chapman snapped. 'Now, get back to wherever you editors gather and do . . . whatever it is you do. I have work to do. And, Gabriel?'

'Yes, Frederic.' Verdon was keeping his temper with difficulty.

'If I ever, *ever* find you in here again, you are to consider yourself disengaged from the employ of Chapman and Hall, longest-serving editor though you may well be. Do you understand me?'

'Yes, sir.' Verdon drooped, as only a misunderstood editor can. 'I do understand, sir.'

'Good. Now, get out. I have some work to do, even if you haven't.'

''Ere, it's that copper again,' Mrs Rackstraw announced.

Chief Inspector Williamson barely waited until she had gone. 'Hasn't got any better, has she?' he sighed.

'We do have offices, Chief Inspector,' Batchelor reminded him, 'if Mrs Rackstraw upsets you so. Just a few doors down.'

'You have *an* office,' Williamson corrected him. 'No, I wouldn't miss the cheerful bonhomie of this place for all the world. And, in any case, the last time I looked, your office was full. Someone was in there trying to swing a cat.'

Batchelor decided to ignore him. Grand, his nose, uncharacteristically, in a book, remarked without looking up. 'Don't tell me James has been upsetting the medical fraternity again.'

'Oh, I expect he has,' Williamson said, sitting down unbidden. 'But that's not why I'm here.'

Batchelor put away his pen and leaned back. Dolly Williamson was the doyen of the Yard detectives these days, now that Whicher and Tanner had gone – one to a nervous breakdown, the other to pour pints in Hampshire. The man's suit marked his calling, the glittering, deep-set eyes even more so. Yes, Mrs Rackstraw had got it right – he could only be a copper.

'So,' Batchelor smiled. 'To what do we owe the pleasure?'

'Arthur Clinton,' Williamson said.

'Who?' Grand and the truth could merely be on nodding terms at times.

Williamson laughed. 'That's what I love about you boys. You enquiry agents are all the same. You'd like your clients to believe you're officers of the law, but that's the last thing you are, isn't it?'

'We prefer "agents of justice", Chief Inspector,' Batchelor said. 'We happen to believe that justice is more important than the law.'

'Hm.' Williamson nodded, clasping his hands across his ample waistcoat, for all June still burned. Almost unheard-of temperatures were no bar to keeping up appearances, to his mind. 'But the problem with that little analogy is that justice is blind. I'm not. Arthur Clinton came here to see you two – or perhaps just one of you – on Tuesday last.'

'You were having him followed,' Grand said.

'Too right I was having him followed. The man's a nob, in every sense of the word. He's due in court soon. I don't want him following his confrères and doing a runner to the continent. He's got dubious contacts everywhere – Rome, Paris. So, what did he want?'

Grand put down his book. 'You *do* know the man's dead, Chief Inspector?' he asked.

'Of course I do,' Williamson said. 'Keeping up to snuff is what they pay me for. And that makes my enquiries – and yours – all the more interesting, doesn't it? My case is ongoing. There are others due to face the high court. It doesn't end with Clinton.'

'I'm afraid, yet again,' Batchelor was patience itself, 'that we cannot divulge—'

'Of course you can!' Williamson bellowed, sitting up and pounding the arms of his chair. 'Your client's dead. All bets are off. I can close you blokes down.'

'No, you can't,' Batchelor told him. 'We've broken no law. We're just doing our job.'

'Yes. And I'm doing mine. You're obstructing the police in . . .'

'All right,' Grand interrupted in a gentle, reasonable tone. 'We'll tell you what you want to know if you answer our questions first.'

Williamson blinked. 'What questions?' he asked.

'What was the cause of Clinton's death?' Grand asked him.

'Scarlet fever,' Williamson said.

'How long had your boys in blue been following him?'

'Three weeks solid, but on and off since the magistrates' hearing. You do *know* he's a Maryanne, don't you?'

'Had they noticed anything odd about him, your boys in blue?' Grand asked, and immediately wished he hadn't.

Williamson roared with laughter. 'Don't get me started,' he said.

'No, I mean over the last three or four days,' Grand explained. 'Did he look unwell?'

'I don't know if scarlet fever shows, does it?' Williamson frowned.

'Well, yes and no,' Grand said. He picked up his book again. 'Wintle's *Pharmacopeia* is a damn good read, believe it or not. James, you interviewed Arthur Clinton. Did he complain of a headache?'

'No.'

'Sore throat?'

'No.'

'Did his neck appear swollen? Did he have difficulty speaking?'

'No, I . . .'

'And what about the rash? It must have been obvious.'

'Matthew . . .'

'My colleague was sitting as close to the man as I am to you, Chief Inspector, and he saw none of the symptoms described by the admirable Wintle in his *Pharmacopeia*.' He tapped the volume again.

'So, the doctor got it wrong,' Williamson shrugged.

'*What*, Chief Inspector?' Batchelor roared with laughter. 'You're doubting the word of a member of the medical profession? Dr Beard would be horrified.'

'That's different,' Williamson said.

'One last question.' Grand leaned back in his chair. 'Have you seen the body?'

'No,' Williamson frowned. 'I have no reason to . . . Why? What are you thinking?'

'He's thinking,' Batchelor said, 'as I am, that a soon-to-be-peer of the realm, accused of sodomy, might consider taking his own life while the balance of his mind is disturbed.'

'That's possible,' Williamson conceded. 'Now it's my turn. And I repeat – what was Clinton's business with you?'

'Oh, that's easy,' Grand said. 'He wanted to know what could be done in the event of his being harassed by police brutality.'

'Brutality,' Batchelor added, 'that may well have led to suicide.'

'Back home,' Grand said, 'that'd be reckless endangerment. You'd get five years hard.'

Williamson was on his feet. 'Yes, well, consider that, Mr Grand.'

'What?' Grand asked him.

'Going home.'

'You young hooligan. Gedoutofit!' They heard the shriek, then a clash of pans and even a squawk as a cat somehow got in on the action.

'Is there a problem, Mrs Rackstraw?' Matthew Grand popped his head out of the upstairs window. It was high noon and the little yard at the back was stinging hot in the heat, the cobbles themselves wobbling and the tarmacadam melting on the road.

'This whippersnapper says 'e knows yer. I told 'im not to be so bloody cheeky. My gen'lemen don't have truck with the likes of 'im.'

'No, no!' Grand shouted. 'It's all right, Mrs Rackstraw. Truck is the order of the day.' He bolted for the stairs. He didn't like the murderous look in the woman's eye and he'd seen what a carpet looked like after she'd used her beater on it. The coiled cane work was in her deadly grip as he ran.

'Isaac?' Grand frowned as he reached the yard. The boy was cowering in a corner, doubled up with his hands over his face. 'Isaac, is that you?'

It was. Isaac Armitage had collected together his savings from Mr Dickens's wages and had ridden the pony to the station. For all he was houseboy to the most famous writer in the country, he had only been to London once before in his life and he hadn't liked it. Mr Dickens had always called it 'town' as if there was only one. To Isaac Armitage, town was Rochester and he felt at home there. The last time he had been in the metropolis, he had been with Mr D, who had taken him to the zoological gardens. This time he had been on his own and crossing Waterloo Bridge he had realized how huge and terrifying the place was.

Nobody – until this mad old besom with the carpet beater – had spoken to him; and him the houseboy of the most famous writer in the country. He had looked at Mr D's books on London in his great study at Gads Hill and had memorized the way to the Strand. The houses, the hotels, the shops, soared above him and a pigeon paid him a compliment, right on his head. He was still trying to remove that when he collided with a crowd on the pavement. A cab horse was down, wilting in the heat, whinnying pitifully in its traces and lolling its tongue. Isaac had never heard language like it – from the cabman, from the onlookers, from the harassed peeler who was trying to move them all on.

He'd got Mr Grand's card tight in his sweaty fist and he'd got the office right, but it was all locked and barred, so he'd flipped the card over and gone to the address on the back. He hadn't realized that Messrs Grand and Batchelor, enquiry agents, shared their lodgings with the inmates of a lunatic asylum.

'Don't you give 'im no 'ouse-room, Mr Grand,' Mrs Rackstraw warned. 'We don't have no riff-raff 'ere in Alsatia.'

'Thank you, Mrs Rackstraw,' Grand smiled rigidly, telling

himself firmly that the woman really would have to go. 'Isaac, are you thirsty?'

'Parched, guv'nor,' the boy said.

'Come with me.'

It was cool in the parlour of the Coal Hole, and the smells of the barrels and the river almost cancelled each other out. Isaac sat with a pewter tankard in front of him, proud that Mr Grand should think him worthy of a pint. Thomas Barnardo, had he been watching, needn't have worried: Isaac's pint had more water in it than the Thames. Which is why Grand was drinking brandy.

'Now,' he said, 'tell me again, from the beginning, why you've come so far,' he jerked his head towards Alsatia and the wide world beyond, 'and risked so much, to come see me.'

'Well,' Isaac looked at the pint, as though the froth would focus his mind, 'like I said, the place was done over.'

'Gads Hill Place?'

'Not the house; just the chalet.'

'When was this?'

'Two days ago. Well, nights.'

'Wednesday.'

'That's right. I got up as usual. Half past six.'

'And?'

'I checked the stables, sponged Dinky's nostrils, gave him his feed.'

Grand supposed that Dinky was the pony and so said nothing.

'I was just on my way to the house to get Georgy's . . . Miss Hogarth's orders for the day and I seen it.'

'What?'

'The chalet door was open.'

'Forced?'

'Yeah. There was glass all over the step and the carpet.'

'What did you do?'

'I went in.'

'And?' This was like pulling teeth.

'The whole room was turned over – cushions ripped, books upended. Mr D's desks pulled open.'

'Anything taken?'

'I don't know,' Isaac shrugged. 'You'd have to ask Miss Hogarth.'

'What happened next?'

'I went to the house. Cook was in the kitchen and I told her.'

'What did she do?'

'Went up to Miss Hogarth and told her.'

'What did *she* do?'

'Come down, told me to stand up straight and close me mouth, like she always does, then went with me to the chalet.'

'Did she send for the police?'

'No, Mr Grand, that was what was so peculiar and why I come here. I offered to saddle Dinky and ride to Rochester but she said no. She said there'd been enough trouble in the Dickens household and she didn't want no more. I helped her put the place straight. Then Mr Brunt come and mended the glass and the lock.'

'You say the glass was smashed?'

'Yes sir. Like crystal, it was.'

'And the chalet turned over?'

'That's right.'

'That would have made a fair amount of noise, Isaac,' Grand said. 'Where do you sleep?'

'At the back, sir, over by the stables.'

'Not in the house itself?'

'Only in the winter, sir, when it's brass monkeys.'

Grand had no idea what time of year that was, so he let it go. 'And it goes without saying, I suppose, that you heard nothing.'

'Not a thing, sir,' Isaac said. 'There was a smell, though.'

'A smell? What, like burning? A pipe, something like that.' It seemed unlikely that a burglar would stop to smoke, but stranger things had happened.

'No, sir, nothing like that. In the chalet, when I first went in, I smelled it. Mr Brunt, he smelled it too. Attar of roses, he said. And he should know.'

'Attar of roses, James.' Grand poured them both a brandy. 'Mean anything to you?'

'Not a lot.' Batchelor raised his glass in a silent toast. 'Perhaps burglars down in Kent are a rather strange lot these days. Or am

I letting the Clinton case get to me? Tell me, why did Isaac come to you?'

Grand shrugged.

Batchelor mulled it over. Grand wasn't most people's idea of a father figure. But in the various interviews they had both had down at Gads Hill Place, there had been no talk of a *Mr* Armitage. Perhaps Isaac was an orphan of the storm looking for someone to rely on; now that Dickens was dead, he was an orphan, pure and simple. It was amazing, taken by and large, that he wasn't known throughout the household as David Copperfield or Oliver Twist, Richard Carstone or Philip Pirrip. Isaac Armitage was perhaps a name Dickens was saving for later. 'Maybe he feels something's not right,' he said. 'If you were housekeeper to the most famous writer in the country and said writer's place is burglarized, wouldn't you be round hotfoot to the nearest law? More, wouldn't you insist Scotland Yard was called in?'

Batchelor nodded. 'Our friend Miss Hogarth is playing her cards too close to her chest, Matthew,' he said. 'Time you did something about that.'

'I can't keep going back to Gads Hill Place,' Grand complained. 'She wasn't exactly welcoming at first last time. I think the next time she will turn the dogs on me.'

'I didn't notice any dogs,' Batchelor said.

'Figure of speech. There's something fishy going on down there, though, and we need to find out what it is. But by a more roundabout route. That's what we need.'

'Sala?'

'Perhaps not the most brilliant idea you have had, James,' Grand observed. 'Since Sala is paying *us* to investigate, asking him questions as to what might be going on may prove to be counterproductive. He might ask for his money back; and I don't know about you, but the cigar and brandy lifestyle is one I could easily come to like.'

'I didn't mean *interrogate* the man,' Batchelor said, miffed. 'I mean, get some more names from him. We've tried Ouvry and Dolby and I can't say they were very useful. We've still got Forster to go, but he's not proving to be an easy man to catch.'

'Might Chapman and Hall be a way in there? I know he doesn't work for them per se, but they might know where he is at any given time. He can't just have had Dickens as a client, surely?' Grand wasn't really sure what an agent actually *did*. He had seen them at work at his father's business, but it always seemed to involve a piece of paper, a hurried walk and a hunted expression; what came of such behaviour, he could never ascertain.

'I should think that he did,' Batchelor said. 'Why would he need another? Dickens far outsold any other ten writers put together; I should think that ten per cent of that would be very nice indeed.'

'Hmm. True. Perhaps Sala could tell us a few others to approach. I've always had a bit of a hankering to meet Ouida, if I'm honest.' Grand was ever a man with a surprise up his sleeve.

'Shall we ask him for a longer list, then? We don't have to tell him we're down a blind alley. We can just say we leave . . .'

'No stone unturned. James, I think you might be able to pull that one off.' Grand sipped his brandy and flipped the lid of the humidor. 'Off you trot then. Look. I can't go; I'm just lighting a cigar.'

EIGHT

'Well,' he said, stroking her hair as she lay beside him, 'if there was nothing at the chalet at Gads Hill, I don't know where else to look.' He pushed himself upright so that he was looking down at her. 'You *sure* you turned that joint over, Beulah? I mean, you *really* scoured it?'

'It's what I do best, Henry,' she yelled at him, stung by the implications. 'I say, it's what I do best.'

'The offices it is, then.' Henry Morford sank back down again. 'You know, this is proving more difficult than I expected.'

'The offices'd be a challenge, Henry,' Beulah purred, snuggling as much of herself as possible under his arm. 'You know, I kinda miss the old days.'

He laughed. 'I knew I did the right thing getting you out of Mount Pleasant, Beulah. Can't let a talent like yours languish behind prison bars.'

He hadn't been quite sure what to expect. The Langham Hotel was in Regent Street – huge, opulent and almost new. He had presented his card at the front desk, the same one he had used at the Rag, and he waited. It was deliciously cool in the marble-columned foyer and a bellhop, or whatever they called them in this country, crisp in white gloves and a shell jacket, showed him to the third floor.

The first room was conventional enough, although a *little* mauve for his personal taste, but the second took him by surprise. He was standing in a lady's boudoir, the velvet curtains drawn against the glare of the sun, the brasswork and the chandeliers glittering with the flames of what seemed like a thousand candles. He was suddenly aware that the bellhop was standing to attention, saluting as only the British did. The boy turned on his heel sharply and was gone.

'He's coming on like a proper little soldier,' a voice like a bow saw came from the huge four-poster bed in front of him, and from the pillows and the floral eiderdown, a little woman lifted her head to look at him. She had an old-fashioned quill pen in her hand and was scratching it over the surface of lilac-coloured paper. 'So, you're Captain Grand,' she said.

'You've heard of me?' Grand had to admit he was a little unnerved by this.

'Mama!' A voice like a knife screeched from the anteroom to Grand's left. 'How often must I tell you?'

'I thought he was a guardsman, dear.' The old girl's wrinkles were more clearly on display thanks to the daylight from the other room. 'It's not fair that *you* should have all the fun.'

'Mama,' the daughter scolded. 'What *must* Captain Grand think of us? Now, off you toddle and get yourself a noggin. I'm sure Captain Grand will tell you that the sun is well and truly over the yardarm.'

'Young man,' the old girl frowned, horrified. 'I don't know the form in whatever country you are from, but here, when a lady alights from her bed, a gentleman turns his back.'

'Oh, sorry.' Grand obliged.

There was much wheezing and rustling of clothes, and a little apparition in white passed the detective, turned to give him a withering stare and disappeared out of the door and down the stairs.

'Now, Captain. Where were we?'

Grand turned back to find the daughter in exactly the same pose that the mother had been in, except that she took one look at the top lilac sheet, screwed it up and threw it into an enormous waste-paper basket.

'You *are* Miss Maria Ramé?' He thought he ought to check. The woman in the bed was a little younger than he was, but not by much. She had poppy eyes, not much of a chin and a nose that not even a mother could love, but she carried them all with such panache that it scarcely registered.

'Call me Ouida,' she purred. 'Everybody does. So,' she waved his calling card in the air, 'Third Cavalry of the Potomac, eh? I believe you're my first. I confess I am a *little* disappointed not to see you in your regimentals. I find those little kepis you fellows wear absolutely darling.'

'I have kept the red tie, Madam.' He flicked it, smiling.

'Very becoming. Very.' She scribbled something down with her quill. 'Come and sit beside me.' She patted the covers.

'Well, I . . .'

'Oh, come, Captain Grand,' she laughed. 'This is 1870. Ladies wear trousers riding in the Row these days, and we've even got women doctors now; well, one, to be precise, but I don't doubt more will follow. I'm not a feminist – *vive la différence*, as my dear old papa used to say, I expect; but I do insist on my little pleasures.'

'But, your mother . . .'

'Won't be back for hours. Her little noggins tend to drag on for longer these days. Someone will find her and wheel her back in time for dinner.' She patted the bed again and, this time, Grand sat on it.

'Actually,' she confided, putting the quill away, 'I have a little confession to make.'

'Oh?'

'The mother–daughter routine is one that Mama and I usually use when a strange man comes to see me, even when he's a Grenadier or a Coldstreamer. As I said, I've never had a Red Tie Boy before; you can't be too careful.'

'I see.'

'In short, if I don't like the look of the man, I signal to Mama who gives him short shrift. If he has never seen me, he will accept that the legend that is Ouida is pushing sixty with a face like semolina and he will leave. It rarely fails.'

'And if it does?' Grand asked.

Ouida smiled. 'Then I engage in a little old-fashioned competition. Drinky?'

From nowhere, the woman had produced a bottle and two glasses.

'It is a *little* early for me,' Grand said.

'Nonsense! I can't write a word without a couple of slugs. Oh, sorry, it's gin, not Red Eye. Is that all right?'

'Fine,' Grand laughed and held the glasses while she poured.

She put the stopper back and clinked her crystal with his. 'Got any cigars, Captain?' she asked. 'I've run out.'

'Sorry,' Grand lied. 'They're in my other coat.' Bad enough that he was swilling gin in a lady's bedroom in the middle of the day, but he drew the line at smoking. Anyway, there were so many candles in the room, it only added to the fire risk.

'Now,' she said, resting her head back on the propped pillows, 'I can understand a colonial wanting to discuss literature with one of the finest exponents of the novelist's art living today, but something tells me you're here for an altogether darker reason.' She pulled a ribbon on her housecoat and a little more flesh crept into view. 'Am I wrong?'

'I too have a little confession to make,' he told her.

'Have you?' she purred, fluttering her eyelashes. 'How simply delicious.'

'*This* is the card I meant to show you.' He produced it and she read it, eyes widening.

She clasped her hands. 'This is too, too exciting,' she said, 'I don't believe I've met an enquiry agent before. What are you enquiring into? A juicy divorce, perhaps? Old Bertie's got himself in the doo-dah with that wretched Mordaunt woman. *And* she's incontinent, you know. No, no,' she shut her eyes, clicking fingers and thumbs in all directions. 'I've got it. White slavery. I've a copy of *The Lustful Turk* somewhere – well thumbed, I assure you.'

'Neither of those things, I'm afraid,' Grand said. 'I'm looking into the death of Charles Dickens.'

'Dear Charles?' Ouida frowned. 'A stroke, surely.'

'Surely not,' Grand said. 'Our enquiries are taking us in another direction entirely.'

'Our?'

'Batchelor.' He pointed to the card. 'My associate.'

'Oh, yes, of course. But,' she was sitting up, frowning, her gin momentarily forgotten. 'Charles? Are you implying that he was murdered?'

Grand nodded. 'Tell me . . . Ouida . . .' he said, 'did you go to the funeral?'

'Lord, no.' She remembered her gin and took a hearty swig. 'No, to be honest, I didn't know Charles all that well. We both wrote for *Bentley's Miscellany*, of course, although in his case rather a long time ago.'

'Your name was given to me by Mr John Forster,' Grand lied. 'He thought you might be able to help.'

'Did he?' Ouida frowned. 'I really can't imagine why.'

'What about Wilkie Collins?' Grand asked.

A strange look came into Ouida's eye. 'Do you like dogs, Captain Grand?'

'I can take them or leave them alone,' Grand shrugged.

'No, no,' she said. 'You must *take* them. I am currently working on an opus – and if I say so myself, it is quite superb – called *Tuck*.'

'Uh-huh.' Grand had already lost the thread of this conversation.

'Tuck is a Maltese terrier, delightful creature. I am looking at society through his eyes.'

'Good for you.' It seemed as if it might be Grand's turn to speak and it was all he could come up with at short notice.

'The point I am making is this.' She leaned forward, beaming, confidential. 'I read a chapter to Wilkie Collins only last week. He was furious.'

'He was?'

'Jealous, you see.' She patted the side of her nose. 'The little green eye.'

'I don't see . . .'

'Wilkie Collins is a bitter, jealous man, Captain. He writes crime fiction. And, strictly between you and me, he's not quite normal.'

'But I thought he and Dickens were friends.'

'Writers have no friends, Captain Grand,' Ouida said, looking into the middle distance, her chin lifted and her lip quivering with emotion. 'We are a breed apart.'

There was a rap at the door.

'Oh, bugger,' she said, dropping her suffering artist look and draining her glass. 'That's Mandeville. I'd forgotten all about him. Be a dear and let him in, would you? He'll probably have cigars on his person.'

Grand obliged and a tall guardsman in scarlet stood there, looking less than enchanted to find a handsome young man in Ouida's rooms.

'Mandeville, darling,' she cooed. 'This is Captain Grand of the Army of the Potomac. You two will have so much in common.'

'Another time, Ouida,' Grand smiled back at her. 'You've been very helpful.'

'Another time, indeed, Captain,' she called. 'You know where I am.' She waved the card again. 'And I know where you are.'

Grand looked at the polished buttons on Mandeville's tunic. 'Pretty,' he said, flicking one. 'So, what are you? Grenadier or Coldstream?'

'Well, really!' Mandeville's monocle plopped out of his eye socket and he swept into the room.

'Got a cigar, Manders, old thing?' Grand heard Ouida say as he closed the door. 'I'm desperate.'

Batchelor had been amazed that Grand had even heard of Ouida, let alone that he was keen to meet her; he had dipped into some of her works and had found them salacious enough, but his authorial eye had not been able to overlook some of her more overblown phrases and he had put her aside. Wilkie Collins, now: there was a writer! *The Moonstone* was a permanent fixture on Batchelor's nightstand and, although he knew perfectly well who had done the deed, it was nevertheless always a thrill to read how Sergeant Cuff had come to the denouement. He decided to walk to Blandford Square. It was a perfect morning, not quite as stifling as the previous week or so, and he had plenty of time before his appointment with the great man; a detour through a park or two would be pleasant and would also give him time to assemble a few sparkling lines of wit and repartee with which to stun the author. Because, who knew? Being an enquiry agent was all very fine and well, but not a job for a grown-up, in Batchelor's opinion, and he was, after all, still working on the Great British Novel.

The door of Collins's house was opened by a rather unexpectedly countrified woman, tall and ruddy, with curls escaping from under her cap. She was also clearly in a very interesting condition, her dress straining across her breasts and stomach. She held one hand under her swollen belly and leaned on the doorjamb.

Despite her obvious discomfort, she was welcoming and smiling. 'You'll be Mr Batchelor,' she told him. 'Come along through into the study. Wilkie is expecting you.'

Batchelor was a little surprised by several things but was too polite to let it show. Firstly, in his admittedly limited experience of the moneyed classes, it was surely unusual to employ a maid or housekeeper in quite such an advanced state of pregnancy. Even thinking the word made him blush; having her taut belly brush against him as she showed him through the hall brought him close to collapse. Secondly, calling one's employer by his given name – no, by his nickname – seemed unusual even in this bohemian household. He made a mental note that when he was a writer himself, he would make sure that his staff were all like this jolly woman, bursting with health and life.

She pushed open a door without knocking and stuck her head through. 'Wilkie? It's Mr Batchelor. Shall he come in?'

'Send him through, Martha, send him through,' a voice called. 'And then go and rest. How many times must you be told?'

Laughing, she pushed the door wide for Batchelor to go in. 'He tells me, Mr Batchelor,' she said, 'but then he doesn't look after Marian nor yet plan his menus. Men!' And with that, she gave Batchelor a friendly slap on the back that sent him flying into the room.

Collins had got up from behind his desk and come round to welcome his guest. He was just as odd-looking as the newspapers described him, with his huge head, thick spectacles and his tiny hands and feet. Batchelor was reminded of nothing so much as a drawing by Edward Lear, and a limerick started to form in his head, quickly damped down. He was here on serious business, after all!

'Mr Batchelor,' the writer said. 'Excuse Martha, won't you? She should be resting in her condition, but it is useless to try and make her lie down.' A twinkle came into his eye, magnified by the enormous thickness of the lenses. 'Although of course,' and he nudged Batchelor in the ribs, 'it's lying down that got her in that condition in the first place.' A reminiscent leer took over his expression for a moment and Batchelor's eyebrows rose. 'These beef-fed country girls, Mr Batchelor . . . are you . . . umm . . . a married man, at all?'

'No.' Batchelor didn't know why, but he sounded as though he were apologizing.

'A housekeeper, something of that nature?'

This time, Batchelor repudiated the idea with some vigour, as an image of Mrs Rackstraw rose in front of him. 'No. Neither wife nor housekeeper,' he said.

'Oh?' Collins's eyes were wide. 'You keep someone tucked up in a nice little apartment, then, do you? Duke Street, somewhere like that?' He leaned forward and dropped his voice. 'Probably the best plan, a man of your years. Keeping your options open, hey?'

Batchelor wasn't sure how the conversation had taken this turn.

'Or . . .' and now Collins looked dubious, 'of course it may be you prefer . . . other outlets.'

'No.' Batchelor laid his cards on the table. 'I don't . . . indulge, Mr Collins. I am saving myself for the right woman.'

'My word!' Collins's glasses fell right off his nose with the shock and it took several minutes to disentangle them from his beard where they had landed. 'That's not something one hears much nowadays. I congratulate you, my boy, and wish you the best of luck and hope she comes along soon. Solitary vices can send you blind, you know.' He turned to Batchelor, his lenses so thick that the weight of them creased his nose. 'Or, at the very least, extremely short-sighted.' He fumbled his way around back to his seat and faced Batchelor across the expanse of paper-strewn desk. 'However, as usual I have taken up too much of your valuable time with my meanderings. What was your business with me this morning?'

Batchelor reached into his pocket for his card, but realized before he even handed it over that Collins wouldn't be able to see the small print. 'My partner and I are enquiry agents and have been engaged by a third party to investigate what we believe to be the murder of Charles Dickens.'

'Murder? Poor old Charles? No, a stroke, surely.'

This was becoming a familiar refrain. 'That is the official reason,' Batchelor said, 'but after exhaustive investigations, we believe that he was in fact poisoned.'

'By whom?' Collins was intrigued. There might be a new plot line here.

'Well, that is what we are still trying to find out,' Batchelor admitted. 'There are certain points about his death that need to be cleared up but, for now, we are trying to find out more about his . . . umm . . . private life.'

'Dearie me,' Collins said, with a smile. 'For an enquiry agent, you are a very prim little miss, aren't you? Are you sure you don't . . . but, never mind that. Charles's private life, eh? I suppose you want to ask me if he had taken that absolute cracker Georgy as his mistress, hmm? Or whether he hunted further afield?'

Batchelor was pleased this was finally proving to be so easy and nodded.

'I suppose you thought you could ask me because I am well known for my rather unconventional views on women and marriage.' The writer looked at Batchelor with a wry smile. 'It was the talk of the town when Caroline left me for the plumber, but she'll be back, she'll be back . . .' A distant look came into the writer's eye then he shook himself. 'Where was I?'

'Marriage. Caroline. Plumber.'

'Thank you. Very succinct. Well, you chose well, my boy. You'll get no mealy-mouthing from me, I can assure you. No, it's all healthy and natural as air. But I'm surprised you had to seek me out. I thought everyone knew about him and Nell Ternan. Been going on a good while, that has. She gave up the stage for him; not that she was much of an actress, I didn't think. But what do I know? I'm just a humble hack writer.' He bowed his head modestly and Batchelor came in on cue.

'Mr Collins,' he gushed, 'who can forget *The Frozen Deep*?'

'Almost everyone, as a matter of fact. Except John Forster, of course – he claws in the royalties for Charles and me wherever it is put on by some poor travelling repertory company. But that was kind, my dear boy. Kind.'

'So . . .' Batchelor felt he was on the cusp of something. 'Miss Ternan?'

'You hadn't heard her name? Come now, I feel very disloyal now. All of Charles's friends had kept his secret? How . . . charming of them. No, Nell is common knowledge if you know where to ask.'

Batchelor remembered the groom, Butler. He was clearly speaking of her when he called her no better than she should be. 'Does she live in Nunhead, by any chance?'

'There you are, you see! You *did* know all along. You were trying to make a fool out of a poor old writer!'

'No, no, not at all.' The short story burning a hole in Batchelor's inside pocket had to be considered. How could he give it to the

writer for his consideration if they parted brass rags? 'I had heard
a rumour from a servant at Gads Hill, that's all. We didn't have
a name.'

'It's not likely to be the only one, I fear. Poor Charles was a
little susceptible when it came to the ladies.'

'Does the name Stella mean anything to you?' Batchelor just
needed to tidy up that final point.

Collins roared with laughter, taking off his glasses and wiping
his eyes. 'Oh, Mr Batchelor,' he said. 'You have cheered a poor
old writer up today and no mistake. Yes, I know Stella. The latest
woman in Charles's life. But, as you are an enquiry agent, I must
leave you something to enquire about. And good luck – I think
you will find the end of the road rather . . .' and he spluttered
with more laughter, 'shall we say, unexpected.'

There were clearly no more revelations to come, so Batchelor
got up from his seat. 'Thank you so much, Mr Collins,' he said.

'The pleasure has been all mine, dear boy, I can assure you.
Please, take this,' and Collins picked up a book from a side table
and wrote in it with a flourish. 'My latest. *Man and Wife*, by an
amusing serendipity.'

Batchelor was overwhelmed. 'Mr Collins, I am overwhelmed,'
he said.

'Of course you are,' Collins replied, already pulling a clean
sheet of paper towards him. A writer's work is never done. 'Can
you see yourself out? Martha needs her rest.'

'Of course,' Batchelor said, almost bowing himself out of the
room. With Dickens dead, it could be said that Collins now wore
the crown.

'Oh, by the way.' The author's voice echoed after Batchelor
as he crossed the hall. 'Don't forget to leave the short story on
the pile near the door. I'll get round to it sooner or later, you
may be sure. Goodbye.'

NINE

There was no doubt about it; Dolly Williamson was becoming something of a nuisance. Not that the great detective pounded the pavements himself – he had people for that, dodgy-looking men in plain clothes who trailed Grand and Batchelor or both in whatever combination they left the Strand. True, the enquiry agents were able to lose them sooner or later, but that took time and ingenuity that could better be spent in tracking down Charles Dickens's killer.

The *really* annoying thing was that Williamson had told them that he too was looking into Dickens's death. How far had he got, they wondered. What were his lines of enquiry? Or was Williamson's only plan to send his flatfeet after them in the hope that they would solve the case and the Yard could take the credit?

No, they had to shake off Williamson's shadows. And how do you rid yourself of a nasty policeman? You go and see a nice one.

Matthew Grand had still not really worked out how London was joined together. He knew lots of bits of it, but not necessarily how it all dovetailed together; it was walking around in London when he most felt that he was a stranger in a strange land; this was a foreign country where they happened to speak English. For this reason, he was often the half of the partnership who dove off the levy that was London into the deep water that was what he always called 'The Rest'; the other towns and cities that filled Batchelor's home country. Even Batchelor had had to get the atlas out to find Alresford, where ex-Inspector Dick Tanner was keeping his hostelry. Tanner's rheumatism had beaten him in the end, and he had taken the route of so many policemen: retirement to run a pub; although his sounded rather a cut above, being the Swan Hotel. It turned out that Alresford was just outside Winchester, connected to it by rail. Batchelor had informed Grand that Winchester was in that direction – a wave of the arm implied that it might easily be to the west; so, accordingly, Grand had made his way to Waterloo. For once, he could do it on foot – even Grand could manage getting around London when all he had to do was walk in a straight line. He went east first, losing his copper shadow before doubling back.

Grand kept a wary eye out for vicars as he took his seat on the train. He had no idea what to expect when he reached his destination, reputedly one of the most beautiful parts of England; though, unlike its American namesake, they made no guns there. Grand had a picture in his head of soaring countryside, the dappling water of the river and a cathedral not far away. He had packed a small valise, in case he should be pressed to stay the night. London was like no other city he had ever known, and he loved it almost like a native, but sometimes he just needed to breathe air that hadn't gone through three million other pairs of lungs before his own.

As he headed further west, he began to sit up and take notice. There were some towns, certainly, bustling stations with market produce piled in teetering ziggurats of lettuce; hens; new potatoes spilling from their burlap sacks. The smell of the countryside came in through the open window and soon, across to his left, he saw the soaring tower of Winchester cathedral, growing as something alive out of the watercress beds of the river. He gathered his belongings around him and sat, excited, on the edge of his seat. He realized all at once how much he needed a holiday; how much he missed his home.

The train to Alresford was steaming quietly to itself in the station when the London train pulled in. A guard screamed in Grand's ear that the train now standing on Platform Two was the . . . something or other to somewhere. It seemed to the American that there was yet another language in this country, along with the ones used by newspaper vendors and chestnut sellers, and it was the most impenetrable of them all – and yet, surely, the most important to be clear and comprehensible to all. He turned to a woman, laden with baskets.

'Ma'am, could you tell me if this train goes to Alresford?'

'Where, my lovely?'

Grand made his voice louder by a notch. 'All-Res-Ford,' he enunciated clearly.

'Oh,' she said, with one foot on the step, 'Orlsfud, you must mean. Yes, my lovely, it's going there. *I*'m going there! I've been marketing, as you can see.' She handed Grand some baskets absentmindedly and used her free hand to haul herself aboard. 'Come on, my lovely. Upsidaisy or you'll miss the train.'

Grand handed her her baskets and followed her into the carriage. It seemed full of women and baskets and screams of delight. 'Ladies.' He tipped his hat.

'Oh, Betty Smithers, you'm a dark horse,' one of them said, poking the woman in the ribs, or where her ribs may once have been, covered as they now were by a comfortable cushion.

'Oh, you leave me be,' she replied, smugly. 'This young gentleman just axed me about the train. He'm going to Orlsfud.'

More shrieks greeted this information. One of the other women leaned forward. 'Who you visiting, my lovely?'

'Richard Tanner,' Grand said. There was clearly no point in trying subterfuge in this carriage.

'The new landlord at the Swan?'

'You be staying?' One of the women had noticed his grip.

'Well,' Grand said, squashing down into a seat between two ample shoppers, 'I may stay overnight, if he'll have me. He's an old friend, from London.'

'Oh, my lovely,' the woman on his left said, chucking him under the chin. 'You'm not old enough to have old friends!' The other women shrieked with laughter again and Grand smiled a desperate smile.

'I've known him since I came to England, more or less,' he explained. Then, before the questions could begin, he gave them a quick potted history of his life thus far, which the women punctuated with clucks and tuts as appropriate. West Point was easy enough and he would gloss over the battlefield casualties as too grim a subject for ladies.

Before he had reached much further than Bull Run, the train began to slow in a series of jerks and the women began to gather their parcels. Grand's first acquaintance passed him half her baskets as though to the manner born, and got down on to the platform with the help of the guard. She looked back at Grand, who was struggling down by himself. 'Are you all right there, my lovely? No, don't bother to put those down, I'm on the way to the Swan,

I can show you.' And she swept out of the station, with Grand staggering under his load, as though she owned the town.

The others watched her go, envy in their eyes. 'That Betty Smithers,' one of them muttered, 'she's never been no better nor she should be.' And with nods of agreement, the shoppers separated to their homes, looking back at Grand, the best-looking man Alresford had seen for many a long year.

'There you are, my lovely,' the woman said, stopping outside a pretty little cottage set back from the road in a rose-filled garden. 'There's the Swan, just down the road, there. Thank you for carrying my bags. It's getting a bit much for me, these days, but needs must. I hope you find Mr Tanner well.'

'Why don't you come and take a drink with us, later?' Grand asked, flexing his fingers to get some life back into them.

'Oh, you and your London ways!' she shrieked, but was smiling nevertheless. 'Me, a respectable widow, drinking with two men. I would never live it down. No, you go and have a nice stop with your friend, my dear. And thank you for your help.'

Grand was smiling as he walked down the dusty lane to the Swan Hotel. He felt as though he had travelled to another country, not just seventy miles from Waterloo. Even if Tanner couldn't help them, it would still have been a worthwhile journey, just to get the stink of the Thames out of his nostrils.

The Commissioner of Lunacy was hard at work when the maid showed James Batchelor into his study. The sun streamed in through the open casement and the noises of Kensington wafted with it. John Forster was in his late fifties, judging by his appearance, thick set and with piercing dark eyes. His dundrearies were magnificent, resting on his lapels, and the quiff of hair at the front disguised to all intents and purposes his incipient middle-aged baldness.

'An enquiry agent?' Forster read the card lying on his desk. 'Well, I suppose you could call me a sort of literary agent. What can I do for you, Mr . . .?'

'Batchelor,' Batchelor said and took the proffered chair. 'My colleague Grand and I have been commissioned to look into the death of the late Charles Dickens, Mr Forster. I understand that you knew him better than anyone.'

'Indeed I did.' Forster put his pen down. 'I am committing it all to paper as we speak.' He waved his hand over the sheaves of manuscript on his desk. 'The Biography.'

Batchelor smiled, wondering how far George Sala had got with his.

'I loved that man, Mr Batchelor.' Forster trumpeted into a handkerchief. 'I'm not embarrassed to admit it. A literary agent is only an agent, but a friend is a friend for life.' He rather liked the sound of that, snatched up his pen again and wrote it down. 'But,' he frowned, 'I'm confused. Charles died of a stroke, surely.'

'Perhaps not,' Batchelor said, having lost count of the times he had heard that. 'We have reason to believe that poison may have been involved.'

Forster sat back in his chair, his eyes wide. 'Dear God!' he muttered.

'You were called,' Batchelor said, 'on the day he died?'

'To Gads Hill, yes. I got there too late, I fear. He was lying on the sofa, looking at peace with himself and the world. I kissed his forehead, the only farewell I could think of.'

'And you went to the funeral?'

'Of course,' Forster sniffed. 'A small circle of family and friends.'

'And no Mrs Dickens?'

'Catherine? Lord, no. That would have been difficult. One of the most awkward chapters I shall have to write, I expect. I next saw Charles, before the funeral, I mean, in his coffin. The undertakers had put this ridiculous ribbon, scarf thing under his chin. Looked just like Marley's ghost, I thought. Perhaps it was some sort of backhanded compliment, but I didn't approve.'

'Since you knew him so well, Mr Forster,' Batchelor went for the jugular, 'can you think of anyone who would want to see him dead?'

Forster exploded with laughter. 'Trollope,' he said. 'Wilkie Collins. Elizabeth Gaskell. That dreadful Ouida woman. If he weren't dead himself, I'd have to add Thackeray to the list.'

'But, surely, they are – or were – his friends?'

Forster looked at the detective's face from under his beetling brows. 'Do writers have friends, Mr Batchelor? Charles and myself apart, I can't think of any. The man was seriously wealthy,

Mr Batchelor, partly through his own brilliance, partly through my, I won't deny it, bullying of publishers. Well, they are tradesmen, after all. But, surely, if Charles were poisoned, wouldn't it have to be someone in the household? Someone with access to Charles and his comestibles?'

'In theory, yes,' Batchelor said, 'but I understand that Gads Hill was a mecca for anybody who had ever read any Dickens. The world and his wife often turned up.'

'That's true, they did. And of course, he had other premises. Broadstairs. His offices in Wellington Street; the place he rented near Marble Arch; Win . . .' and his voice tailed away.

'Win?' Batchelor took it up.

'Win or lose, Mr Batchelor, I'm intrigued to know for whom you are working.'

'Sorry, Mr Forster,' Batchelor said. 'Client confidentiality.'

'Of course, of course. I'm just trying to think. Charles was a bit of an imbiber, to tell you the truth. Brandy, sherry. Then again, he did love his egg and anchovy rolls. You know, I suppose, about the laudanum? That's another chapter I'll have to be careful about. It was his lameness, you see. In his heyday, Charles thought nothing of twelve-mile hikes, at a steady four miles an hour – I'm amazed he had time for that, bearing in mind his astonishing output. Said it was while walking he got his best ideas. *Drood* was getting him down, though. He told me it wasn't going well. I don't suppose the opium helped.'

'The laudanum?' Batchelor checked.

'No, no, that was just for daily fitness. No, Charles would sneak off to Bluegate Fields now and then to smoke the stuff. Said it did him the world of good, but I'm not sure. You don't suppose poor Charles could have poisoned himself, do you? By accident, I mean?'

But James Batchelor didn't answer. Because James Batchelor had gone.

The Swan Hotel seemed to sleep in the dusty sun, standing wrapped in its midday silence at the edge of the road. The walls were whitewashed and cast back the glare so that Grand had to shield his eyes to look at the name above the door. 'Richard Tanner, prop.,' it said, 'licensed to sell intoxicating liquor.' Grand

smiled; this was all rather a long way from feeling villains'
collars in Shadwell. He pushed the door and went in and was
immediately struck blind, or as near as made no difference. After
the glare outside, the inside was like being down a mine. Grand
could see a chink of light in the distance, which seemed to sparkle
and quiver. But everything between him and it – and it was even
difficult to judge how far that might be – was a mystery.

He took a tentative step forward and felt uneven slabs under
his feet.

'Oh!' A voice came from within the quivering light. 'Be careful,
young sir. The floor's uneven and we don't want you going a
purler.'

Grand stopped in his tracks. He had no idea what a purler
might or might not be, but it was clearly something to avoid if
possible.

A girl came out of the light and crossed the gloom towards
Grand. 'I keep telling Mr Tanner we must put the lights up on
days like this. That white wall outside, it makes folks as blind
as bats in here. Wait there a minute, sir, and your eyes will
accustom.'

Grand raised his hat. 'Thank you for the warning, ma'am,' he
said, laying the accent on a bit thick. It worked with women of
all ages, but most of all on those under twenty, which this one
clearly was, though only by a little. She was pretty and buxom
and spilling out over her bodice, in best barmaidly tradition.

'You're not from round here,' she told him. 'I expect you're
here for Mr Tanner.'

'I am, yes, but . . .'

'Oh,' she said, flapping at him with a damp tea towel she wore
over her shoulder like a stole, 'Mr Tanner gets all sorts coming
to see him. He was famous, so they say. When he was a policeman,
I mean.'

A familiar voice sounded from a doorway in a corner which
was still dark, despite the fact that Grand's eyes were fully
acclimatized now to the gloom. 'I'm still a policeman, Molly,'
Tanner said. 'Once a policeman, always a policeman. Is that
Mr Grand I see?'

Grand stepped forward. 'It is, Inspector Tanner. How are you?'

'Just mister now, please. Just plain mister.'

'What about once a policeman, always a policeman?' Grand laughed.

'Oh, that's just for the visitors,' Tanner explained, coming forward to shake Grand's hand. 'They like to think they're brushing shoulders with a bit of genuine East End thuggery when they come to see me. Like to think they're shaking the same hand that felt the collar of Muller the Railway Murderer, back in the day. But I'm a landlord now, am I not, Molly?'

She smiled up at him. 'He is, Mr . . . Grand, is it? And the best landlord in Alresford.'

'I'm sure he is,' Grand agreed politely.

'Get along with you, Moll,' Tanner said, slapping her backside in a casual manner. 'She's having a joke with us, Mr Grand. There is only the George in Alresford apart from my Swan, and nobody goes there unless they want to end up with a nice attack of the flux. It's said they don't wash the glasses there, just leave them out in the rain. Our Moll, here, she's always polishing ours, to make sure they're clean as a bosun's whistle. Speaking of which, would you like to wet your whistle, Mr Grand? It's a dry old day out there.'

Grand was delighted to find his old friend in such a good humour. He and Batchelor had worried for the man when they heard he had retired and that he was unwell. Try as they might, they couldn't imagine him in any other setting than London. And yet, here he was, a landlord to his fingertips. 'I would love a drink,' Grand admitted. 'The journey wasn't long but it was hot.' He amused Tanner, while Molly poured their beer, with the story of the shopping women of Alresford. The girl laughed. 'You'll be the talk of the town by nightfall,' she told him, 'if you aren't already. Not much happens around here.'

'You have custom, though?' Grand asked, looking around. Although it was as clean as a new pin, there wasn't a soul in the place.

'Evenings, evenings are our busy time,' Tanner said. 'We even have people coming in their carriages, out from Winchester. It's a pleasant drive and they can stroll along the river before they come for a bite to eat and a drink before setting off back home. It's quite the thing, isn't it, Moll?'

'Mr Tanner has made this place lovely,' the girl said. 'It was a dirty hole before he took it over.' She beamed at him and pushed the drinks across the bar. 'I'll leave you two to talk. I've got a pile of potatoes in the scullery I need to get ready.' And dropping a bob and flashing a dimple, she was gone.

Tanner took a deep drink from his beer, holding it up to the light like a connoisseur. 'She's a good girl, is Moll,' he said.

'And quite a draw in her own right, I would imagine,' Grand said, smiling.

'We do get a lot of the young bloods in,' Tanner agreed. 'The younger masters from along at the school, they do like to see if they can catch a glimpse of her ankle. But I don't think you've come all this way just to see what kind of a barmaid I've managed to find for myself, Mr Grand.'

'As always, there's no fooling you, Mr Tanner,' Grand agreed. 'James and I . . .'

'How is Mr Batchelor? Well, I hope.'

'James is well. He is currently . . . pursuing our enquiries.'

'That was my next question, but now I don't need to ask – your business is flourishing, I can see.'

'It would flourish even more if it weren't for one of your erstwhile colleagues.'

'Not that idiot Field!' Tanner said, almost spilling his drink. 'I wondered when your paths would cross.'

'We have met him, yes, but he isn't the reason I'm here. While we're on the subject, though, do tell me what you know about him. He does a lot of skulking in shrubberies and that seems to be about it.'

'Charlie Field is an idiot, pure and simple. I expect he's given you the chat about being a professional and how that makes all the difference.'

'Umm . . . yes, he has, as a matter of fact. But then, so has—'

'Take no notice. He's had more official warnings than I've had hot dinners. Don't tell him I said so, but he couldn't catch a cold. Never could. But, he's not the reason for your visit, you say.'

'That's right. Adolphus Williamson is our problem.'

'Dolly?' Tanner sucked the froth from his upper lip. 'Ah, now there's a real copper. Breathing down your neck, is he?'

'In a manner of speaking.'

'That'll be because of the file, I'm afraid.'

'The file?' Grand frowned.

'There's a file on you and Batchelor at the Yard. As there is on Field and Polliak; on every private detective agency. No doubt Dolly's been rummaging through the shoe boxes and he'll have come across you. Which reminds me . . .' Tanner raised an eyebrow and nodded in the direction of Grand's chest.

Grand sighed and opened his coat. No shoulder-holster. No gun.

Tanner laughed. 'Glad you took my advice,' he said. 'We'll make an Englishman of you yet.'

'I was hoping,' Grand said, 'I could persuade you to rat on your former colleague and tell us how to get Williamson off our case.'

'Lie through your teeth,' Tanner shrugged. 'It was always the bane of our lives at the Yard, but it works. If you've got a trasseno – er, that's villain to you, Mr Grand – that's hard as nails and sticks to his story, however implausible that story may be, there's not much we can do about that.'

'What about "falling down stairs"?' Grand asked.

'Beg pardon?' Tanner was innocence itself.

'I understand that quite a few . . . trassenos . . . fall downstairs in English police stations. Leaves them with nasty lacerations.'

'Ah, well,' Tanner smiled, winking. 'It's a fatal combination, isn't it? Careless villains and badly designed buildings. What are you going to do?'

'Williamson's having us followed.'

'Is he now?' Tanner took another swig. 'He's got it in for you right enough. But there are two of you, aren't there?'

'There are,' Grand agreed.

'Split your command. Double back on yourselves. If you've got time, go on pointless journeys. Unless he wants you for murder, Dolly hasn't got the resources to go outside the Met area, and there are all sorts of jurisdictional issues. If he realizes he's getting the run-around, he'll back off.'

'That's good advice, Mr Tanner.'

'It is, Mr Grand,' the landlord nodded, 'but it doesn't come cheap, I'm afraid.'

'Ah.' Grand reached for his wallet. 'No, of course not.'

Tanner laughed. 'I don't want your money, Mr Grand. I want

information. Why is Williamson nosing into your affairs particularly? Yes, there's the Yard file but, in theory at least, you and he are on the same side. There has to be a reason. What case are you working on?'

For a moment, Grand hesitated, and was about to come out with the usual client confidentiality claptrap, when he realized who he was talking to. 'The murder of Charles Dickens,' he said.

Tanner whistled through his teeth. 'Get away!' he murmured. 'Who've you got in the frame?'

Grand shrugged. 'Nobody,' he said. 'Everybody.'

'There's a woman involved, of course.'

'There is?' Grand's eyes widened.

'Oh, yes.' Tanner was sure. 'There's *always* a woman involved. There is a Mrs Dickens, isn't there, if memory serves?'

'There is and we haven't talked to her yet, but I can't see a motive. He left her years ago.'

'Hell hath no fury, Mr Grand, like a woman left years ago. And revenge is a dish best served cold. I can let you have a whole load of other platitudes if you like.'

'There was a mysterious woman at the funeral,' Grand was thinking aloud. 'We haven't been able to identify her yet. And another – or is it the same one? – called Stella. We don't know who she is either.'

'I think I can promise you she won't be what she appears to be,' Tanner said.

'What does that mean?' Grand had not travelled seventy miles and been jostled and poked by the ladies of Alresford to be given platitudes *and* cryptic.

'I don't know,' Tanner said. 'Call it an old copper's nose. If I were you,' he leaned forward and became conspiratorial, 'I'd call in the Yard. I hear that Dolly Williamson's a good bloke.'

Fortunately for Matthew Grand, the beds at the Swan Hotel were comfortable and reached by a single staircase. He was quite the hero of the hour that night, with the ladies who had rapidly adapted to his London ways just happy to listen to his accent whilst buying him drinks, and the teachers from up at the college all quizzing him on the recent hostilities, whilst also buying him drinks. Moll helped him up the stairs and then left him at his door, despite mild protestations from him that he needed help taking his boots off. In the morning, still booted, he awoke to a tremendous headache, not helped by the mad Hampshire bird sitting on his windowsill that was not so much singing as shouting 'tweet' down its own personal megaphone. He crept downstairs, refused breakfast and made his way to the train. His plans to visit Winchester Cathedral were all put aside in favour of sitting rocking slightly with closed eyes on the platform of the city's station, waiting with tensed muscles for the London-bound train to arrive with an almost preternaturally loud scream of whistles, howl of engine and yell of brakes, applied with what he considered unnecessary vigour. A sleep in his corner seat made him a little more human, but even so it was fully evening before he felt able to share his findings with Batchelor, or fully understand what his partner had discovered. A bath and a plate of something greasy concocted by Mrs Rackstraw and he was finally fit to face the world, the world of Canton Kitty.

TEN

Batchelor felt quite ill at ease, following so precisely in the footsteps of Charles Dickens. As they walked down Cable Street towards Canton Kitty's he could almost sense the author by his side, excited at the prospect of a pipe of the poppy in the dark of the den. Batchelor hadn't been keen to knock his idol from his perch, but the facts were stacking up against him now; just because he was a womanizer and a drug addict didn't stop him from being the world's greatest writer. After Edgar Allan Poe, no author's life nor death could be considered that dissolute or peculiar; although there was clearly something not quite right about the last days of Dickens, at least he was wearing his own clothes when he died. Or was he? Batchelor made a mental note to find out.

'This must be it.' Grand broke into Batchelor's thoughts.

Batchelor looked at the door, discreetly lit by a gas jet in a cage above it. There was no sign, no door knocker even, just a small grille set at approximate head height. Could this really be the place? How could a drug-addled visitor ever find it?

Grand tapped on the door and the grille immediately swung open. In the shadows within, a face loomed closer. 'Yes?' It was hard to tell from just one word, but it didn't sound like the rough patois of *Edwin Drood*'s opening. Still, the night was young.

Before setting out, Grand and Batchelor had agreed the form of words they would use and had also decided that Grand should do the talking. A foreign accent would probably stand them in better stead than Batchelor's local but well-spoken tones. Grand laid it on a bit thick.

'Hi y'all.' Batchelor poked him in the back and he toned it down. 'I'm new in town and I'm as desperate as a porcupine in a melon patch for a pipe of the good stuff.' He felt rather silly saying that, and avoided Batchelor's sardonic eye, but it did the trick and the door eased open just far enough to let them in. The hall was dim but clean and tidy. They had expected to stumble over bodies as soon as they were inside, but the only person living, unconscious or dead, that they could see was the one who had let them in. It was a woman, that much they could tell, small and dressed simply. Her hair was tightly wound into a bun at the nape of her neck and her evening dress was dark in colour and fitted like a glove. She stood, hands folded in front of her, and she seemed to be waiting for something. The agents shuffled their feet; this wasn't what they were expecting and their thoughts were the same: could this possibly be Canton Kitty's, the most notorious opium den in London?

The woman sighed. 'Do you gentlemen have the password?' she said, in genteel tones.

'Hell no,' Grand said, keeping up his subterfuge. 'We jest heerd . . .'

The woman sighed again and held up a hand. 'Please,' she said. 'We really don't need theatrics, do we? Has someone sent you here or are you just here on the trail of Edwin Drood? Um . . .' The woman bowed her head momentarily. 'You do *know* it's fiction, do you?'

Grand and Batchelor were frankly amazed. It was as though the woman had read their minds. Batchelor was first to recover. 'It's more the trail of Charles Dickens we are on,' he said. 'We were friends of his.'

'I am very sorry for your loss,' the woman said. 'If you were friends of Charles's then you are welcome, of course, and you won't be expecting all that five passed-out sailors in one bed nonsense. That will save us a lot of time.' She stepped into the light shed by the candelabra discreetly placed around the hall. She was about Dickens's age, but very well preserved. Her cheek was olive but she had clearly never been nearer Shanghai than the two enquiry agents had. She saw their expressions and chuckled. 'I see Charles didn't share my little secret. No, I am not, nor ever have been, Chinese. My father, God rest his soul, was a librarian in a private house in Ashby-de-la-Zouch. My mother died when I was very small, but was a very cultured woman, by all accounts. But a librarian doesn't leave enough for a daughter to live on and I had a flair for business and so . . .' she spread her arms and smiled, 'here I am. Now,' she stepped forward and linked one arm through Grand's and one through

Batchelor's, 'how can I amuse you two gentlemen today? Not personally, of course. Those days are *very* much behind me, thank heaven. Are you *really* here for the poppy?' she asked Grand, 'or do you have more exotic tastes? Many of our gentlemen who are not used to smoking prefer to take their poppy in more palatable form. We stock all the best laudanum brands; I must say I recommend that if you have a favourite you already use at home, it's best to stick to that here. It saves . . .' and she gave another of her little deprecatory head bobs, 'incidents.'

Batchelor, remembering his visit to Gads Hill, said, 'I personally favour McMunn's.'

'An excellent choice,' she said, squeezing his arm in a friendly manner. 'Now, the only other thing I need to know is, do you want to indulge together?'

'Or?' Grand wanted to hear the options.

'Well, or separately, of course,' she said. This time it was Grand's arm which had the little squeeze. 'Other options are whether you want to have one of the girls to join you, again, together or separately or, and this is quite popular, would you like to join the small party I have in my own apartments. I would warn you, though, that the party is more for . . .'

Batchelor filled in the gap. 'Addicts?'

She dropped his arm. 'Addicts?' she said. 'I fear you *have* been reading dear Charles's book. Or *Silas Marner* – you look like a reader.' She made it sound like an insult. 'And what I always say is,' she said, drawing herself up in outrage, 'what Mary Ann Evans doesn't know about laudanum could be written on the back of a very small envelope. However,' she came down off her high horse and pushed open a door, 'I think we'll start you two young gentlemen off easily, until you find what you want. After that, we'll see.'

With a light push, they were in the room and the door was closed firmly behind them. In the silence, they could hear muffled piano music and also conversation, with the occasional high-pitched shriek, quickly stifled. The room itself was small and dark; in the corner there was a bed, unmade but clean-looking. A single candle burned in a sconce on the wall.

'Not what I was expecting at all,' Batchelor muttered to Grand.

'What was you expecting?'

The voice, coming from the shadows beneath the candle, made them both jump.

'I expect you was expecting lascar sailors and young university gents with yellow skin and eyes like dark pools, wasn't you?' The owner of the voice stepped out and a pretty young girl came into view. She was deliberately dressed to look much younger than her actual years, but her eyes were knowing and her voice tired. 'Well, Kitty don't allow that sort of thing and, anyways, how could they afford it? Talking of which, that'll be a half-sovereign, gents, if you both wants the works. If it's just one of you, it's still a half-sovereign.' The girl broke into a throaty laugh. 'You'll excuse my little joke, I know.'

Batchelor swallowed hard. 'And if we don't want the works?' he said. 'If we just want some laudanum?'

'It's still half a sovereign,' she said, getting surly. 'A girl has a living to make. Kitty's kind enough as they go, but she ain't a charity, you know.'

Grand fished out the money and passed it over. It disappeared faster than winking inside her bodice and she started to haul up her skirts. 'Well, now,' she said. 'That's more like it. Who's first?'

'Neither of us,' Batchelor said, quickly.

'Oh, it's just the drops, then?' she said, going over to a small table under the light. 'How much d'you want? You don't have to take it all at once . . .'

'No,' Grand said. 'Not drops either. We were wondering if you had ever met Charles Dickens.'

'Blimey,' she said. 'You paid me money just for that. It's a quick answer. No. None of us girls met him. He used to go straight through to Kitty's private party. Him and the woman.'

'Woman?' Grand and Batchelor looked at each other. This could prove fruitful.

The girl stood with her back still to them, the drops measured in a small glass. 'Are you sure you don't . . .'

Grand grunted.

'Then, may I . . .?'

'Be our guest.' They watched as she knocked back the double dose and waited a moment for them to take effect.

'Oh, that's better.' She plumped down in the chair. She lifted a hem and revealed an expanse of bare thigh. 'You sure?'

'Positive,' they chorused.

Her hand went slack but the skirt stayed where it was. 'No,' she said, her eyelids drooping. 'We never got to see Mr High-An'-Mighty Dickens. He'd come round the back, him and the woman . . .' her head lolled.

'Wake up!' Batchelor said, leaning forward to slap her hand and accidentally getting thigh.

'Sorry . . .' she pulled at the hem again. 'I thought you said . . .' And this time, she was asleep beyond any waking, a smile on her face. She really did look like a child, with all the worry wiped from her face by the poppy's caress.

Batchelor looked at her with wide eyes. 'Matthew?' he breathed. 'Is she dead? That was a hefty dose she took.'

Grand went closer and felt her wrist, then lifted an eyelid. The pupil rolled up into her head and she tried to bat him away. 'She's alive,' he said. 'But we'll get no more out of her.' He lifted her effortlessly and carried her across to the bed, where he tucked her in. He dropped a featherlight kiss on her forehead. 'She's had an easy night of it tonight,' he said, looking down at her.

'This is probably a good enough place to ply her trade,' Batchelor said. 'It beats under the arches for the price of a bed, any day.'

Grand looked at him and smiled. 'That is so like you, James. Always see the ointment, never the fly.'

Batchelor tried to work out whether that was a compliment or not, but couldn't be sure. 'Shall we go?' he said. 'Before Kitty comes back.'

'I think that may be a good plan,' Grand agreed. 'A tactical withdrawal. And we did more or less get what we came for. Even if that wasn't quite what Kitty was expecting.'

'Did we?' Batchelor whispered. He had opened the door and was peering out. The coast was clear, so they edged out and tiptoed across the hall.

'Yes,' Grand said as they eased the thick oak door closed behind them. 'Dickens did go to Kitty's and went to the parties for the more – shall we call them – *committed* opium eaters. And, he went with a woman.'

'We still don't know who.' It was a fair point.

'True. But the chances are that the lady in the case has a fair amount of laudanum about her person. Perfect for slipping into Dickens's food or drink or even just feeding to him as a treat. We're getting closer, James. Closer all the time.'

The old church clock of St George in the East was striking three as Grand and Batchelor left Canton Kitty's. There was no moon to splash the gravestones with silver, only the pale slab of the river to their left where the lighters bobbed black. Both of them had heard the footfalls that were not their own and both of them had imperceptibly speeded up their walk. Matthew Grand's strides usually had James Batchelor scrabbling to keep up, but tonight he matched him step for step. Bluegate Fields was not a place to be after dark and it was that hour in the metropolis when the dark was at its blackest before dawn. Soon the cabmen and the costers would be about, trudging to their carts for another long, sweating day. The labourers would be swarming to the dock gates of St Catherine's and the Black Eagle to wait in hopeful line for news of a cargo ship that would bring them work. If not, and the ships only needed a handful each time, they would have to find their tommy where they could and crawl back to the arches in Pinchin Street to catch some sleep. Until the next time, when the only social round they knew would begin all over again.

'How many?' Batchelor whispered out of the corner of his mouth.

'I count three,' Grand whispered back. Of all the nights to leave his thumb-breaker at home. If push came to shove, fists were all they had. Fists, and the perfectly timed boot.

'Is that the three behind us or the three in front?' Batchelor's question was louder now because there suddenly seemed no point in subterfuge. Blocking the path that ran between the graveyard and the river wall, three large roughs in fustian stood with folded arms.

Grand and Batchelor stopped. There was a shed to their right, a rickety, single-storey building that had seen better days. Batchelor read Grand's mind. 'No hiding place there,' he murmured. 'That's the mortuary. If you're hoping for help from anybody inside there, you'll have a rather long wait. Who are they? Williamson's boys?'

'Now, we're not looking for trouble, fellas,' Grand called out to the men ahead.

Batchelor turned so that the two men stood back to back and he was facing the three who had been following them since Cable Street. 'Honestly,' he said. 'No trouble at all.'

'Right,' the man in the centre facing Grand said. 'We'll start with the wallets.'

'Oh, you're Irish,' Batchelor beamed, changing places with Grand. 'That's refreshing in this part of London.'

'We've got a joker, Sean,' another man grunted. 'A regular comedian.'

'He's an idol of the Halls,' Grand said to the men in front of him. 'Always tries out his new material on riff-raff from the bogs.'

The silence was tangible.

'I said, the wallets,' Sean repeated.

'Oh, darn,' Grand drawled, patting his jacket. 'I've been and gone and left the dang thing at home.'

'What a coincidence,' Batchelor said. 'So have I.'

'It's a double act, Sean,' Sean's man observed. He was sliding a club out of the wide sleeve of his coat.

'So it is,' Sean grunted. 'I particularly like that one's fake American accent.'

All six of the roughs were closing in now, and Grand wasn't about to let them get any closer. He drove his boot into Sean's groin and caught the man next to him with a left cross. Batchelor ran forward, driving his shoulder into somebody's chest and sending them both sprawling. A club whizzed past Grand's head and he grabbed the man swinging it and butted him, the Irishman screaming in pain as the blood spread over his face. Batchelor was back on his feet, trading punches with a man who stood a head taller. He felt a crack to his temple and his vision blurred as he staggered under a cudgel blow. Grand poleaxed another of them with both fists to the man's chest, but he wasn't ready for the club that caught him on the shoulder and he dropped to one knee.

'No time to rest on your laurels now, Matthew,' Batchelor hissed, and he lunged at the nearest man, bowling him over and grappling with him in the grass. Grand was on his feet again and he ducked below another flying club before bouncing its owner's head against a gravestone. He tried to grab the club itself but he felt his arms pinioned and he was forced to the ground. Any second now, he knew, the boots and the clubs would rain down and it would be all over.

Batchelor heard it first, as a huge Irishman was strangling him with his own tie. A deafening, staccato rattle that was getting nearer. 'Over here, boys,' a voice called.

The rattle continued and a dark figure was suddenly amongst them, cracking heads and throwing men about.

'Another time,' Sean grunted in Grand's ear before slapping him around the head and the roughs pulled back.

'Come on, lads,' the voice shouted. 'They're getting away!' And the rattle died as the men vanished into the darkness. When Grand and Batchelor stood up, shaking and bloody, where they had expected to see a small army of policemen, they saw the rotund bulk of ex-Chief Inspector Field.

'Lads?' Batchelor said, looking around.

Field laughed. 'Never fails,' he said. He swung his wooden rattle once more with its deafening clatter that echoed through the graveyard. 'I'm glad I kept this little souvenir of better days. You must be Mr Batchelor.' He held out his hand. 'Charlie Field.'

'Impeccable timing, Mr Field,' Grand said. 'A few more minutes there and we might really have hurt them.' He held something up in the light of the creeping dawn. 'One of yours, James?'

Batchelor felt his jaw. 'No,' he said, running his tongue around his mouth. 'Not mine.'

'Nor mine,' Grand said and he threw the bloody tooth away. 'Something else for the charnel house, then.'

'We're grateful, Mr Field,' Batchelor said, trying to straighten his tie. The knot was pulled so tight it was hard to move. 'And what luck you happened to be passing.'

'What's luck got to do with it?' Field chuckled. 'I've been trailing you boys for the last twelve hours.'

'You have?' Batchelor frowned. 'Why?'

Field looked at him. 'I'm afraid you're in over your heads, gentlemen,' he said. 'This isn't the West End with doilies and tea parties. Look at a man funny here and he'll rearrange your face. As you almost discovered. I thought you'd end up at Canton Kitty's eventually.'

'You knew about her?' Grand asked, stooping as best he could to retrieve his hat.

'Everybody knows about Canton Kitty. I remember when she used to starch the collars for her old man's laundry. More innocent days, then, of course. I assume you went there in search of Dickens, as it were.'

'You know about that, too?' It was Batchelor's turn to ask a question.

Field laughed. 'I expect Dolly Williamson will have made some observations to you two about amateurs and professionals; and, pain me though it does, I'm afraid I have to echo him.'

There was a sound of running feet and a helmeted copper was hurtling towards them, swerving around the headstones, his boots clattering on the flags.

'What's the trouble here?' he said, trying to catch his breath.

'Whatever it was,' Field told him, 'it was all over five minutes ago. You'll have to do better than that, boy.'

'Oh, it's you, Chief Inspector. Sorry, guv. I couldn't place the rattle's direction.'

Field closed to him. 'What's your name, lad?' he asked.

'Berryman, sir,' the copper answered, standing straight with his thumbs down the seams of his trousers.

'How old are you?'

'Nineteen, sir.'

Field chuckled, then frowned. 'You're on point, aren't you? Cable Street?'

'Yessir.'

'Then what the Hell are you doing here, lad?' Field shouted. 'Point is point and you never leave it even if all London's burning. Is that clear?'

'Yessir.' Constable Berryman stood to attention even more, if that were possible. He hadn't been born when Chief Inspector Field was doing his rounds, but somehow that made it all the worse.

'Cut along back there, then,' Field said quietly.

'Yessir, thank you, sir. Er . . . you won't be mentioning this to the sarge, will you?'

'Who is it?' Field asked.

'Gallagher.'

'God, no,' Field grunted. 'I'd rather gouge my eyes out. Run along, now.'

And Berryman saluted and was gone.

'J Division!' Field tutted and his eyes rolled skywards.

'Do you know *all* the policemen in London?' Grand asked.

'Hardly know any of 'em these days,' Field confessed. 'But whippersnappers like young Berryman there need to think I do. I wouldn't know Sergeant Gallagher if I fell over him.' He looked at them both, sliding the rattle into his pocket. 'No, the reason I know about Charles Dickens going to Canton Kitty's is that I took him there.'

'You did?' Batchelor asked.

'Of course. You can't expect a man like Dickens to go alone to places like that. He insisted, though. He wanted local colour for the opening of *Edwin Drood*. Have you read it, either of you?'

'Every word,' Batchelor assured him.

'Hmm,' Grand said, with much less commitment.

'I have to say, old friend that I was and one of his greatest admirers, I don't think he *quite* captured an opium den, do you? And if the old crone he's writing about is supposed to be Canton Kitty, he's woefully wide of the mark there, I'd say.'

'Did anything happen there?' Batchelor asked. 'Anything . . . untoward?'

Field laughed. 'What, apart from the hallucinations, the visions of Hell and falling over a couple of dozen Jack Chinamen? No, it was just like tea with the vicar.'

'Sorry,' Batchelor muttered. 'Silly question, really.'

Field drew a cigar from its leather case and offered the rest of the contents to Grand and Batchelor. They declined. Batchelor couldn't feel his jaw and Grand was having difficulty raising his right arm. 'I think old Charles regretted going to Bluegate Fields myself. Venomous place. A lascar held a knife to his throat; if I hadn't intervened, he'd have been done for. So, all joking apart, how's your investigation coming along, then?'

ELEVEN

Batchelor and Grand presented an unusual sight the next morning. There was marginally more flesh colour than bruise on each face, but it would take a good set of measuring callipers to decide by what margin. Batchelor's lip was split and Grand's left eye was half closed in what looked like an ironic wink. Every limb hurt to a greater or larger extent and they had both taken extra cushions to the table with them to address their breakfasts.

For once, Mrs Rackstraw had cooked them something suitable. The porridge she dished up as a rule was more lump than not, but she had managed things better and the oatmeal was as smooth as silk, slipping past sore mouths like mother's milk. She had even cut the crusts off the toast and the coffee and tea was not anything like as scalding as normal. She spoke in lowered tones and it occurred to Grand and Batchelor that appealing to her maternal side was perhaps something they should do more often. Sitting still for too long was not really an option; each of them had an appendage that would seize up in cramps after just a few minutes, and so they decided that they would take a short stroll, to loosen up and perhaps quietly plan their next moves as they took the air.

Mrs Rackstraw helped them down the steps one at a time and stood, a mother hen to the last feather, in the doorway, looking after them with anxious eyes. They were good boys, taken all in all, if only they didn't keep getting visits from such disreputable characters.

As they strolled down the Strand, Grand's leg and Batchelor's back started to loosen up, and within not too many yards from their front door they began to feel more human. The porridge coated their stomachs pleasantly, a slight northerly breeze had sprung up and so even the smell of the river was just a faint rumour instead of something that could stop a clock. Their strides lengthened and Batchelor even began to hum a snatch of a song. They couldn't see any trailing Yard men either, which had to be a bonus.

Just as he got to the chorus, the peace of the morning was shattered by a heart-rending wail from immediately above their heads. Looking up, holding on to their hats, they could see nothing. The wail rose up the scale and then stopped suddenly. So suddenly that the silence was more foreboding than the wail, though that had been enough to turn their spines to water. Grand looked around him and saw a brass plate next to an imposing door. 'Chapman and Hall,' it said in ornate Gothic script. 'Publishers.'

Grand nudged Batchelor and pointed. 'Isn't that . . .?'

'Dickens's publisher? Yes. It is.'

'And did that wail . . .'

'I would call it more of a screech.'

'If you will.' Grand was always happy to leave lexicographical detail to his partner. 'Did it not come from that window, there?' He pointed again, to a frosted window that had some white letters painted on it: the H A L of 'Hall'.

'Shall we go and see what it's all about?' Batchelor asked, rhetorically.

'I daresay Williamson will object,' Grand said, 'but I don't see how we can let it be.'

And, rather gingerly, they climbed the stairs.

The scene that met their eyes when they pushed open the door at the top of the stairs was unusual but also explained the sounds they had heard. A wild-haired, wild-eyed woman was sitting sobbing on the floor, cradling one cheek in a wrinkled hand and leaning heavily against a door. Another door was open in the further wall and a flock of startled editors with inky fingers and eyeshades were looking out like guinea fowl, checking on where the fox might be hiding. Above the woman stood a man in his early twenties, dressed in the height of fashion and with hair just so; his immaculate clothing made the crouching woman look even more dishevelled by comparison. He was reaching down with one hand and speaking to her in soothing tones.

'Come on, Em, now do. There's no need to get in such a bait

about it. We don't know if Young Mr Frederic is in there, even, let alone that he's dead. And, frankly, I don't believe that the human nose is sensitive enough to smell blood, even close to, let alone through an inch of mahogany. So, be a good woman and stand up and calm down, in any order you choose. I've sent a boy round to Mr Frederic's house and he'll be here in a jiffy, I feel sure.'

This speech, which seemed reasonable to everyone listening, had no effect, unless possibly the woman began to sob even more heartbreakingly.

'Em!' The man had tried a quick slap. He had tried cajoling. Now it was time to try a little authority. She looked up, the tears making her rather piggy and red-rimmed eyes even piggier and redder. Above her receding chin, her lips trembled and quivered, her nose dripping tears.

'Mr Frederic!' she howled, and was once more incoherent with grief.

The man standing over her whirled away in frustration, and noticed Grand and Batchelor for the first time. After the first shock of their battered faces, his innate good breeding took control. 'I'm terribly sorry,' he said, raising his voice a little to be heard above the wail. 'We're not actually interviewing new writers at present. Miss Jones isn't very well.'

'Is there a problem?' Batchelor asked, realizing as he spoke that perhaps the question was more than a little redundant.

'Well,' the fashionable gent looked over his shoulder to where the secretary sat alone with her grief, 'we are known for being a little less formal than some other houses, but this is unusual, even for Chapman and Hall.' He smiled at them. 'I'm Trollope, by the way. Henry Trollope, one of the partners here. Miss Jones,' and he waved an arm, 'is under the impression that Frederic Chapman, the other partner still living is . . . well, not to put too fine a point on it, no longer living. The door to his office is locked, she says she can smell blood and that Mr Frederic is never late. Only one of those facts is correct and I must say that I cannot comprehend for the life of me why we suddenly need to start locking doors in premises where even the stamp money only ever comes to a few shillings. However, Mr Frederic demanded it and so it had to be.'

'Where is the key?' Grand thought it was a reasonable question.

'This is another of Miss Jones's cause for alarm,' Trollope said. 'It should be in her desk drawer, but it is missing.'

'Is her desk locked, as a rule?' Batchelor asked.

'No . . . I say, chaps, you don't mind my asking who the Hell you are, do you? Only, today is proving a little trying and it isn't even ten o'clock yet.'

'Sorry.' Batchelor fished out a card and handed it over. 'We hadn't intended to pay you a visit, but we heard the noise.'

'I should think they heard it in Whitehall. She's got a good pair of lungs on her, Em, I'll give her that much. May I introduce you?' He walked up to the woman and bent from the waist. 'Em,' he said, speaking clearly and slowly as if to a child. 'Em. These nice gentlemen are detectives. Look,' he pointed. 'Mr Grand and Mr Batchelor. Don't they look nice? Hmm? Now, if you get up, Em, away from the door, either Mr Grand or Mr Batchelor – or for all I know both of them together – will open the door and then we can show you that Mr Frederic isn't in there. Now! How does that sound? Hmm?'

The woman stayed crouched in her doorway, looking with frantic eyes at each of the three men in turn. Whichever one of them it was, it was not possible to tell, but she saw something in one of their faces which she could trust and she slowly scrambled to her feet and edged along the wall, away from the door. Grand reached into his pocket and pulled out his wallet of trusty lock-picks. This was something else of which Richard Tanner would disapprove, he felt sure, along with his Colt .32, but he felt that his reputation as an enquiry agent rested on his ability to undo this door, right here, right now. He had had lessons from Fingers O'Flaherty, the famous safe-cracker, lately released from a stretch in the Scrubs and who owed Grand a favour, but he had never had a chance to put his new skills to the test. He bent down to the lock and looked through. As he had always suspected when reading fiction, when you look through a keyhole, the most you see is a small amount of the inside of a door. He thought that perhaps he could also see a small chink of light, such as would be coming in through the next frosted window.

'Sniff,' Miss Jones hissed, leaning forward to poke Grand in the shoulder. 'Sniff. You'll smell blood if you do.'

Grand obliged and could only smell recently drilled wood and oiled lock wards. He looked at her with a comforting smile and chose a pick, which he inserted into the lock. Remembering his lesson with Fingers, he manipulated the pick around, keeping the sections of the lock out of the way with more picks, introduced one by one. After only a moment or two, and to his immense surprise, the lock clicked and, when he turned the doorknob, the door swung open, displaying the room for all to see.

Miss Jones batted Grand aside and was in there first. For those who didn't get a clear view – all of the editors had now surged into the room – there was a clue to the contents of the leather chair in front of the swept and cold fireplace. The scream seemed to bypass their ears and hit them right in the brain, like an icicle falling in winter.

Trollope took her by the arms and spun her round and, before anyone could stop him, he dealt her an uppercut that had her unconscious instantly. He handed her inert form to a sub-editor.

'Lay her down somewhere, someone,' he muttered. 'I really can't stand this screaming another minute.' He turned into the room. 'God strewth!' he said, and went white. 'She was right.' He beckoned Grand and Batchelor into the room.

The three men looked into the room towards the fireplace, some innate sense keeping them at bay. An arm hung limply down, the knuckles of the hand grazing the floor. Congealed blood made a pool around the fingers and had soaked into the carpet, obscuring its rather ornate pattern and creating an obscene mirror of gore. A leg stuck out at a rakish angle and a head lolled on a shoulder. Any one of the parts of the puzzle would have been enough to show that the man was dead. And yes, there was a metallic smell of recent death in the room; in that respect, Miss Jones had been quite right. But, in another, quite wrong.

'What the devil's going on here?' a voice demanded to know. 'Why is Miss Jones lying across her desk? Why is my office door open against my explicit instructions?' Frederic Chapman had arrived and was not in the mood to be messed about. He barged through the little knot of men in his doorway and strode into the room. He looked at the man in the chair and turned to stare at Trollope, Grand and Batchelor. 'And who in blazes has crushed Gabriel Verdon's skull?' And, with a small groan and an elegant fold at the knees, Frederic Chapman fainted dead away.

Grand and Batchelor stayed around the offices of Chapman and Hall for as long as they could without exciting comment. Miss Jones had revived for long enough to look through the doorway and see Young Mr Frederic prone on the floor. Her second collapse was more permanent and she had been carted away to Charing Cross Hospital in Agar Street. Frederic Chapman had also recovered and had immediately taken charge, demanding police and explanations in any order they liked to arrive. Henry Trollope, explaining to his partner, turned to introduce Grand and Batchelor, but they had gone. A gruesome murder like this, of a prominent member of a famous publishing house, would attract the instant attention of Scotland Yard, and so it was inevitable that Dolly Williamson would be the police who arrived and sufficient unto the day was that evil; they could always go back later and poke around, should the latest death prove to have any bearing on the cases currently in hand. They both had a feeling that being banged up in a cell by an irate Williamson wouldn't help their aches and pains any, so they turned for home and made a good pace along the Strand, back to Mrs Rackstraw and safety. Before they got home, Grand put out a restraining hand.

'James,' he said, 'it has just occurred to me that Miss Jones may be able to help us. Should I follow her to the hospital, do you think?'

'Do you really think she knows anything?' Batchelor was doubtful. The woman had looked as mad as a hat-stand as far as he could tell.

'It's hard to say,' Grand said, 'but I got the impression that she has a responsible position in Chapman and Hall, when she isn't delirious, of course. Perhaps if I visit her now, when her guard is down, she may be able to tell me a few titbits. Gossip, you know.'

'I suppose . . .'

'I'll take her some flowers.' Grand stopped by the old woman who sat on the corner, selling wild blooms from a battered bucket at her feet. 'Cornflowers, look. She'll like that.' He gave the woman a coin.

'Thank you, guv'nor. You've got a lucky face.' The old crone didn't look up; had she done so she would have had to reword her thanks, as Grand's black eye was developing nicely.

'You may be right,' Batchelor said. His back didn't take to standing on street corners at the moment, and he knew of old when Grand got one of his bright ideas, it was easier by far to let him go along with his hunch. 'I won't go out anywhere until you get home. We need to talk things through, see where this case is taking us. It may be that we will have to tell George Sala that we have hit a brick wall.'

'Admit defeat? Never!' and, brandishing his cornflowers, Grand set off along the Strand in the opposite direction, albeit with a slight list to starboard.

Batchelor watched him go. He hoped Mrs Rackstraw wasn't going to be too angry that he had let him wander off on his own; he walked back towards home, already composing a number of excuses, ready against the day. Mrs Rackstraw was not angry about Batchelor having mislaid Grand, but she was rather riled at having been treated like a skivvy – as she put it – by another nob knocking on the door when she was in the middle of her pastry. She'd sent him round to the office and no mistake; he didn't look very reputable in her experienced opinion and so she had got him out of the house, sharpish. Batchelor had noticed a rather irate-looking gent as he passed by on his way along, and turned on his heel on the step and hot-footed it back. Just because they were currently investigating two cases, had been beaten practically to a pulp and had Scotland Yard on their tails, didn't mean that they could turn work down.

The man waiting for Batchelor outside 41 The Strand looked pale and drawn. He had tight curls and a cherubic face but the eyes burned with an inner fury and it was clear that he didn't like being kept waiting.

'Are you Grand?' he asked, 'and whatever happened to your face?'

'No, I'm Batchelor,' Batchelor told him, 'and please, don't ask.'

'I was hoping for the senior man.'

Batchelor fumed inwardly. It had been his idea originally to set up in the enquiry agency business, and in his mind's eye the signboard was to read 'Batchelor and Grand'. Still, it was too late now. 'We have no senior men,' he said. 'Grand and I are equals.'

'Lovely,' the man said. 'You'll have to do, then.'

'Come in, Mr . . . er . . .'

'Boulton,' the man said, and waited while Batchelor unlocked the street door. The sun had not come around to their side of the road yet and only the steeple of St Clement Danes was gilded by it, a promise of heat still to come. Soon enough it would creep down the walls of the publishers' and the counting houses, flash and dazzle off the harness of the cab horses and the drays, drive the window shoppers into the cool of premises to be pounced on by salespersons who gave daily thanks for the weather.

Batchelor led the way along the corridor and up to the half-floor back. The odd little clocksmith who shared the building was not in yet, and no one had picked up his mail for days.

'Would you like some tea?' Batchelor asked, hauling open the curtains to let the day in. 'I have a spirit kettle here somewhere . . .'

'Thank you, no,' Boulton said with a shudder, and whipped a hip flask from his pocket before sitting down. He took a swig and a deep breath, as if to compose himself. 'I won't mince words,' he said. 'I know that Artie came to see you recently.'

'Artie?' Batchelor looked suitably vague.

'Come, come, Mr Batchelor. Coyness won't get us very far now, will it? Arthur Clinton.' Boulton had met people like Batchelor before. Enquiry agents spied on people. They listened at doorways. Peeped through keyholes. They collected soiled bedsheets to prove infidelity. And they were all impressed by money, so Boulton added, 'Lord.'

'I'm terribly sorry, Mr Boulton,' Batchelor said, 'but I cannot divulge . . .'

'For God's sake, man!' Boulton shouted, taking another swig from his flask. 'We'll get nowhere if you shilly-shally like this.

Artie was a friend of mine – a very dear friend – and somebody killed him.'

Batchelor had been hunting vaguely for the kettle, but now he stopped and sat down opposite Boulton. 'They did?' he said.

Boulton took several deep breaths to control himself.

'I heard . . . scarlet fever.' Batchelor followed the established line.

'If Artie Clinton died of scarlet fever, I'm a Turk's arse. He was murdered, Mr Batchelor. "By persons unknown", I believe is the phrase.'

'It generally is,' Batchelor said. 'Unless of course you have a known person in mind.'

'I believe I have.' Boulton crossed one elegant leg over the other. 'But first, I need to know what Artie came to see you about.'

'Mr Boulton,' Batchelor spread his arms. 'I thought I made it clear . . .'

'Artie is dead, Mr Batchelor,' Boulton said loudly. 'Client confidentiality flies out of the window with his soul . . . oh, that's rather good, isn't it? Poetic. All right, let me help you. In his conversation with you, did he mention Ernest? And Frederick? John? Hugh?'

'Er . . . he may have done,' Batchelor said, regretting again that he had made no notes of Arthur Clinton's visit.

'I am Ernest,' Boulton said. 'So, you see, I know what Artie knew.'

'The Strand Theatre,' Batchelor nodded as the details flooded back. 'The private box. The conspiracy and inciting of persons to commit an unnatural offence.'

'Don't get me started,' Boulton's eyes flashed fire. 'Who decides what's an unnatural offence, eh? You? Me? The Lord Bloody Chancellor?'

'Well, I was under the impression it was the joint wisdom of the Houses of Commons and Lords,' Batchelor said. 'But I could be wrong.'

'I was subjected to the *roughest* of handling,' Boulton bridled at the memory of it. 'That police surgeon had no idea how such things are done. I couldn't sit down for a week. And Fanny . . .'

'Fanny?'

'Funnily,' Boulton corrected him. 'I said "Funnily". I was about to say, funnily enough, I found I could stand it. Worked through the pain.'

'What is it you do, Mr Boulton?'

Boulton looked a little outraged. 'I am an actor.'

'Ah. Would I have seen you in anything?'

An odd smile flitted across the man's face. 'I have no idea,' he said. 'But we have more pressing matters now, Mr Batchelor.'

'Indeed we do,' Batchelor agreed. 'I have to say, Mr Boulton, that, if you suspect foul play, you should go to the police. Scotland Yard.'

'Hah!' Boulton roared.

Batchelor remembered the gist of Arthur Clinton's tale of woe. The police were clearly not Ernest Boulton's best friends. 'Ah, no, perhaps not, then.'

'Not indeed,' Boulton said. 'But not for the reason you're thinking. You asked a moment ago if I had a "known person" in mind for Artie's murder. I have.' Boulton paused for effect, the actor in him coming to the fore. 'His name is Adolphus Williamson and he is a chief inspector at Scotland Yard.'

Matthew Grand didn't exactly chase the cart which ferried Miss Jones, still twitching and screaming every once in a while, to Charing Cross Hospital, but he wasn't far behind. She was not hard to locate; the nurses had seen all sorts, but not all that many women in such a state of exhausted hysteria. He spoke to a doctor in the corridor outside the ward and didn't bother to disabuse him when he assumed he was the patient's son.

'Does your mother have these turns often?' the doctor asked.

Grand told the truth. 'No, sir, my mother enjoys excellent health as a rule.' This was quite literally true. He had seen his mother remove all manner of critters from the larder in his time, although even she had called the outside help when a bear had got into their mountain retreat that time. As for Miss Jones's general health, he had no clue.

'She seems a little confused,' the doctor said, a little confused himself by Grand's clearly American accent. It wasn't often that parent and child were so unlike each other, either. But the science of genetics could be a strange bedfellow. 'She keeps saying someone called young Mr Frederic is dead but he had someone else's legs.'

'Yes, I can explain that,' Grand said, hopefully. 'You see, she saw someone who had been beaten to death, in the office of . . . young Mr Frederic. It wasn't him, though, so she . . . well, rather than accept it wasn't him, she seems to have assumed that it was someone else's legs he had on . . .' He looked up at the doctor, aware he sounded as mad as the secretary. 'Look, doc, it's a police matter. I'm just worried about my dear old maw.' Grand had found in his years in London that a hick American accent could take him a long way.

'You can go and see her for a while,' the doctor said, pulling out his watch from a waistcoat pocket. 'I was in surgery when she was brought in. I must get back. Legs don't amputate themselves, you know! Good luck with Mother. If she doesn't improve overnight, we'll have her in Colney Hatch as soon as winking. Goodbye.'

Grand found himself thinking that would be handy. He could visit his dear old maw and his dear old ex-housekeeper at the same time and save a journey. Then he reminded himself that his dear old maw was terrifying ladies' soirees back in Boston, pushed open the door to the ward and went in.

Forty pairs of eyes raked him as he walked down the ward, looking for Miss Jones. She wasn't hard to spot, being strapped to the bed by leather bindings and still thrashing her head from side to side. 'Mr Frederic,' she muttered. Then, 'Legs!' she would shriek. Two nurses were tucking her in under the covers so tightly that the straps were almost redundant, but he was glad of them all the same.

'Hello,' he said to the nearest nurse's back. 'The doctor said I could visit with . . . my dear old maw.'

The woman spun round. She had a face very much like a currant bun, not helped by the ludicrous starched bonnet above it. Her eyes were kindly, though, and she had Grand summed up in a moment as someone who would be able to pay for as many extras as they could put on his mother's bill. 'It isn't visiting time,' she pointed out.

'No. But she has had a nasty shock and I wanted to see if she was all right.' He lowered his voice. 'It's a police matter. I need

to know if she can be interviewed later. You know how it is . . .
stressful for the poor old soul.'

The nurses' eyes widened. The one on the further side of the
bed mouthed, 'Police?'

'I fear so. A horrible murder, bludgeoning, blood. The works,
in fact. She . . . well, she saw the body. It turned her head.'

The nurses both stepped back. It was all very well for this rather
personable young man to say she *saw* the body, but the woman
was clearly raving. What if she *caused* the body? The one nearest
Grand gave the straps an extra tug and they both scuttled down to
the foot of the bed.

'Stay as long as you like,' the bun-faced one said, and they
hurried away, with the regulation nurse's walk-don't-run gait.

Grand pulled up a chair and leaned near to the stricken woman,
who now seemed to be aware of him. 'Hello, Miss Jones,' he
said, softly. 'Are you feeling a bit better now?'

'Who are you?' she whispered. 'You were there, weren't you?
There when they found Mr Frederic with the wrong legs.' Her
eyes were widening and getting frantic. She opened her mouth
for a wail, but he forestalled her with a gentle finger across her
lips.

'Sshh, Miss Jones,' he said. 'Sshh. It wasn't Mr Frederic. He
is well. I saw him before they brought you here. He is very well
indeed.' Grand cast his mind back to the prone body on the floor
and thought that perhaps the lie wouldn't count, being for the
general good. 'Yes, perfectly well.'

She lowered her chin and looked at Grand, truculently.
'Mr Henry hit me.'

'Yes,' Grand had to agree. 'He did. But it was for the best.'

'He hit me *twice*.'

'Well, I only saw him do it the once. But if you say so . . .'

'I *do* say so! He hit me *twice*.' She tried to beckon Grand
nearer and realized that her hands were tied. She tugged at the
straps but they were firm. 'Why am I tied down?'

'You . . . you haven't been well,' Grand said. It was all
he could manage at short notice. 'Just lie still and they will untie
you.'

'Hmm.' She was dubious, but nothing really had been quite
normal so far today, so why should it be any different now?

Unable to use her hands, she beckoned with her head for Grand to move closer. She dropped her voice even more to an all-but-inaudible whisper. 'I never liked him, you know,' she said.

'Who?' Grand needed to be sure. There were three men in the case as far as he knew: Chapman, Trollope and Verdon. It was difficult enough, but it would be a lot worse if the woman insisted on just using pronouns.

'Mr Henry. He doesn't deserve to be a partner with Young Mr Frederic, just because his father bought him a share. His father is nothing but a common hack.'

'His father . . .?'

'Trollope.' A thought occurred to her and she narrowed her eyes. 'Are you foreign?'

'American, yes.'

She sighed and rolled her eyes. 'Anthony Trollope,' she said, speaking louder, as one must to foreigners. '*Barchester Towers*? Have you read it?'

'In a busy life . . .' Grand began.

'You haven't missed much,' she said, tartly. 'He didn't even buy his dratted son into his own publishers, you might like to take notice. And so he came to Chapman and Hall and he *hit* me.' She glowered. 'Twice.'

This could become wearing. Grand was about to ask her for more detail of what had transpired before he arrived, but he was forestalled by the arrival of a woman carrying a large bowl of water and a rather unappetizingly grey sponge and towel.

'Step aside,' the woman growled. 'I got to bathe everyone what comes on to the ward. Miss Nightingale's instructions.'

'But I was visiting . . .'

'Sister says you can wait outside. Won't be long.' And the woman rolled up her sleeves to reveal water-reddened forearms that wouldn't disgrace a docker.

Grand felt sorry for Miss Jones, cowering there in the bed, but went for a walk along the corridor outside, trying to ignore the various screams and cries which came from the wards along his route. Finally, on his sixth perambulation, he bumped almost literally into the woman with the bowl, the water within it now just a little more scum-flecked than before.

'She's all tidied up now,' the woman said. 'Waiting for you to go back. Your dear old mum, is she?'

'Yes,' Grand lied. He almost believed it himself by this time.

In the ward, the eyes followed him again and he was soon settled by Miss Jones's bed. A nurse had taken the opportunity of the bathing to slip the woman a hefty dose of laudanum. The stained glass was still on the side and Grand could tell, drawing on his experiences at Canton Kitty's establishment, that she had had enough to fell a buffalo. She was still awake, though drowsy.

'Who are you?' she asked again.

'A friend,' he said. He could tell she was at the stage when she didn't need extraneous detail.

'You're very good to visit me,' she said, smiling. 'Who are you again?'

'Matthew.'

'That's a nice name. Not like Henry. That's not a nice name. Frederic, that's a nice name. Gabriel. That's a funny name, that is. Like a n'angel, don't you think?' Her eyelids flickered and Grand poked her gently on the arm. 'Who are you?'

'Matthew.'

'That's right.' She dropped off to sleep for a full five minutes and Grand got up slowly, preparing to leave. Suddenly, her eyes flew open and she stared at him. 'Don't go,' she said. 'You're Matthew. In the Bible. Like Gabriel. Henry isn't in the Bible though.'

'No. Why don't you like Henry?'

She looked at him, puzzled. 'He hit me,' she said as if that were explanation enough.

'Any other reason?' Grand was getting into the pace of this now and with any luck would get all the information he needed before she lost consciousness altogether. She did seem to have an iron constitution; his lie to the doctor was not so inaccurate after all.

She shook her head. 'No' really. Whippersnapper. Young Mr Frederic calls him the idiot.' She shrugged her shoulders. 'But no harm in him, s'pose. He can't help it if his father's a postman.'

'And what about Gabriel?'

She had dropped off again, but he was used to it and waited.

'Gets a lot of money,' she said, suddenly.

'How much?'

She shrugged again and smiled. Grand patted her hand. It was rather like reasoning with a child. 'More 'n he should get, I can tell you that. The other editors wouldn't like it if they knew.' She looked straight at Grand and her eyes were frightened. 'Is that why they killed him?'

'Do you know who killed him?' Now Grand felt he was getting somewhere.

'Who's dead?' she asked. 'Not Young Mr Frederic . . .' She struggled against the straps. 'It's Young Mr Frederic's tea time . . .'

'No, no, calm down. Everyone is well and there is no need to do the tea. Umm . . . Mr Henry is doing it.' It was a desperate ploy but it worked.

'I hope he makes sure the kettle boils properly. Mrs Halfbrackett doesn't always. Young Mr Frederic . . .' and she drifted away on pink clouds of dreams of the love of her life.

The gaps were getting longer, but she fought the opium's grip through the long afternoon. The nurses made it their business to check things down the far end of the ward more often that day than they usually did in a week. Matthew Grand was the most decorative thing that they had seen in there for many a long shift, and they wanted to make the most of him while he was there, the dusty sun just touching the tips of his eyelashes and a curve of his manly cheek as he sat there, holding hands with his dear old mum.

As the sun began to sink below the rooftops, Grand got up and stretched his long legs, reaching above his head with both hands to get some life back into his arms. With a final pat of the woman's hand, he left the ward, leaving the nurses to twitter and sigh in his wake. He didn't have much to tell Batchelor, but the titbits he had managed to glean were better than nothing. He had rather enjoyed spending time with his mother, even if only by proxy. That matron would have raised an eyebrow if she had seen her stand-in; but as minor Boston royalty, she knew how to behave and Grand was sure she would be gracious.

TWELVE

He was still smiling, thinking of his mother, his father and his home on the wild Atlantic shore when he trotted happily along the street towards his other home, Alsatia. Batchelor was pacing back and forth in the road, his watch in his hand, his hat jammed firmly on his head, a couple of evening cloaks over his arm.

'Matthew! Where in the world have you been? Get your glad rags on; we're going to the theatre and I have a lot to tell you on the way.'

'Don't you want to know . . .?' Grand was being bundled up the steps.

'Later. We need to get going and there's a lot *you* need to know.'

As they hurried along towards the theatre, cloaks flying in the warm evening air, Grand could hardly believe his ears. 'Williamson?' he exploded. 'You can't be serious!'

'I'm not,' Batchelor told him, 'but Ernest Boulton is.'

'Who?' Grand asked.

'I knew you weren't listening,' Batchelor said. 'The chap I've just been talking about. Arthur Clinton's friend. He's sure that Dolly Williamson murdered him.'

'Don't I know that name from somewhere?'

'Yes, I just told you . . .'

'No. I've seen it written down. But where?'

Batchelor chuckled and slapped his friend on the shoulder. 'Just a few more corners to turn and you'll remember, for sure.'

Grand had a blissful moment of realization. 'Of course!' he said, snapping his fingers. 'So *that's* why we're off to the theatre!'

An extremely large man filled the doorway at the back of the Strand Theatre. There were any number of Stage Door Johnnies loafing about, most of them in white ties and elegant tails, but two of them in particular seemed more persistent than the others.

'I've told you already,' the bouncer said. 'Mrs Graham and Miss Park don't give personal interviews. And *never* after a show.'

'Oh, I'm sure they'll see us,' Batchelor said. 'We're all friends.'

'Alphonse?' A French accent by way of Bermondsey rang down the passageway. 'Is there a problem?'

'These . . . gentlemen . . . claim to be friends of Mrs Graham and Miss Park.'

'Yes, well, that's what they all say, isn't it?' A little man with a shock of white hair bustled past the bouncer and shooed the detectives into the alleyway. 'You'll have to excuse Alphonse,' he said. 'He's new. Now, I really must ask you to move on, gentlemen. I've had no instruction . . . Ooh, they're nice.' He snatched a bouquet of roses from a Johnnie and smiled at him. 'Fanny's favourites,' he said, and vanished inside with them. Alphonse filled the doorway again and Grand sized him up. He was big, that much was certain, but there was a school of thought which believed that the larger they were, the harder they fell. However, there were other ways to skin cats, preferable perhaps to an international incident outside a London theatre. And he was still feeling a tad tender after that little business in the churchyard of St George in the East.

It was about an hour later that two elegantly dressed ladies left the Strand. The Johnnies had gone by then, denied their audiences, and their cards had been personally ripped up and dumped by Alphonse as soon as their backs were turned. The pair were nattering together, swaying their hips as they came around the corner and they hailed a waiting cab.

'Thirteen Wakefield Street, heart,' the taller of the two trilled, and they climbed in. They had just settled themselves when the door flew open and James Batchelor jumped in. He tipped his hat. 'Room for a little 'un?' he asked brightly.

It *was* cramped in the hansom, knees to knees all round, and it occurred to Batchelor that there was less room here than in a private box in the theatre.

'*Do* you mind?' one of the ladies snapped. 'This is a private cab.'

'No, I don't mind,' Batchelor beamed, and reached up to knock on the cab's roof. With a jolt, the horse lurched forward and they were soon rattling along the Strand. 'Left,' Batchelor shouted. 'Make for Kingsway.'

'We don't give interviews,' the taller woman said.

'I'm not surprised,' Batchelor nodded, 'but I must admit, you're *very* convincing. Now, let's see; I think introductions are in order.' He glanced out of the window. 'No, *left*. Not there. The next . . . oh, all right, then, you'll have to take the first right.'

'What the bloody Hell is going on?' the tall one asked. She caught sight of her companion. 'Am I the only one to have noticed that there's a maniac in the cab with us?' she screeched.

'You can drop your voice, Fan,' the other one said. 'This is Mr Batchelor – the detective I told you about.'

'Oh, bugger,' the taller one said, several octaves lower, 'in a manner of speaking.'

'Now, you, Mr Boulton, I know. You must be . . .'

'Frederick Park,' the taller one said. 'My friends call me Fanny.'

'I'm sure they do. Now, Mr Boulton . . . or is it Mrs Graham?'

'A stage name,' Boulton said. Neither man had removed his makeup and showed little sign of intending to do so.

'Indeed,' Batchelor said. 'But it's your other stage name I'm more interested in. Stella, isn't it?'

The cab lurched to a halt.

'Oh, for God's sake!' Park hissed. 'What *is* the matter with this cabbie?'

A head peered in through the open window and it tipped its hat. 'He's foreign, I'm afraid,' Batchelor said. 'When it comes to the Knowledge, he hasn't got any. My associate, Matthew Grand.'

Fanny Park smiled and pouted at Grand. True, he had had a lot of rebuffs in his time, but it sometimes worked.

'Ladies,' Grand beamed.

'When you came to see me earlier today, you were less than candid, Mr Boulton.'

'Was I?'

'Well, yes,' Batchelor said. 'For a start, you weren't wearing a frock.'

'Dress,' Park corrected him. 'The cavalry wear frocks.'

Grand was about to deny it, then remembered that the man was talking about the British cavalry.

'And you didn't tell me about the Dickens connection either.'

'Dickens?' Boulton frowned. 'What's Dickens got to do with it?'

'That's sort of what we'd like you to tell us,' Grand said, and squeezed into the cab as well. 'We don't want the world and his wife to overhear this, do we?'

'No,' Park said, looking Grand up and down. 'Anyone passing will just assume that we are a pair of courting couples out for a night on the town.'

'Fanny!' Boulton growled at him, and Park subsided, at least to the extent of getting his compact out and powdering his nose. 'I didn't tell you about our little peccadilloes because it has no bearing on poor Artie's death. At least, not directly.'

'And indirectly?' Batchelor asked.

'Indirectly, it gives Williamson his motive.'

'It does?' Grand asked.

'Unaccountably,' Boulton said, 'what Fanny and I like to wear in our stage act – what we like to wear during the day – seems to upset some people.'

'Call us naughty,' Park chipped in, 'but we do *so* like outraging society.'

'You do?' Grand asked.

'Oh, yes,' Park told him. 'When our case comes up, we shall be wearing all the latest Paris fashions. It'll turn a few heads, I can tell you.'

'I have no doubt of it,' Grand said. 'Tell me, did you wear this get-up on the night you were arrested?'

'No,' Boulton said, 'and there's the irony. Others in our party that might have already absconded. Fanny and I have decided to face the music. We have a point to make.'

'That point being . . .?' Grand was a *little* out of his depth. Men dressed in the latest Paris fashion was not yet the coming trend in Washington.

'That if a man wishes to dress as a woman, he should be allowed to.'

'And if a woman wants to dress as a man?' Grand asked.

'It already happens, dear boy,' Park said. 'On the Row of a morning, you'll find half a dozen of the *grandes horizontales* wearing trousers under their habits.'

Grand had heard this from Ouida already.

'No, it wouldn't matter what we wore,' Boulton said. 'We could dress up as Christmas trees and Dolly Williamson would still be on to us.'

'That's why he killed Artie,' Park said, his lip trembling a little. 'Why, beforehand, he came to see you.'

'Like all his kind,' Boulton sneered. 'Like the upright copper he pretends he is, he loathes anything remotely different. Finds Biblical quotations to damn our kind. Well, there is a day coming when the Williamsons of this world won't be able to touch us. Because there will be no law against what we do.'

'Until then,' Park said, 'we must have justice for Artie. We're relying on you two to bring him down.'

'Easier said than done,' Batchelor sighed.

'How did you know, by the way,' Boulton asked, 'about the Dickens connection?'

'You can thank the genius that is my partner in crime for that,' Batchelor said, and tipped his hat to Grand. 'The name Stella came to light in the course of our enquiries into the death of Mr Dickens.'

'You're enquiring into the death of Dickens?' Boulton's eyes were wide. He fumbled in his reticule for his flask and took a huge swig. 'My God, the world's gone mad.'

'I knew I'd heard that name somewhere before, but I couldn't place it. We were on our way to the theatre before I put two and two together. James told me that Ernest Boulton had been to see him and it all fell into place. I had seen your handbills and the hoarding outside the theatre – it's only a stone's throw from where we live and I pass it most days. "Ernest Boulton is Mrs Graham in 'Stella and Fanny Go Wild'". Sorry we missed it, but it is impossible to get in without booked tickets, the box office told us.'

Boulton and Park looked at each other and then at Grand, smiling the smile of the successful actor. 'It is going rather well,' Park added, smugly. 'We're moving to better rooms shortly, on the strength of it.'

'So,' Batchelor asked, leaning forward but feeling it was inappropriate to pat a knee, 'you are *that* Stella, are you? You knew Charles Dickens?'

'Of course I am and of course I did,' Boulton chuckled. 'Such a lovely man. He told some people that I was the new woman in his life.'

'You were at the funeral?' Grand asked.

'God, no. That would be chancing my arm a little *too* far, I think. No, Fanny and I outrage society enough as it is, but in the abbey, for a friend? No, even I have my limits. No, I drank a little sherry in Charles's memory, but that was all.'

'So . . .' Grand was trying to sort out the tangle in his own mind. 'Charles Dickens was . . . a *friend* of yours?' He wasn't sure how to put it; there must be some form of words, but he was blowed if he could think what it might be.

'Lord, no!' Boulton frowned, swigging from the flask again. 'I mean, yes, he was a friend, of course, but he was strictly a ladies' man.'

'*Real* ladies, he means,' Park thought he ought to clarify.

'Quite. No, Charles saw our act, didn't he, Fan?'

'Loved it, Mr Batchelor. Loved it. Insisted on seeing us after the show – rather as you two did, you naughty boys.'

'We were chuckling, you know,' Boulton went on, 'about drag and so on, and I said that Charles should put me in his next book.'

'*Edwin Drood*?' Batchelor wanted to be sure.

'That's the one.'

'But there's no Stella in that,' Batchelor said. 'There's Pussy and Rosebud . . .'

'He hadn't got round to it when the great landlord in the sky called time,' Boulton said. 'I was due to appear in Chapter Twenty-Four, I believe, when the twist in the tale first appears.'

'The twist being . . .?'

Everybody in the cab looked blank.

'Well, *I* don't know,' Boulton trilled in his Stella voice again. 'You can't second-guess the master. He had something in mind, that was for sure. No, I just gave him a bit of local colour.'

'You visited Gads Hill, though,' Grand checked. 'Talked to the houseboy, Isaac.'

'Was that his name?' Boulton asked. 'Yes, I remember: sweet lad. A trifle on the simple side, but well meaning.'

'And you went with Dickens to the opium den?'

'Where?' Boulton looked horrified.

'Bluegate Fields?' Batchelor said. 'Canton Kitty's.'

'God, no,' Boulton bridled, emptying his flask with a final swig. 'That stuff'll kill you. I look after myself. My body's a temple; what is it, Fan?'

'A temple, Stell,' Park nodded approvingly.

'There you are,' Boulton said. 'Can't both be wrong.'

'Did you have any reason to want Charles Dickens dead?' Grand had to ask.

'Me?' Boulton shrieked. 'That's a terrible thing to say, Mr Grand. He was a sweetheart, that man. A brilliant, funny, dazzling sweetheart. I wouldn't have hurt a hair on his genius head, would I, Fan?'

'Certainly not,' Park agreed. 'But, clearly, Mr Grand, from what you're saying, *somebody* would.'

'Somebody would,' Batchelor nodded.

'One case at a time,' Boulton said. 'Artie Clinton is our priority, gentlemen. When our case comes up, Fanny and I are likely to be going away for rather a long time.'

'If Williamson doesn't get us first,' Park chipped in.

'Exactly,' Boulton nodded. 'We're not rich, Mr Batchelor, Mr Grand, even allowing for our very healthy ticket sales. But we'll give you *our all* if you get the man who killed Artie Clinton.'

Grand looked at Batchelor and vice versa. Neither was sure they could handle the all that Ernest Boulton had in mind.

'We'll be in touch, la . . . gentlemen,' Batchelor said. 'In the meantime, I suggest you hail another cab. I can't drive one of these things and we've already established that Matthew, though he can handle any horse you care to put in front of him, doesn't know Wakefield Street from his elbow.'

'You won't let us down?' Park squeezed Grand's arm.

'Not even lightly,' Grand assured him, and they all got out. When Boulton and Park had rattled off into the starry, starry night in their newly hailed cab, Batchelor turned to Grand. 'Better get this rig back to its rightful owner, Matthew. He'll be worrying.'

'That's a good idea,' Grand said, climbing up on to the perch again. 'Where I come from, a man can get hung for horse-stealing.'

'Hanged,' Batchelor corrected him.

'Whatever.'

*   *   *

The town house of Lord Arthur Clinton was tucked away in Eaton Mews, behind the elegant Georgian facades that every investigator, journalist, policeman and enquiry agent knew covered a multitude of sins. Grand and Batchelor were together on this one, in the fond hope that they stood slightly more chance that way of battering down the brick wall they expected to meet.

Lord Albert Clinton was a taller, leaner, less stooped version of his late departed brother. He had the same petulant mouth, the languid eyes, the thinning hair.

'Enquiry agents?' The man was dressed in black, puffing on a large cheroot. Servants in the Newcastle livery dashed hither and yon carrying books and bundles of letters, many of them bound in pink ribbon. 'What are you enquiring about, specifically?'

'Specifically, my lord,' Batchelor was better with the aristocracy than Grand, whose leanings were altogether too Democrat, 'your late brother's demise.'

'We're not Catholic, you know,' Clinton said, offering his visitors seats. A huge spaniel padded hotly into what had clearly been Lord Arthur's study, panting and wheezing in the heat. He looked at Grand and Batchelor, didn't like what he saw, and flopped across Lord Albert's feet. 'God, Fauntleroy, you weigh a ton. Cook's been feeding you leftovers again, hasn't she?'

'I don't follow, sir,' Batchelor said.

'The dog,' Clinton explained. 'Getting fat.'

'No, I mean your reference to Catholicism.'

'Well, isn't that why you're here? Looking into Artie's suicide?'

'Suicide?' Grand spoke for the first time.

'Gentlemen.' Clinton freed one of his feet with difficulty and placed it gently on the spaniel's back. 'I don't mean to seem uncooperative, but what the bally Hell has all this got to do with you?'

'We have been engaged by a client,' Batchelor said. 'A client who believes that your brother was murdered.'

Lord Albert paused before removing his other foot and placing it on the dog's back. 'The client's name?' he asked, his voice hard, his eyes furious.

'I cannot divulge . . .' Batchelor began, but Grand had other ideas.

'Ernest Boulton,' he said.

Clinton got up, stepping off the spaniel with reasonable alacrity, but not until the animal had yelped in pain. 'That degenerate!' Lord Albert muttered. He looked at them both. 'You know the wretch passed himself off as Artie's wife, don't you? Lady Clinton! It's a good thing for Stella they don't allow duelling in this country any more, or I should have called him out and put a bullet through his brain.'

'Can we assume you didn't approve of your brother's friends, my lord?'

'Assume what you like,' Clinton said, pouring himself a brandy. 'Oh, Stella does have a marvellous soprano voice, it's true. But as for the rest of it . . .'

'It's the rest of it we're concerned with,' Grand told him.

'Don't be,' Clinton said. 'It's all too late now. The police had charged Artie with unmentionable crimes that would make a docker blush . . . although, come to think of it, Eton and the Navy – *de rigueur* in both of those institutions. This *is* 1870, I suppose. But no, Stella and Fanny took the whole thing too far. Thrown out of Burlington Arcade more times than I've had hot dinners. The point is that Artie is dead. He'll have to answer to a higher judge now.' Clinton pointed solemnly to the ceiling.

'The official line is scarlet fever,' Grand said.

'Yes, well, that's just for public consumption. No. I believe this wretched Stella business had got Artie down.'

'Did he say as much to you?' Batchelor asked.

'No, he didn't, as a matter of fact. *Au contraire.* Seemed very combative. Wanted to sue everybody – the police doctor, the old fart of a magistrate, the police themselves.'

'Would that be Chief Inspector Williamson?' Grand asked.

'Yes, I believe that was his name.'

'Tell us, my lord,' Batchelor followed up, 'did Mr Williamson come here, to interview your brother personally?'

'I believe he did, yes. I live across town, of course, so I'm unaware of the precise comings and goings. I know he raged about the whole thing. What was it he said? "Those bloody chief inspectors, they're all the same."'

'Met a few, had he, over the years?' Grand felt obliged to ask.

'Haven't we all?' Clinton sighed, and Grand and Batchelor thought they ought to let that one go. 'There is a rumour,' Clinton went on, 'a wicked, despicable lie, I assure you, that Artie is not actually dead at all, but that he has fled to Paris – the Bois de Boulogne to be precise – to escape the full rigour of the law. I have seen his body, gentlemen, and I can assure you that that is nonsense.'

'My lord,' Batchelor said, 'I can see that you have much to organize here and you have been patience itself, but would it be in order for us to interview your late brother's staff?'

'Interview away, gentlemen. There aren't many more skeletons hiding in the Pelham-Clinton cupboards, I don't think. And if there are, I don't want to know about them. Come on, Fauntleroy, walkies! Let's run some of that fat off you.'

The dog had not moved and didn't now, simply rolling a yellowed eye at the detectives as they set off to stop the staff in their scurrying and find out what they knew.

The late Lord Arthur's staff had been as helpful as Grand and Batchelor could expect. The butler, Griswold, had been with the family since Queen Anne's reign (or so it seemed to Batchelor) and was loyalty itself. Yes, the attack had come on suddenly. One minute he was right as rain; the next, dead. No, there was nothing funny about Lord Arthur. Yes, the police had come calling, but it was all a case of mistaken identity and Lord Albert was sorting it all out.

Talbot, the gentleman's gentleman, was altogether more forthcoming. Yes, Lord Arthur kept the company of dubious people. They came to Eaton Mews sometimes, wearing clothes that could only be described as extreme. Were they men or women? Who could say? Talbot only picked up snippets of gossip. Fanny, he knew, was a law student, so, surely, he had to be a man. But as a woman, he was very convincing. That American chappie, the one from Scotland, certainly believed he was a woman – Fanny, that is, not the American chappie. All in all, it was very confusing. And, strictly between Grand, Batchelor and Talbot, the gentleman's gentleman was only too pleased to be looking for employment elsewhere, where men were men and women were glad of it.

Grand paid particular attention to the cook. While she was overfeeding Fauntleroy, what else might she have been feeding his late lordship? While the American quizzed her minutely on Lord Arthur's dietary intake on the days before his death, Batchelor quietly rummaged in her cupboards. There was nothing there – except perhaps tapioca, a personal hatred of his – that could be construed as poison.

They had left the under-butler, Mason, until last, simply because he was up to his eyeballs in moving Lord Arthur's personal effects. There was a will to be probated, bequests to be sent to various beneficiaries. Mason, it turned out, had no loyalty towards his late master; nor, in fact, to masters generally. Lord Arthur, apart from his little peccadilloes involving day dresses, was a declared bankrupt. The Eaton Mews house would have to go towards his debts and all of them, even Griswold, the pompous old arse-licker, would be out on the streets come Thursday.

'He shook, you know,' Mason muttered, careful that old Griswold shouldn't hear. 'Lord Arthur, in his last moments. Shook from head to foot. I know. I was there.'

'You called the doctor?' Batchelor asked.

'I did. Bugger all he could do, of course. Family retainer, like all the rest of them. About as qualified as Fauntleroy, if you ask me. Stuck leeches behind His Lordship's ears. "Violent delirium" he said, looking at Lord Arthur twitching and writhing on the bed. Well, I could see that. When he died, with the doctor right there, taking his pulse, the old quack said, "Scarlet fever". Have you ever heard anything so ridiculous?'

'So,' Grand became confidential, leaning nearer to the man. 'What's your opinion on it all, Mr Mason? What do *you* think caused Lord Arthur's death?'

Mason became confidential too. 'He was poisoned.'

'Who by?' Grand asked.

'One of his Pretty Boys, I shouldn't wonder. They should hang them all, if you ask me. Not natural. Not natural at all.'

'Tell me, Mr Mason,' Batchelor said. 'The day of Lord Arthur's death. Or perhaps the day before – did he have any visitors?'

'No, not that I can . . . oh, wait. Yes, there was one bloke. Not the sort to have a calling card and I'd never seen him before. He was a policeman. From Scotland Yard.'

THIRTEEN

The lights burned blue in Alsatia that night and Grand and Batchelor were sitting alongside each other in their respective armchairs, looking at a blank wall. And this time, it really was blank.

'I just can't believe she did that,' Grand said. The shock had still not passed.

'Don't fret yourself, Matthew,' Batchelor clucked. 'All the pieces are still here. You know Mrs Rackstraw never actually throws anything away. It'll just take a little longer, that's all.' He was tacking the pieces of paper that Mrs Rackstraw had carefully placed in a pile back into position. 'Actually,' he said, brightly, looking over his shoulder at his despondent colleague, 'she may have done us a favour in an odd sort of way; given us a chance to re-evaluate, reassess, recap.'

'Re Mrs Rackstraw,' Grand was lighting a cigar. 'Williamson's right, you know. She'll have to go.'

'Well, if Williamson thinks she ought to go, that's a damned good reason to keep her, isn't it?'

'Point taken,' Grand shrugged. 'Tack away, James. You're better at this sort of thing than I am.'

For a while, Batchelor fussed around, holding the scraps of paper to the lamplight, turning them this way and that. Finally, when Grand was well into his second cigar and draining the last of his second brandy, order, of a sort, stood before him. Batchelor sat back down, heavily, and took a swig of his own neglected tipple. 'Right,' he said. He had a pen and yet more pieces of paper, still on a pad, to his right. 'You first.'

'Charles Dickens and his dark side.' Grand was reading the papers now back on the wall.

'He has a mistress in Nunhead,' Batchelor said, adding scribblings as he spoke. 'Name of Ellen Ternan.'

'What do we know about her?' Grand asked.

'Nothing, other than what Wilkie Collins told us.'

'She's an actress.'

'Never heard of her, though,' Batchelor shook his head. 'Can't be very good.'

'It's how good she was in the sack that probably interested Dickens. You're guessing she was the woman in the veil at the man's funeral.'

'Stands to reason,' Batchelor said. 'We need to find her.'

'Nunhead, Collins said.'

'Yes, and so did Butler, the groom.'

'What's in Nunhead?' It was not a part of the country that Matthew Grand had knowingly come across.

'Apart from Nell Ternan, not a lot,' Batchelor told him. 'It's got a station and a cemetery. That's about it.'

'A backwater, then.' Grand was thinking aloud. 'Somewhere out of the way where he can stash his mistress.'

'A woman,' Batchelor said, in dark, meaningful tones. 'Didn't Dick Tanner raise that? Didn't he tell you that there's always a woman involved?'

'In the general scheme of things, that's likely.' Grand blew a final smoke ring and stubbed out the remains of his cigar. 'But in this case, we've got three of them.'

'Nell Ternan, Georgy Hogarth . . .'

'And Catherine Dickens, the wife scorned. And if you throw in Dickens, as we must . . .'

'The eternal triangle becomes a square,' Batchelor reasoned.

'Actually a rhomboid, if I remember my Conic Sections from West Point.'

'So what are you thinking?' Batchelor asked.

'They all love dear old Charles.' Grand leaned forward, scanning the papers in front of him. 'Chronologically, Catherine comes first in that Dickens married her. They may or may not at one time have been passionately in love.'

'But Georgy, the little sister, is waiting in the wings. She has eyes for Charles as well.'

'And becomes their housekeeper.'

'And remains *his* housekeeper when big sister moves out.'

'That seems to be something of a trend here, I notice.' Grand was still trying to complete his understanding of the Englishman's home life, which was so very different from that of the average

American. 'The Reverend Moptrucket had his sister-in-law stashed away in the kitchen, too.'

Batchelor shrugged. He had not had that much experience of housekeepers, apart from those here in Alsatia, and surely *they* couldn't be the norm.

'Then along comes little Nell,' Grand continued, 'unless I'm mixing my characters too much.'

'And Dickens falls for her. Was this, I wonder, before Catherine moved out or afterwards?'

'It must have been before,' Grand reasoned, 'hence the need to keep her quiet. Dickens didn't have a brass neck about mistresses like Wilkie Collins does.'

'Even so,' Batchelor was frowning as he spoke, 'these three women would have a motive for killing each other – jealousy. But why kill Charles?'

'It's his fault, isn't it?' Grand was trying to get in touch with his feminine side and see things from the distaff point of view. 'He's over-affectionate, perhaps, with his sister-in-law and leads her on. That annoys Catherine.'

'Then Nell comes along and takes Georgy's place.' Batchelor moved the story on.

'Which annoys Georgy. Hell, they might all have been in it together, taking turns to mix the potions that killed him.'

'No, no, that wouldn't work. Our problem is that we haven't met Nell or Catherine yet. Two points of our rhomboid, or whatever you said it was, are missing. But the only woman we know for certain visited Gads Hill in the run up to Dickens's death wasn't a woman at all. It was Ernest Boulton.'

'All right.' Grand leaned back and focused as Batchelor took up his pen again. 'The *other* dark side of Dickens's life; the rouge and lipstick brigade.'

'Dickens intended to put Stella into *Edwin Drood*, although for the life of me I can't see how she'd fit. There could be a Landless connection, I suppose.'

'Who knew about Stella?' Grand asked.

'Isaac Armitage – he'd met her at Gads Hill.'

'Yes, but he thought she really was a woman. I mean, who knew about the cross-dressing?'

'Wilkie Collins,' Batchelor nodded, remembering. 'He wished

me luck and said I'd find the end of that road rather unexpected.'

'He got that right!' Grand chuckled.

'But there's nothing funny about Dickens,' Batchelor reminded them both. 'No skeleton of the unmentionable kind in his cupboard.'

'No,' Grand agreed. 'I just think old Charles got a kick out of it all. "Latest woman in his life", that sort of thing.'

'Which might explain Canton Kitty's too.'

'Important if, as we believe, it was likely laudanum that killed him.'

'It's the notes I haven't written that are hurting my head at the moment.' Batchelor refilled their glasses.

'Lord Arthur Clinton and Gabriel Verdon,' Grand nodded.

'Both of them die within three weeks of Dickens,' Batchelor was piecing it together. 'Clinton comes to see us trying to get Scotland Yard off his back on charges of immorality.'

'And dies the next day of a disease that doesn't kill you that quickly.'

'According to Stella and Fanny,' Batchelor took over, 'poisoned by Chief Inspector Williamson, who is annoyed by the fact that Clinton's money – or at least Clinton's connections and social standing – will get him off the hook.'

'Links between Dickens and Clinton?' Grand's eyes narrowed in the lingering smoke of his last cigar.

'Stella,' Batchelor said, scribbling it all down. 'The friend of one; almost certainly the lover of the other.'

'Coincidence?' Grand had to raise it, but neither man believed in coincidence and neither therefore answered.

'Gabriel Verdon.' Batchelor committed the name to paper. 'Long-serving editor at Chapman and Hall, Dickens's publishers.'

'Cause of death, though, James.' Grand was shaking his head. 'Totally different. Dickens, we've established, was probably poisoned, though short of digging the poor bastard up in the abbey, we're never going to be able to prove that. Likely Clinton was too – same lack of proof and also, like Dickens, a family who don't really want us to pry. If we're looking at one killer for all of them, he's sure changed his tune.'

'You're right,' Batchelor sighed. The smoke, the brandy, the pieces of paper were all beginning to whirl in his brain, a mixture as heady and bewildering as anything that could be found at Canton Kitty's. 'I suggest we sleep on it. Then we need to talk to the ladies. Call it.' He spun a penny in the air.

'Tails,' Grand said.

'Sorry,' Batchelor caught the coin and revealed it triumphantly. 'It's the dear old Queen, God bless her, I'm afraid. I'll take the gorgeous, smouldering spitfire that is Nell Ternan. You can have frumpy old Catherine Dickens. Fair?'

Frumpy old Catherine Dickens didn't live in such splendour as Grand had seen at Gads Hill Place, but she wasn't doing badly. Dickens had obviously stopped short of leaving her to starve in a garret; in fact, judging from her general build, she hadn't been left to starve anywhere and, as if to prove the point, she immediately rang for tea and buns as soon as Grand had come into the room.

'Having a nibble of something at this hour always sets you up, I feel, don't you?' she smiled, and settled herself comfortably back in the overstuffed armchair.

Grand wasn't sure which meal or snack this could possibly represent, but he knew that this was potentially a sticky sort of interview to conduct, so if she needed sugar, she should have sugar. He hadn't decided, even now when he was sitting on her itchy horsehair sofa in her drawing room, waiting to drink her tea, how to refer to Dickens. Your husband? Your former husband? The artist formerly known as Mr Dickens? They all sounded wrong.

'Mr Grand,' the woman said, suddenly, from the depths of her chair. 'You have a look of a rabbit in thrall to a stoat. Please don't concern yourself when it comes to referring to Charles. Mr Dickens will do as well as anything else.'

Grand was stunned and had to make a special effort to close his mouth.

'I have been living apart from my husband now for over twelve years, Mr Grand; the feeling of loss and grief has never left me. In common with all who loved him, I mourn his death, of course I do. But more, I mourn for my lost hopes.' She smiled, a shy, small smile. 'Although I knew it was fruitless, every morning, as I awoke and dressed and ate, walked, went about my daily tasks, I could hope that today might be the day that he came back to me.' She looked down at her hands, folded calmly in her well-upholstered lap. 'Foolish, I know. But it was my private foolishness.' She looked up at him, suddenly, her eyes sharp. 'It has kept me alive, Mr Grand. That, and my children.'

Grand had had the impression that the children had sided with Dickens, and this placed him squarely on the horns of another dilemma. So far, this interview was not going terribly well.

'I know that the Press and even dear Georgy choose to give the impression that the children spurn me, but they do nothing of the sort, Mr Grand. Dear Charlie came with me, of course, but the others visit, when they can. I may not have been the best housekeeper in the world, Mr Grand and I suppose it could be laid at my door that we had far too many children, but . . .' her smile this time was mischievous, 'I think you are man of the world enough, Mr Grand, to know that these things do take two. But sadly, my intellect is not equal to that of dear Charles and so, I had to go.'

Grand cleared his throat. It really was time he contributed to this conversation. 'I understand that he—'

'My word, yes!' Catherine Dickens rocked back and forth, her hands slapping her knees. 'Like a weasel. With any woman in sight when he was younger; then, latterly, just that absolute strumpet, Ellen Ternan. No better than she should be, of course. Actress.' All was delivered in a quiet, no-nonsense tone; she might just as well have been ordering the weekly vegetables.

Grand was flustered. That hadn't been what he had intended to ask at all. Although now he was pressed to remember what he had been going to ask.

'I'm sorry,' Mrs Dickens said, contritely. 'I am teasing you, Mr Grand. I see so few people and they have such . . . ideas of me, the ones that come. They expect me to behave like one of Charles's heroines, the stupid ones, the ones that don't get their man. He did put a lot of his life into his books, the lamb, even . . .'

'Even?'

'I beg your pardon?' She opened her eyes wide and looked like an elderly child, all innocence.

'You said, "even".'

'Did I?' She looked up as the door eased open and an elderly maid came into the room, pushing a laden trolley. 'Tea and buns, how lovely.' The maid laid everything out in front of her mistress and left the room, all without speaking a word. 'Nice woman,' Catherine Dickens said. 'Been with me since . . . before. Couldn't stand Georgy, one of the few people who doesn't like her. She really is *very* likeable, my sister. Have you met her?'

'I have,' Grand said.

'And you found her charming, of course.'

'I did.'

'What a gentleman you are indeed, Mr Grand. But remind me again why you are here.'

'I am an enquiry agent, Mrs Dickens,' Grand decided to bite the bullet on the mode of address. 'My colleague and I are investigating the death of your . . . Mr Dickens.'

The woman laughed again, but quietly. 'Not *my* Mr Dickens, though, surely. You are investigating the death of the famous author, the spellbinding performer, the womanizer, the liar, the . . .' She took a sip of tea. 'Excuse me, Mr Grand,' she said, dabbing at the corner of her mouth with a napkin. 'I don't always take things so well, as you might realize.'

'I think you deal with your unusual situation with considerable fortitude,' Grand said politely, and as he spoke he realized, to his surprise, that he meant it.

'Why, *thank* you, Mr Grand. That is very kind.' She took an enormous bite of sugared bun and gave it her full attention for a moment. 'I find that people do tend to side with Charles. He was no prize, you know, not back in the old days, or indeed now . . . when I say now, of course, I mean recently. The constant tapping – tap, tap, tap – always three times on anything he passed. And vain! Oh, Mr Grand, I could tell you such stories! He combed his hair hundreds of times a day. Even when my poor dear sister was dying – he based his Little Nell on her, you know – even then, as he loomed like some ghoul over her last breaths, he was still combing his hair. I don't believe he even realized he was doing it, in the end.'

'We understand that there may be . . . women . . .'

'Women, yes, Mr Grand, in the past, as I said, certainly many women. But of late, just Ellen. He has kept her for years in far more comfort than I enjoy. Ever since he began to see some success, he has kept several premises for . . . writing . . . in, and so it has always been easy for him to disappear for days on end, with everyone assuming he is somewhere else; somewhere he should be, that is.'

Grand was beginning to see a pattern to the woman's speech. She wasn't telling him everything – of that he was certain. When she lied, or left something unsaid, there was a little muscle that jumped and kicked in the corner of her left eye. It was jumping and kicking now.

'I understand that you called in a detective, to watch your husband.'

'It did become necessary,' she said. 'It was when I found the bracelet, you know.'

'The bracelet?' Grand didn't know there was any jewellery in the case.

'Yes. I thought it was a present for me, but then I saw the legend inscribed on the clasp.' The muscle wasn't twitching now, but her eyes filled with tears. 'I had heard no words of love from dear Charles in such a long while that I knew at once it was meant for another. I cared then, Mr Grand. Please, don't get me wrong,' and she held up a sugary hand, 'I care still. But then it was raw. Plorn was only six. I myself was only forty-three. I hoped even then for more children . . .' She looked stricken again and comforted herself with a bun. 'So I engaged a man, a policeman . . .'

'Inspector Field?'

'I believe that is his name.'

'And do you still hear from him?'

'I have engaged him, from time to time. I don't wish to be rude, Mr Grand,' she said, suddenly leaning forward and topping up his cup, 'but could you tell me quite why you came to see me? Charles and I have not exchanged a word for many years. I'm not sure . . .'

Grand was caught on the hop. He wanted to get information by stealth, but this woman had made so much of the running he wasn't sure whether he had even asked her anything. 'I suppose I just wanted to know if Mr Dickens had any enemies,' he blurted out.

'Enemies?' she chortled. 'Everyone loved Charles, of course they did. Everyone.' Her face darkened and she looked truly malevolent, sugar-dusted as she was. 'I loved him. I love him still.'

There seemed little else to say. Grand got up and put his cup and saucer back on the trolley. 'Thank you for your candour, Mrs Dickens,' he said. 'I'm sorry to have troubled you.'

'No trouble at all,' she trilled and watched him go. When his hand was on the doorknob, she spoke again. 'But, Mr Grand?'

He turned. 'Yes?'

'Just because everyone loved him, doesn't mean that many of us didn't also want to see him dead.' She smiled. 'Goodbye.'

As soon as he rang the bell, James Batchelor understood. The Nunhead sun flashed on the brass plate alongside the door and it explained that odd slip of the tongue that John Forster had made when he was listing Dickens's properties. 'Win,' he had said, and turned it into the meaningless 'Win or lose'. Yet, here it was – Windsor Lodge. And he understood something else too; as soon as the door opened, he smelled something – attar of roses.

'Not today.' The attractive chestnut-haired woman who had just opened the door was already closing it.

Batchelor hated jamming his foot in the door, especially as it carried with it a certain amount of pain, but it was an essential part of the armoury of the private detective and he used it now. 'Miss Ternan?' he raised his hat. 'Miss Ellen Ternan?'

She blinked for a moment. 'Are you the Press?' she asked. Her eyes were a clear, sparkling blue. Her day dress was deepest black with a little purple trim on the cuffs. Full mourning, Batchelor observed, and yet . . .

'No, madam,' he said and passed her his card. 'My colleague and I are looking into the death of Mr Charles Dickens.'

Again the blink and perhaps – or had Batchelor imagined it – a hint of a blush. 'What has that to do with me?' she asked.

'Well, to begin with, Mr Dickens pays rent on this house – or, at least, he used to.' It wasn't like James Batchelor to be so blunt. First the foot in the door, now the rude assumption. He'd be accusing the woman of murder next. But that was precisely the point, wasn't it? For all James Batchelor knew, he was looking now at a cold-blooded, blue-eyed murderer.

'You'd better come in,' she said, and once he was in the passageway she checked the road in both directions before closing the door.

Windsor Lodge was nowhere near as palatial as Gads Hill, but it was large, light and airy. There was the inevitable piano in the drawing room, aspidistras in the corners and paintings and photographs everywhere. But none, Batchelor noted with his trained detective's eye, of Charles Dickens.

'Are you Grand or Batchelor?' Ellen Ternan asked, looking at the card in her hand.

'I am Batchelor, Miss Ternan.' He took the soft chair she offered him.

'Ter*nan*.' She stressed the last syllable. 'It's pronounced Ter*nan*.'

'I see,' Batchelor smiled. Kept women were vain by the nature of their calling. By definition, they felt themselves superior to at least one other woman in the world – in this case, Catherine Dickens. 'You were a little hard to find,' he said.

Something close to a smile flitted across Nell's face. 'Charles would have it so,' she said. 'We found solace when we could. He called me his magic circle of one. We nearly died together even if we couldn't live together.'

'You did?' Batchelor frowned. Could the whole thing be a mare's nest, a suicide pact gone wrong?

'The railway accident at Staplehurst, Mr Batchelor. Back in sixty-five. Do you remember it?'

James Batchelor had been a boy reporter then on the *Telegraph*. He had not yet met Grand and was up to his journalist's neck in the Haymarket stranglings. A train crash had barely registered.

'It was five years exactly,' Nell went on, 'to the very day that he died. He was heroic, Mr Batchelor. Saved my life as well as those of several passengers. Of course, he had to play it down to avoid the scandal of my presence.'

'Was it such a scandal?' Batchelor felt bound to ask. 'Wilkie Collins.'

'Dear Wilkie.' She laughed, and the sound was odd in the

stillness of Windsor Lodge. 'Such a degenerate, but he adored
Charles. We all did.'

'Even Mrs Dickens?' Batchelor thought it time to mention the
other woman to the Other Woman.

Nell's face fell. She got up and crossed to the window, looking
out over the long lawn that ran behind the house. 'What do you
want to know?' she asked.

'Everything,' he said, simply.

'How do *I* know,' she turned to him, 'that what I am about to
divulge will not appear in some lurid yellow press tomorrow and
be sniggered about in salons and public houses alike?'

'You have my word, Miss Ternan,' Batchelor said, taking care
to stress it correctly.

Nell looked at him. The face was boyish, the eyes honest and
steady. He was younger than her by a year or two, but they
breathed the same air, walked the same streets. And here they
were, from their different perspectives, talking about the same
man. She swallowed hard and took a chance.

'I come from a theatrical family, Mr Batchelor. Charles first saw
me on stage when I was eighteen. He was forty-five. It wasn't love
at first sight; I suppose I grew on him, with time. He of course,
was the great writer . . . or so I thought. We became intimate,
although I know he agonized long and hard over what to do about
Catherine. He confided in a few select friends. John Forster advised
caution. Wilkie Collins said, "Follow your heart, Charles". William
Thackeray . . . in fact, I don't believe I can remember what
Thackeray said, but then, who can? Charles and Catherine separated
in the May of 1858. I was shunted around, discreetly, to Broadstairs,
Slough, various French and Italian resorts. Oh, it was wonderful
. . .' She smiled at the memory of it, then she sighed. 'But I was
not Mrs Dickens. Nor, it transpires, will I ever be.'

'You went to the funeral?'

'Yes,' she said. 'Widow's weeds, although I was not, strictly
speaking, a widow. Veils are all-disguising, aren't they? And
George Dolby was so kind. But, Mr Batchelor, I really don't
understand. Dr Beard said that the cause of death was a brain
haemorrhage, a stroke. Why are you looking into it?'

'We have reason to believe, Miss Ternan, that Mr Dickens was
poisoned.'

Nell sat down hurriedly, her hand to her mouth. 'No,' she whispered. 'That can't be.'

'You knew that Mr Dickens took laudanum?'

'For his gout, yes, but always in small doses. Not enough to kill him.'

'We believe that an extra-large dose was given to him on the day before he died.'

'Where?' Nell asked, sitting upright and lacing her fingers tightly together.

'Er . . . probably the chalet,' Batchelor told her, 'at Gads Hill.'

'I suppose . . .' she began. 'But, no, it couldn't be.'

'What couldn't be?' Batchelor asked.

'Charles took me once to an opium den, a frightful place in Bluegate Fields. He needed to see for himself, he said, because it was part of the plot of *Edwin Drood*. Some Americans came with us, some friends he had made on his American tour.'

'Did you get the impression that that was Mr Dickens's only visit to such a place?'

'I did,' Nell said.

'Then we're back to Gads Hill,' Batchelor shrugged.

Nell stood up. 'Would you come with me, Mr Batchelor?' she asked, and he followed her along a winding passageway into a second drawing room, smaller than the first and crammed with books, most of them by Charles Dickens Esquire.

'Do you like it?' she asked, waving her hand around the room.

'Very nice,' Batchelor said. He was not much of a connoisseur of interior décor but, having suffered in many a teeming garret where the cockroaches were larger than he was, he could at least appreciate cleanliness.

'Charles adored it,' she said, quietly, as the memories flooded back. 'He saw it as his retreat. More than Gads Hill, it was a magic place to hide from the world. Tell me, Mr Batchelor, are you a fan of Charles's work?'

'Certainly,' Batchelor said. 'I'll let you into a secret, Miss Ternan; I used to be a newspaperman.'

She gasped and recoiled.

'Oh, don't worry.' He held up his hand. 'That was then, I assure you. Now I wouldn't give journalists the time of day. No, I only mention it because I have had to wrestle with the written word. And when you've done that, you realize what a genius the master was.'

'Indeed,' she said, with a strange look on her face. 'That's just as well, Mr Batchelor; because you are standing on the very spot where a genius fell.'

If Batchelor had not been a man, it would have been his turn to gasp and recoil. As it was, he just let his jaw drop. Instinctively, though, he stepped to one side, as if the great man still lay sprawled on the carpet.

'Charles was with me for the two days before he died,' she said. 'He had dinner with the Prince of Wales and the King of the Belgians and came straight here.'

'But . . . Miss Hogarth . . .'

'Georgy and I came to an arrangement years ago,' Nell said. 'You know, I suppose, that she loved Charles too?'

'I had heard a rumour,' he said.

'She told the world nothing,' Nell went on, 'because that was what Charles wished. When he was supposedly at Broadstairs, at his offices in Wellington Street, at Gads Hill, he was usually here with me. So it was on the eighth of June. He became unwell a little before breakfast. I wanted to send for the doctor.'

'Beard?'

'Anyone,' she said. 'But Charles wouldn't hear of it. He knew he was dying. He said he was expecting it, but not this soon. His overriding anxiety . . .' Nell paused, her fingers pressed to her lips as the memories of Dickens's last day flooded her mind, '. . . was that he should not be found dead here. He must go to Gads Hill. I sent Georgy a telegram and she sent Butler . . .'

'The groom.'

'Yes. He came in the closed chaise. The dear man must have lashed the horse almost to death to get here so quickly, and somehow we bundled poor Charles into the cab.'

'You went with him?'

'No.' A tear rolled down Nell Ternan's cheek. 'He insisted I didn't. It was the last time I saw him alive.' She sighed, fighting her demons of regret, and she pulled herself together. 'Georgy sent me a telegram later that night. Dear Charles was still alive then, barely, but the family had gathered and I felt I couldn't intrude.'

Batchelor waited until he felt she could go on. 'What did he mean?' he asked her. 'That he was expecting it, but not this soon? He wasn't such an old man.'

The strange expression had returned to Nell Ternan's face. 'No, Mr Batchelor, Charles didn't mean the grim reaper, except in the most general sense. Someone wanted to kill Charles Dickens and he knew why.'

'He knew why but not who?' Batchelor's pulse was racing. At last, after weeks of brick walls and obfuscation, here it was. And he only felt a *little* smug, having solved the case ahead of Williamson, ahead of Field and without Grand.

'If he knew that,' Nell said, 'he didn't confide in me.'

'The "why", then,' Batchelor perched on the edge of a sofa, on the edge of a solution. 'I'll settle for that.'

Nell smiled. 'He was a loving man, was Charles Dickens,' she said. 'Kind and considerate. He was a loving friend to his friends, a loving father to his children, a loving lover to me. So loving, in fact, that he put the people he loved into his books. I was Estella in *Great Expectations*, Bella in *Our Mutual Friend*. I was even, unfinished though it is, Helena Landless in *Edwin Drood*.'

'That was nice of him,' Batchelor said, 'to write so lovingly of you.'

'Yes,' she said. 'Except that he didn't.'

'I'm sorry,' Batchelor frowned. 'I don't follow.'

'Charles Dickens never wrote a word,' she said.

It took a while for James Batchelor to say another and, when he did, it merely turned out to be, 'What?'

'Oh, he longed to *be* a writer, certainly, and he tried hard in that respect, God knows. But he couldn't do it. The words just would not flow.'

'So . . .?' Batchelor was confused.

'So he got his friend Trollope – the elder, I mean, not that idiot son of his, to write for him. Old Trollope was a postman, when it comes right down to it; needed the money. He didn't really care if it was his name or Dickens's on the weekly instalments. After Trollope, Wilkie Collins wrote one – I forget which – and then, of course, Gabriel Verdon took over.'

'Verdon?' Batchelor mouthed.

'Only a *very* few of us know,' Nell said. 'Reputation was

everything to Charles, which is why I had to linger in the shadows. Had it come out that Fagin, Martin Chuzzlewit, Nicholas Nickleby – all of them – were the creation of somebody else, Charles would have been ruined. He wrote up the instalments when he felt threatened, so that Verdon's handwriting would not become apparent. And, of course, he wrote some of the short stories, even a play, I believe, with Wilkie Collins. He could manage shorter pieces, but full-length novels were simply beyond him. And he gave some of the ideas for the plots, although not that in his later works, if I can use the word "his" at all.'

'So *that's* how he could be so prolific,' Batchelor said as realization dawned.

'Exactly. A man who gives so much to charity, who gives his time to good causes, who goes on holidays with his friends and family, who spends so much time with me – such a man could never have written the millions of words attributed to Charles. Gabriel Verdon did all that – the angel Gabriel, as Charles called him. More angelic than he knew.'

She closed to Batchelor and dropped to her knees, cradling his face in her hands. 'Oh, Mr Batchelor, I beg of you. Don't let this become public knowledge. Those of us who know have kept this secret for years – Charles's secret; our secret. Think of the millions around the world who read him, who hang on his every word. Charles Dickens is a god to them, a literary genius above all others. You cannot destroy that. You cannot!' And she collapsed on his knees, sobbing wretchedly. He lifted her up and sat her on the sofa beside him.

'Miss Ternan,' he said softly. 'Nell. Please don't worry,' and he teased an errant lock of hair from her face. 'If it lies within my power, none of what we discussed today will ever reach the outside world. You have my word on that.'

FOURTEEN

'You gave her your word and yet you've told me,' Grand teased, passing Batchelor a much-needed brandy.

'Don't enlarge your part, Matthew,' Batchelor scolded. 'You're not the world, just a speck in the floating detritus of eternity.'

Grand sucked his teeth in mock admiration. 'What a loss you are to journalism,' he said. 'Stuck in this God-awful day job.'

'Puts a different complexion on things, doesn't it?' Batchelor winced as the brandy hit the spot. 'All that outpouring, all those dazzling characters and wonderful stories – most of them Gabriel Verdon's.' Grand was still puzzling it out. 'So why did Verdon have to die?'

'I've been wrestling with that one all the way back from Nunhead,' Batchelor said, 'and I haven't the first idea. Did somebody find out that he was the real Dickens, as it were? An outraged fanatic who lost his temper and killed him? Did somebody else at Chapman and Hall learn the truth and have a row with him?'

'Had to be somebody on the inside,' Grand said. 'All that business with the keys. I can't believe anybody could walk right in to Chapman and Hall, just like that.'

'So, you're Henry Morford?' Henry Trollope beamed. 'Should I have read anything of yours?'

Morford grabbed the man's arms and quoted from himself, '"Thrilled ye ever at the story, how on stricken fields of glory, men have stood beneath the murderous iron hail?"' He waited for a response, but got nothing but the ticking of Chapman and Hall's clock. 'The *New York Times* can barely function without me,' the American went on, undeterred.

'So,' Trollope was still smiling, though for the life of him he didn't know why. 'You're here because . . .?'

A distant look came over Henry Morford's face and he held his head high. 'I just wanted to stand in the office of the publisher of the world's greatest writer,' he said. 'You know, for posterity's sake.'

'Er . . . I see,' Trollope said. All his life he had been used to the adulation of crowds; perhaps if Henry Morford knew the truth about Charles Dickens, he wouldn't have been so impressed. There was a sudden commotion and Frederic Chapman hurled himself into the room with a woman in tow. Her hat sat at a rakish angle across her head and both of them looked shaken.

'Well, *there* she is,' Morford beamed broadly, displaying a fine set of teeth. 'Beulah, honey, where've you been?'

'You know me, Henry,' she smiled just as broadly, straightening her hat. 'In this maze of passageways, I just got lost. This kind gentleman, I say, this kind gentleman . . .'

'. . . was about to call the police.' Chapman was clearly seething. 'Caught her ferreting about in the offices. What the Hell's going on?'

'Er . . . Mr Morford,' Trollope felt obliged to explain.

'Henry Morford, sir,' the journalist half bowed and handed Chapman his card. 'I'm guessing you must be Sir Frederic Chapman.'

'No, I . . .' The accolade had not come Chapman's way as yet, but he lived in hope.

'Beulah and I are over from the States and we heard about Mr Dickens's death. Well, I am a devoted fan; we both are, aren't we, Beulah?'

'Sure are,' she winked at Chapman, 'I say, we sure are.'

'You'll have to forgive us kinda barging on in here, but we just couldn't resist. We Americans are pretty impulsive folks, you've probably heard.' He held his wife to him, hugging her around the shoulders. 'I told Beulah that it was likely Mr Trollope and Sir Chapman would be this way, but she will go exploring. I'm sorry about that, Sir Chapman.'

'Er . . . just Chapman,' Chapman said, subsiding a little. He looked at Beulah again and she certainly did seem a little on the simple side. Perhaps he had misjudged her.

'Well, that's mighty democratic of you, Chapman,' Morford said, 'and thanks for letting us tread on this hallowed ground. We'll see ourselves out.' There were handshakes all round. 'Now, you stick with me, Beulah, y'hear? Can't have you getting lost again.'

Everybody laughed and the Americans made for the stairs and the Strand.

'Well?' Morford asked out of the corner of his mouth as Chapman and Hall's door closed behind them.

'All the safes are Chubbs,' she hissed back. 'Fort Knox'd be an easier nut to crack. What now? Wellington Street?'

Morford looked around him to get his bearings. St Clement Danes and Temple Bar loomed one way; Charing Cross and Trafalgar Square the other. 'If we have to,' he said, 'but since we're in the Strand, why don't we pay a courtesy call on those enquiry agents? One of them's a goddamned Yankee, for Christ's sake.'

'I do love your railroads,' Grand remarked to Batchelor, 'and you know that I do, so you'll understand that I am not being rude to a very well-meaning body of plate-layers when I say I never want to take this train again.' The train to Higham had gone over yet another set of bone-jarring points and Batchelor could only nod in agreement, his teeth still rattling in his head.

The train pulled in with a savage jerk at Higham Station, and Grand and Batchelor alighted, the only passengers to do so. The guard, comatose as ever, waved them through like old friends and they set off up the lane towards Gads Hill Place. The hot summer had not abated at all as July approached over the horizon, and soon their boots, the bottoms of their trousers and even their hats were rimed with soft dust, kicked up by their passage. Batchelor was a townie through and through and, although no one could call London clean, he remained very suspicious of floating detritus once he was outside its limits. Grand was at home with dust; his blue uniform back in the day had often been indistinguishable from the grey of his opponents, until a quick brush-down had revealed his true colours. He spat to clear his mouth and took a swig from the water bottle he carried with him whenever on the road, through force of habit. He held it out to Batchelor, who shook his head. He knew it was probably a good idea, just not very British.

'How antagonistic is Georgy Hogarth likely to be, do you think?' Batchelor asked Grand.

Grand thought for a moment. 'She has been caught out in at least one lie and I suspect has a lot more that she has told but we don't know about. So, on the principle that no one likes to be found out, I should say . . . very.'

'There's something odd in that house,' Batchelor said. 'Something strange about the household, perhaps I should say. The gardener's wife keeps having children by person or persons unknown; the groom knows far too much about his employer's private life, and I wouldn't be surprised if there wasn't some blackmail involved there somewhere; the cook is demented . . . her kitchen is as hot as Hell.'

'Come along, James,' Grand admonished, and clapped him on the back, raising a new dust-cloud. 'All cooks are mad; we of all people should know that. And . . . Butler, is it, the groom?'

Batchelor nodded.

'Butler, like all grooms, knows everything. You can't have someone carting you all over the countryside without them knowing where you go. It just isn't possible. You can't blindfold your coachman.' Grand gave it some thought. 'Not for long, at any rate. And if he was blackmailing him, it wouldn't do any good to lie about his death, unless he expected Georgy to carry on paying him.'

'Or Nell.'

'Or Nell, true. And she has no doubt come out of all this very nicely. From what we've learned of Dickens, he was lots of things, but not mean.'

'We could always ask Ouvry, I suppose.' Batchelor was doubtful. They hadn't exactly parted on the best of terms.

'I just don't see money as the motive here,' Grand said, as they turned into the drive. 'Dickens was certainly worth more alive than dead.'

The house looked peaceful in the hot sun. The shrubbery was rustle-free and the lawn baked in the heat. It was almost possible, to the intent listener, to hear the paint on the windows bubble and the glass to creak as the sun took its toll. But there wasn't a sound, from the garden or the house. Not a ghoul in sight. Grand stepped up and rang the bell with a flourish.

They could hear it echo back and forth. There was no scientific reason for it, but they knew that the house was empty, just by listening to the lonely peal of the bell. There were no scurrying footsteps, no calling voice. Just a silence, which wrapped around their ears and deafened them with its intensity. A shiver ran up Batchelor's spine.

'Is everything all right?' he asked Grand. 'There should be someone in, surely?'

A crunch of boot on paving made them turn. Brunt was approaching around the corner of the house and he stopped when he saw them there. 'Oh,' he said, without enthusiasm. 'It's you.'

Batchelor stepped forward. 'That's right, Mr Brunt.' He thought by using his real name rather than the Dickens-given one, he might improve the man's mood. 'We were just wondering where everyone was.'

'Well, Catherine'll be a-lying down,' he said, looking squint-eyed at the sun to assess the time. 'Emma'll be . . . well, I dunno where she'll be. Along of Butler, if I knows anything. Isaac's down in the village, I s'pect.' He stopped as though that explained everything.

'And Miss Hogarth?' Batchelor prompted.

'Oh, Miss Georgy and Miss Caroline, they're down at my cottage. Missus is whelping. They like to give a hand, but if she don't know what's what by now, I dunno who does.'

Grand's eyes nearly fell out of his head. 'Your wife's having a baby?' he asked. 'What, right now?'

The gardener nodded.

'Why aren't you down there?' Grand asked. He wasn't sure how things were done in England, but where he came from, the father was usually at least in hailing distance.

The man shrugged. 'Wasn't there when the babby was begun,' he said, with no malice in his voice. 'Don't need to be there when it's born. Any road,' he said, as an afterthought, 'Missus is certain it's another girl. Carrying it low. Or was it high?' He thought for a moment. 'Still and all, none of my business.'

Batchelor was stuck for words, but Grand found plenty. 'So, let me get this right,' he said. 'You *know* this child isn't yours?'

'Tha's right.'

'And yet you don't seem to mind too much.'

'Mr Dickens, he allus seen us right.'

'Is the child Mr Dickens's child?' Batchelor almost groaned with the thought of yet another motive.

'Nah!' The man was horrified. ''Course not. I s'pect my missus knows who'm it be, but it ain't Mr Dickens's, no how. It'll be one of them visitors of his, I s'pect. That funny little bugger . . .'

'Wilkie Collins,' Batchelor added out of the corner of his mouth.

'Or that one with all the hair.'

'Forster.'

'Or that writer. Could be him.'

Batchelor was stumped; that was rather a large field, in this milieu.

'Or it could be Butler again, feeling his oats. Any road, the missus, she does like to spoon and I don't mind it. T'ain't the little 'uns' fault, is it? They didn't ask to be born.' He glanced up at the sun. 'Well, I must be getting on. The cottage is down there aways. You'll find Miss Georgy and Miss Caroline there, right enough.' And he ambled away.

Grand and Batchelor walked off down a path which skirted the lawn and led in the direction of the gardener's pointing finger. Before they had got very far, they heard the sound of voices, coming nearer and around the next piece of shrubbery, then saw Georgy Hogarth and, with her, Caroline Moptrucket. Grand rapidly caught Batchelor up with a potted history of the girl and greeted them both by name as they got within a yard or so.

'Good news for Mr Brunt, I assume,' Grand said, taking in their smiling faces.

'Mr Grand,' Caroline gushed. 'I had never seen a child come into the world before. Such a beautiful thing. Beautiful.'

'Brunt has a lovely daughter,' Georgy said, rather less fulsomely.

'Does he?' Batchelor raised an eyebrow.

Georgy smiled knowingly and the daughter of the vicarage looked puzzled. 'Well, someone certainly has, shall we say?' she said. Then, she frowned. 'Why are you gentlemen here again? Surely, last time . . .'

'We have discovered rather more since we last spoke,' Grand said, solemnly. 'And I am not sure any of it is for Miss Moptrucket's ears . . .'

'Anything you can say to me, you can say to Caroline,' Georgy said, linking her arm through the girl's and pulling her close. 'She is like a sister to me.'

Grand looked at the girl's open, innocent face and wondered. Nevertheless, he had been given carte blanche, so he took it.

'Shall we sit somewhere?' he said. 'The sun is a little hot here in the open.'

'Perhaps the chalet?' Batchelor suggested.

Georgy led the way. 'The chalet will be being dismantled and moved soon, when dear Charles's will is proved. He has left it to a friend.'

Batchelor grasped the opportunity. 'Mr Dickens has been generous . . .?' he began. No need to tangle with Ouvry again, which was a very real relief.

'Charles has been very fair in his dispositions,' Georgy said, flatly. 'This house is to be sold, but only when we can arrange other accommodations for me and the staff. I understand Charlie may be considering it, but of course that will depend on the auction. I am to have . . .' She shook herself. 'I think you must ask Mr Ouvry for details.'

Darn! Grand looked at Batchelor and set his mouth in a rueful line.

'But for now,' she continued, 'you are quite right. The chalet is cool and, happily, completely restored to order after our little incident.'

Caroline Moptrucket fluttered along beside Georgy, making noises of comfort and general confusion. Her father might well have advanced views on the education of girls, but she already had a feeling that much of this conversation was going to trawl waters new to her. She suppressed a delighted shudder. The handsome American was a welcome visitor and, if his friend was perhaps a tad on the weaselly side by comparison, he was not unattractive.

In the chalet, all was tidy and it would need a practised eye to know what was different from when Dickens used it. The two women sat together on the small sofa, Grand perched on the edge of the desk, and Batchelor took the chair. Georgy Hogarth folded her hands calmly in her lap and smiled up at Grand. 'What would you like to know, Mr Grand?' she asked, her tone even.

'First of all,' Grand said, 'we would like to know why you didn't tell us that Mr Dickens was brought back here to die, having collapsed at Windsor Lodge, where he was spending some time with Miss Ternan?'

Caroline Moptrucket's eyes were like organ stops as she turned to look at her friend.

Georgy took a deep breath in through her nose, her mouth clamped shut. 'I see,' she said, so quietly she could hardly be heard. 'Who told?'

'Does that matter?' Batchelor asked.

'It does to *me*,' she hissed, leaning forward. 'It does to *me*. So I can no longer speak to the snake in the grass, whoever it was.' Then, remembering herself and her position, she straightened up and was calm once more. 'The reason I didn't tell you, Mr Grand, Mr Batchelor, was that it had no bearing.'

'But, Georgy . . .' Caroline Moptrucket might be an innocent abroad, but she could tell a hawk from a handsaw. 'But Georgy, *surely*, if these gentlemen are investigating dear Mr Dickens's death, it must . . .'

Georgy turned on her. 'If you wish to stay, Caroline,' she snapped, 'I must ask you to keep your opinions to yourself.'

The girl shrank away as far as she could on the small sofa and tears came to her eyes.

'Miss Moptrucket is quite right,' Grand said, quietly. 'It may have given the killer time to escape, while we have been chasing our tails.'

'Killer? There *is* no killer!' Georgy Hogarth had had just about enough. 'Charles was . . . over-extending himself. He was racing hither and yon – here one minute, Nunhead the next; writing every hour God sent . . .'

'And that's the other thing,' Batchelor said. 'We understand from Miss Ternan that Mr Dickens didn't in fact write his own books.'

Caroline Moptrucket shrugged her shoulders at that revelation. 'Goodness me, Mr Batchelor,' she said, at last given the chance to appear as a woman of the world. 'We all knew *that*. Gabriel Verdon has been writing them for years.' She blushed. 'Dear Gabriel . . .'

'. . . is dead,' Grand said, rather brutally, Batchelor thought.

Caroline Moptrucket put a hand to her breast and fainted elegantly away, folding forward and pitching on to the rug at her feet.

Georgy Hogarth looked at Grand with real annoyance on her face. 'Thank you very much, Mr Grand,' she spat. 'Caroline has carried a torch for Gabriel for years, despite the fact he could easily be her father. Like all of us here, she appreciates genius, and Gabriel was, indeed, a genius. But he lacked Charles's story-telling flair and so, together, they became one perfect writer, each dependent on the other. Indeed, the original title for *Barnaby Rudge* was to have been Gabriel Verdon: their little joke. But we all advised against it; a nosy journalist,' Batchelor bridled, 'or just loose lips could have uncovered what was, at the end of the day, an innocent deception, and all would have been ruin.' She poked Caroline lightly with an extended toe and the girl groaned, but didn't get up. 'As it was, we all made sure that the publishers didn't know; it was easier that way and, if there had been trouble, they could have honestly claimed to be blameless. Henry Trollope knew, of course, because of his connections; his father had also helped dear Charles out from time to time, before he found his own fame and fortune.'

'But . . .' Grand was puzzled. 'Why did these other writers let it go on? Why didn't they step out of the shadows and tell the world they had written the books? Then they could have all of the money instead of just . . . how much? Half?'

Georgy laughed. 'Half? Mr Grand, how naïve of you. No, the usual stipend was ten per cent. Charles was the genius in the eyes of the public. Without his name on the cover, who would have bought the books at all?' She leaned forward, 'I must ask you to be honest,' she said. 'If Charles Dickens had not been the author, would you call *Hard Times* a novel of genius?'

'Well . . .' Grand was over a barrel, having never even heard of the book.

'*Barnaby Rudge*?' she persisted. 'So, Charles's name was vital. He did write his own short stories and articles, of course; he was actually a perfectly able journalist. But that didn't put the gilt on the gingerbread and Charles did love to have all the trimmings.'

'So . . . *Edwin Drood* . . . was Gabriel Verdon writing that?'

'Well, no,' the woman replied, with another fruitless poke at her recumbent companion, 'Charles actually *was* writing that one. He was finding it nigh on impossible, though, what with his commitments and Ellen, of course. He also didn't have the staying power and had come to the end of his imaginative road; he had no idea how to end it. He and Gabriel had had a falling out and, apart from that, he was too proud to admit he was wrong.' She sighed and put her head in her hands. 'I can hardly believe that everything has gone so wrong, so fast. Poor Gabriel. I kept the news from poor Caroline. She had such hopes. But Gabriel didn't just write like Charles. He had the same . . . appetites.'

'Mrs Brunt?' Grand ventured.

She looked at him sharply. 'You're not an enquiry agent for nothing, I see,' she said. 'Yes, Mrs Brunt had caught his eye. That was one of the reasons for the argument. Charles . . . came upon them and, for a man of his tastes, he could be something of a prude. He threw him out of the house.'

'I see.' Grand looked down at Caroline Moptrucket, who was beginning to stir. 'Well, thank you for your candour, Miss Hogarth.'

Batchelor put in his oar. 'If indeed this time you have told us everything.'

'Mr Batchelor,' she said, quietly. 'My life is in ruins. The only man I ever loved or will love is dead. No doubt his sordid failings will soon be a matter of public record. His books will cease to sell. Frederic Chapman, a decent person who has done nothing wrong, will be ruined. *We* will all be ruined. So, if you wouldn't mind, I would be grateful if you would go now, while I tend to my friend.'

On cue, the girl at her feet gave a groan and began to struggle to her feet, hampered by her enormous skirt. In the interests of decency, Grand and Batchelor averted their eyes and left the chalet, their minds whirling. There would be a lot to add to their wall of paper tonight, and no mistake.

In America, they called it 'casing the joint'. In Britain, it was loitering with intent. Either way, Henry and Beulah Morford spent most of the day doing it. On the trail of Dickens as they were, they had discovered a great deal about the great man, and among their discoveries were Messrs Grand and Batchelor of 41 The Strand. The rumour went that there were some questions about Dickens's death and that Grand and Batchelor were asking most of them. Perhaps, then, Grand and Batchelor had what the Morfords were looking for.

Number 41 posed no problems. It was locked, but Beulah Morford had cut her teeth on Elder and Crutchley Impregnables and once again gave the lie to the company's advertising by picking the lock and walking in. She was wearing widow's weeds she had hired from a costumier near the Adelphi, and had a convoluted story ready should either Grand or Batchelor turn up. As it was, they didn't, and she took an hour to ransack the drawers, scatter the contents of filing cabinets and clean out the safe. Nothing. But there *was* another address; further along the Strand to the east, in the area known as Alsatia. With his years of nosing into other people's business, the man from New York instinctively knew that this was another Bowery, another Hell's Kitchen. There were murkier people wandering the sidewalks here and, as dusk was falling, there were no lights shining in the home of Grand and Batchelor, enquiry agents. The Morfords assumed they were out turning stones and, with a flick of her nail file, Beulah was inside, Henry her shadow in the passageway.

It was nearly dark by the time the pair had concentrated on the study under the eaves. The heat of the day still lingered here and they could see the lights of Southwark winking at them from beyond the river, the wharfs and warehouses black against the purple of the sky. There were pieces of paper stuck to the wall with incomprehensible scribbles all over them. Some referred to Charles Dickens, but they were not what they were looking for.

They were just about to go down to what seemed to be an office-cum-sitting room on the floor below when they heard a click. Morford reached the door in one stride and grabbed the brass knob. Nothing. It wouldn't budge.

'We're locked in,' he hissed.

Beulah had got out of tight places before. There was only one other exit – the skylight overhead. She hauled a chair into place and gathered up her skirts. Not dressed for a rooftop getaway, she had to admit that this wasn't going to work.

'They're in here!' they heard a female voice shriek from beyond the door. 'I've locked them in.'

Feet thundered on the stairs and the door burst open. A large man with a gun stood there. And the gun was pointing at them.

'You've got three seconds,' he said, clicking the hammer back.

The Morfords had their hands in the air. 'My name is Henry Morford,' he gabbled. 'I'm a journalist from New York. This is my wife, Beulah. We were looking for Mr Grand, a fellow American.'

'One,' the fellow American began his count.

'We always look up fellow Americans when we're on our travels, don't we, Beulah?'

'Two.' The man wasn't listening.

'Just like finding a friendly face, you know. Shoot the breeze, that sort of thing.'

'Three.'

The hammer clicked on to an empty chamber.

'Son of a bitch!' Morford hissed, his heart still firmly in his mouth.

'Give it up, Henry,' Beulah advised. 'I say, give it up.'

'I'm Matthew Grand,' Grand said, 'and I *never* shoot the breeze with anybody caught ransacking my rooms by my housekeeper.'

The Morfords saw her for the first time. Peering out from the darkness of the stair, her face flickering in the candlelight, Mrs Rackstraw scowled at them both. James Batchelor was checking the notes on the wall, to make sure nothing was amiss.

'And I'm going for the police,' she hissed at them, and was gone.

'An empty gun,' Morford was still complaining. 'Son of a bitch.'

'Suppose you tell us,' Batchelor said, 'what you're doing here.'

Grand may have had no bullets in his gun, but he was still blocking the door, and Henry Morford saw no safe, painless way past him.

'The police are already on their way,' Batchelor said.

'London's finest,' Grand added. 'I don't know what experience you've had of the inside of jail cells, Morford, but here, I got to tell you, they throw away the key.'

'The crank, eh, Matthew?' Batchelor sucked in his breath.

'I was thinking more the treadmill, James,' Grand nodded with a knowing look. 'Three hundred and sixty-five steps to nowhere.'

'One for every day of the year,' Batchelor was philosophical. 'Of course, there *is* a way out of this, Matthew, for our American friends, I mean.'

'What?' Morford blurted out. 'Tell us what.'

Grand's eyes narrowed and he took a step forward. 'Suppose,' he said, 'you tell us the truth.'

Morford looked at Beulah.

'Like I said, Henry,' she said, 'give it up. I got nothing.'

Morford sighed. 'All right,' he said. 'Beulah and I were already in London when we heard of Dickens's death. And we really *are* fans.'

'We are,' Beulah agreed.

'We heard that *Edwin Drood* was left unfinished, that Dickens hadn't completed his instalments before he died. Can you imagine the prestige, the kudos?' Morford looked up, his eyes bright; he could see his name writ large, flickering in the limelight over a thousand stage doors. He sketched it out with a wave of his arm, 'Henry Morford, the Man Who Finished *Drood.*' He sighed and looked around the room, flushed with pleasure.

Grand and Batchelor looked at each other. Both of them could think of a thousand better epitaphs to leave to the world.

'We've seen you before,' Grand said. 'You made a ruckus outside Westminster Abbey at Dickens's funeral.'

''Fraid so,' Morford said. 'I figured if I could talk to the family and friends, I'd find out where Dickens kept his notes – some clue as to how he intended to finish the God-damned book.'

'Nobody'd talk to us,' Beulah threw in. 'I say, nobody'd talk to us, Henry.'

'We . . . er . . .' Morford was searching for the right words, wringing his hands in a perfect Uriah Heep. 'We'll have to ask for a few other incidents to be taken under consideration, in the court, I mean.'

'Oh?' Batchelor raised an eyebrow.

'Well, Dickens's chalet at Gads Hill for one,' Morford said.

'I done that,' Beulah confided.

'Then, there's your offices along the street, there.'

'You've ransacked our office?' Batchelor was furious.

'Well, now, ransacking's a bit strong, Mr Batchelor. Mr Grand, you'll understand this – I'd say Atlanta was ransacked, wouldn't you?'

'No, Mr Morford,' Grand shook his head. 'I'd say Atlanta was destroyed.'

There was a thunder of hobnailed boots on the stairs and a fierce and red-faced woman was at the still-open door, two very large bobbies at her back.

'Ah,' Grand beamed. 'The cavalry.'

FIFTEEN

Mrs Rackstraw was still vibrating with righteous indignation when Grand and Batchelor left the house to call in at the police station. Although the Morfords were clearly rather challenged in the 'what belongs to who' department, the enquiry agents felt that they probably weren't malicious, simply rather single-minded. The housekeeper, however, was of the opinion that flogging was too good for them; hanging, with optional drawing and quartering, was the very least they deserved. With empty promises to make sure that the pair received the full punishment the law allowed and then some, Grand and Batchelor made good their escape and headed towards E Division Station, just along the road from their house.

'Afternoon, Mr Grand, Mr Batchelor.' The desk sergeant was an old friend of theirs, who had often earned an extra half a crown or so by putting dog owners in distress their way. 'How can I help you?'

'Mr and Mrs Henry Morford,' Batchelor said. 'I believe they were brought here a little while ago. Can we see them, do you think? Also, I think we need to make it clear we won't be pressing charges.'

The sergeant brought his palms down on the desk with an audible crack and sucked his teeth regretfully. 'I'm very sorry, gents,' he said. 'I am afraid that the miscreants in question are answering to a higher authority.'

'They're *dead*?' Batchelor was horrified. Whatever could have happened? Could they *both* have fallen down the stairs?

'Dead?' The sergeant was perplexed. 'Oh, no, I see what you're thinking there. No, not *that* Higher Authority. I just mean that Mr Williamson's had them away to the Yard. I'm not sure what you gents have done to annoy him, but all stations north of the river – and south, for all I know – have had a memo to say that anyone who has any connection with you two must be sent direct to the Yard.' He raised his hands and let them go again. Grand wondered how the desk could stand the constant pounding. 'So, off they went. They should be there by now.'

'But . . . they shouldn't be under arrest . . .' Batchelor began.

'Sure they should,' Grand interrupted. 'They tried to burgle our house.'

'Burgalries,' the sergeant said. 'Bane of modern living, in my opinion, burgalries. String them up, like in the old days, I say. My old granddad was hanged for stealing a loaf of bread,' he said, 'not that I tell everyone that, o' course. But those were the days, all right. Riots in Hyde Park, bloody Fenians blowin' things up. Mind you, Mr Field always had them on the run.'

'Did he?' Grand somehow doubted that.

'Yes. Holy terror was Mr Field. I had the honour of serving under him in Lambeth. Trassenos the length and breadth of the manor were terrified of him. Look at him funny; he'll have you. Not like today. Today it's all about helpin' old ladies across the road. That Mr Whicher went mad because of it. I tell you – and I know I'm speaking against myself here – they don't make coppers like they used to.'

'Amen,' Batchelor smiled.

Scotland Yard in Whitehall Place always put the willies up James Batchelor. He had no idea why. Despite his calling, he had never really gone even close to the wrong side of the law but, even so, he always felt that a heavy hand was about to descend on his shoulder and consign him to the hulks – Australia or somewhere equally horrendous. True, they'd abolished all that after complaints from the Australians, but Batchelor felt they might bring it all back, just for him. So he kept quiet and let Grand do all the talking. He had managed to get past the desk sergeant on the door, the desk sergeant on the first floor and also on the second, but was having difficulty with the custody sergeant. He was spinning ever more fantastic tales when a voice they knew rang down the corridor and Batchelor almost jumped out of his skin.

'Mr Grand! Mr Batchelor! How very fortuitous. This saves me from having to send a constable to bring you here. Such a nasty thing to happen to gentlemen in your position, don't you think? To have the police knocking on your door.'

The two turned round slowly. Williamson stood in the door of his office, beaming like a nightmare borne of the pen of John Tenniel. He beckoned with an implacable forefinger and they

walked slowly to his door and were reeled inside like unwilling
salmon caught by a cunning fly. The inspector closed the door
behind them, the smile still in place.

'I'm glad to see you,' he said, his tone friendlier than usual.
'I was wondering if either of you had any skill with cyphers.'

'What happened to amateurs and professionals?' Grand simply
had to ask it.

'Ah-ha, Mr Grand. Perspicacious as ever, of course,' Williamson
beamed. 'But as well as my perfectly sound beliefs in that quarter,
I also believe in horses for courses, and we just don't seem to
be getting anywhere with this . . . let's call it "document", for
the moment, shall we? And I know that Mr Batchelor was once
a journalist and also that he is endeavouring to write the Great
British Novel . . .'

'How the . . .?'

'Now, now, Mr Batchelor. Let's keep this civil. So, I thought
to myself, here's a literary gent, who may be able to help me
with this little problem.' He leaned down and pulled a small,
green-covered book from a drawer in his desk. 'This is the diary
of the late Gabriel Verdon. We found it in his office, hidden
inside a copy of *Barnaby Rudge*. The pages of the bigger book
had been cut out to accommodate this one and, in our experience,
no one does something as fiddly as that except for a very good
reason.' He didn't hand the book over, but took his seat behind
the desk, tapping the diary on the pile of papers in front of him.

Grand and Batchelor tried hard not to look too eager, but failed.

'Many of the entries are quite straightforward, meetings and
so on. But others are more . . .' He smiled at Batchelor, a disqui-
eting experience for the enquiry agent. 'Is "arcane" the word I
am looking for?'

'It could be,' Batchelor said. He reached out a hand. 'If you
let me look through it, I could tell you.'

Williamson suddenly threw the book at Batchelor, who, to his
own surprise, caught it deftly. 'Howzat,' Williamson said, softly.
He watched as Batchelor scanned the pages, frowning from time
to time. 'Does it mean anything to you?' he asked, after a moment
or two had passed.

'This is quite a simple cypher,' Batchelor said. 'It is just a
matter of transposition of letters.' He held the book out to

Williamson and pointed. 'See, here, there are only so many letters in English that occur in pairs. For instance, you don't often have two "kays" and I can't think of a single example of two "aitches". So you can discount that. E is the commonest letter, so that transposition is easy to work out . . . hmm . . . do you have a piece of paper and a pencil, please?'

Williamson pushed over a pad and a pencil. Batchelor got to work, occasionally biting the end of the pencil and humming to himself. Grand watched proudly, as a parent might when their child first learns to walk. He was himself adept at cyphers – most civil war officers had come across them back in the day – but had decided early on in their partnership to let Batchelor be the official expert. Finally, Batchelor put the pencil down and sat back, prepared to read out his results.

'Quite a lot of this is . . . personal, shall we say. Mr Grand and I have met some of Mr Verdon's conquests, or at least have heard about them, and so I think we know who it refers to.' He turned to look at Grand. 'I think if I just say I am no longer surprised that Miss Caroline Moptrucket fainted when she heard of Gabriel Verdon's demise, you will understand what I mean.'

Williamson and Grand nodded sagely. Williamson had never heard of Caroline Moptrucket, but the implication was clear enough.

'But there are some other references here which are not as obvious. "FC came to see me again this afternoon. He is very insistent and offered violence if what he requires cannot be done." And here, "I fear that FC is having me followed. I was buffeted violently in the GR station today . . ." GR? It could be RG, I suppose . . .'

'Gloucester Road,' Williamson said. 'It was on his way home, certainly.'

'Right. ". . . the GR station today and was nearly hurled on to the track. I begin to fear for my life." This final bit sounds desperate. "Told FC that I cannot do the impossible. He hounds me night and day. I fear he is mad, or close to mad. If this does not end, I will do something desperate." And that's the last entry.'

Williamson and Grand sat, thinking. 'FC?' Williamson spoke first. 'Frederic Chapman, for my money. We know that he and Verdon often clashed. In fact, the locks had been added to the office doors because they had had words.' He jotted a note. 'I'll send someone round to escort the gentleman in for a few questions.'

'We've discovered that Dickens . . . ow.'

'Mr Grand, did you just kick Mr Batchelor?' Williamson wanted to know.

'Cramp,' Grand said, smoothly, as Batchelor rubbed his shin.

'You've discovered that Dickens . . .?' Williamson looked penetratingly at Batchelor.

'Dickens just had a stroke,' Batchelor said. 'After all our work, too. But enquiring doesn't always come up with the answer the client wants.'

'So you can stop following us now,' Grand ventured.

Williamson's eyebrows rose. 'Following you?' he said. 'I haven't been following you.'

'Not *you*, not personally,' Grand persisted. 'But your men. There's someone behind every tree. To be honest, Chief Inspector, it's starting to get us down.'

Williamson leaned forward. 'Gentlemen,' he said, solemnly, 'on my mother's grave, God bless her, I swear I have not followed you, nor have I had you followed. And, for avoidance of doubt, I do not plan in the future to have you followed. Unless you give me cause, of course.'

The detectives looked at him. He wasn't an easy man to read, but he seemed to be sincere.

'Boulton and Park gave you cause, though.' Batchelor felt he had to raise the subject. 'You had them followed.'

Williamson's smile vanished. 'I cannot discuss other cases, gentlemen,' he said.

'They'll go down, though, surely?' Batchelor wouldn't let it go.

'The law is a funny thing,' the chief inspector mused. 'The late Mr Dickens said it was an ass and I can see his point. Messrs Boulton and Park offend society's sensibilities, but there is actually no law against men wearing frocks. Sodomy, now, that's different.'

'Is that what they're guilty of?' Grand asked.

'That'll be up to a jury to decide,' Williamson shrugged.

'But the problem was Arthur Clinton, wasn't it?' Batchelor asked. He watched the chief inspector carefully. There was no twitch of the jaw, no flicker of the eyes, but this was a seasoned copper, hard as nails, crafty as a fox, and a whole raft of similes that Batchelor had never thought of.

'Oh?' Williamson said. 'In what way?'

'The Boultons and Parks of this world are cannon fodder,' Batchelor explained, 'but *Lord* Arthur Clinton could cock a snook at the law. And the upholders of the law. You.'

'Is that why you killed him?' Grand asked.

For a moment, a thunderous silence held sway on the third floor of number 4 Whitehall Place, then Williamson roared with laughter. 'It is easy to become a little nervous, in your profession, gentlemen,' he said. 'Start seeing crimes and criminals where there are none. If you take my advice,' he said, coming round from behind his desk and laying an avuncular hand on each man's shoulder, 'I should take a nice holiday by the sea. Breathe in some of that lovely fresh air.' He hadn't removed the hands, which seemed to weigh a ton. 'And, meanwhile, I shall let your American friends go. Shortly. It won't do light-fingered Beulah any harm to spend an hour or so behind bars; although I fancy she isn't a stranger to the setting.' With a final pat which nearly broke their collarbones, he ushered Grand and Batchelor to the door; before they had reached the top of the stairs, had a couple of constables on their way to Chapman and Hall.

'Wait up, Mr Grand, Mr Batchelor.'

The enquiry agents turned at the mention of their names. The light was failing across Whitehall Place as they left the Yard and the July days were still long in the land.

It was a very different – and diffident – Henry Morford who had called to them and he and Beulah looked the model of American tourists abroad, albeit ones who had narrowly escaped a prison stretch.

'The desk sergeant explained,' Morford said, 'that you guys intervened on our behalf and refused to press charges. That's mighty New York of you.'

'Our pleasure, Mr Morford,' Batchelor said. 'You may have to finish *Edwin Drood* on your own now.'

'Oh, I intend to, I intend to,' Morford grinned. 'Anyhow, it's time I made an honest woman out of Beulah. Now, honey, give Mr Batchelor his watch back.'

Instinctively, Batchelor felt his pockets. The watch was still there.

'Just joshing, Mr Batchelor,' Beulah said. 'I say, Henry was just joshing.'

There were awkward chuckles all round. The arrival of a Black Maria pulled by sweating, snorting horses turned Morford's thoughts again to his recent ordeal. 'I knew about Scotland Yard, of course,' he told Batchelor, 'but I wasn't ready for Chief Inspector Williamson. That guy is one helluva bastard, isn't he?'

'Oh, he is that,' Batchelor had to agree.

'Especially when Chief Inspector Field had said there was no harm in our little pursuits.'

'Who?' Grand blinked.

'Charlie Field,' Beulah said. 'He's a big friend of Charles Dickens's.'

'He is indeed,' Grand said. 'What he is not is a chief inspector.'

It took most of the next day to find Chief Inspector Field. And they did it by a rather circuitous route. Kelly's Street Directory in the Westminster Public Library threw up the current address of Ignatius Paul Polliak, consulting detective, and he was still at 13 Paddington Green. The dapper little man with the waxed side-whiskers and thick Hungarian accent by way of north London, had not seen his former colleague Field in years, but he knew where he could be found of an evening; he'd be feeding the ducks in St James's Park.

A solitary copper wandered the rhododendron bushes, the bullseye lantern at his waist sending odd shafts of light darting into the shrubbery. He saluted the portly gentleman sitting on the park bench, throwing breadcrumbs to the squawking mallards, and by the time Grand and Batchelor had joined him, the copper had moved on at his stately two and a half miles an hour.

'Well, well,' Field said. 'Didn't expect to see you boys among the Park people.'

'Park people?' Grand was unfamiliar with the term.

'Maryannes,' Field explained. 'Shirt-lifters. The name won't mean anything to you, Mr Grand, and it might not mean much to you, Mr Batchelor, but the first example I heard about was Lord Castlereagh.'

'Foreign Secretary—' Batchelor *had* worked for the *Telegraph* once upon a time and some information had stuck – 'under Lord Liverpool. Committed suicide in 1822.'

'Before my time,' Grand sat alongside Field.

'Mine too,' Batchelor agreed and sat on the other side. There wasn't much room on the bench.

'Ah, but not before mine,' Field chuckled. 'You could say it was the revolting crimes of Lord Castlereagh that put me in uniform in the first place. I was a mere lad at the time, had my heart set on a career on the stage. Then I read about Castlereagh.'

'"I met murder in the way,"' Batchelor quoted. '"He wore a mask like Castlereagh."'

'Castlereagh was a killer?' Grand checked. They had their shortcomings, it was true, but Grand couldn't think of a single American Secretary of State who actually murdered people.

'Figure of speech.' Field lobbed the last of his bread on to the troubled waters and the ducks flapped madly. 'No, Castlereagh's crime was of engaging in unnatural activities with a man dressed as a woman, here, in this very park. Oh, those were different days, of course, and we all have to move with the times. Actually, I find the Park people very helpful.'

'You do?' Grand asked.

Field checked his hunter in the gathering gloom. 'Jingling Janet will be along soon. One of my narks, Mr Grand. I'm sure your American policemen have them too – a mine of information, I assure you.'

'Sure our American policemen have them,' Grand said, 'but the point at issue here is that you're no longer a policeman, are you? You're a private detective, just like us.'

Field chuckled. 'I'm *nothing* like you, gentlemen,' he said. 'What do you want?'

'When we exchanged confidences,' Batchelor said, 'when we told each other how our Dickens investigations were going, you failed to mention the Morfords.'

'Did I?' Field smiled. 'How remiss of me.'

'You told them,' Grand took up the tale, 'that it was fine to burglarize premises at will and that the police would turn a blind eye.'

Field was outraged. 'I did no such thing,' he said.

'You posed as a serving officer,' Batchelor went on. 'Not the first time you've done that, it's true. But now it's starting to get in our way.'

'*Your* way?' Field heaved his bulk upright. 'Listen, sonny. I was sorting crimes and bagging murderers before you were born. The Manor Place Murders; the Daniels – Good and McNaghten; James Greenacre; Frederic Muller . . . and don't get me started on the bloody Fenians. They're my collars – *mine*. And if anybody's going to get the bastard who killed Charles Dickens, it's going to be me.'

Field was on his feet now and the ducks had gone. 'So, let's put all this another way, shall we?' he said. 'No more co-operation. No more exchange of information. And the next time I see some Irish bastards kicking the shit out of you, I'm just going to walk on by.'

'I don't appreciate it, sir.' Frederic Chapman was on his high horse. 'I don't appreciate it at all. I am dragged from my home by your blue-coated oafs and dumped in a cell. *Me*. Chapman, of Chapman and Hall. I'll have your badge, Mr Williamson.'

'I don't actually have a badge, Mr Chapman,' the chief inspector pointed out. 'No policemen do. I've got a tipstaff lying around here somewhere – you're welcome to that, if you like.'

Chapman was outraged. 'You're being flippant with me, sir. I assume all this has to do with Gabriel Verdon. Well, I've already told you all I know on that score.'

Williamson smiled. 'I wonder if that's actually true,' he said.

'I beg your pardon?' Frederic Chapman was turning a richer shade of crimson.

'What can you tell me about this?' Williamson had produced a small book from his desk drawer.

'What is it?' Chapman asked.

'Gabriel Verdon's diary,' Williamson told him. 'My boys found it in his office. That would be one of your offices, Mr Chapman.'

'So?' Chapman became nonchalant. 'I had no idea Verdon kept a diary.'

Williamson smiled again. 'No, I'm sure you didn't; but it makes very interesting reading. It's all in code, of course, but I've cracked that – easy when you know how. This entry, for instance – "I fear that FC is having me followed."'

'What?' Chapman blinked.

'And this one – "Told FC that I cannot do the impossible. He hounds me night and day. I fear he is mad or close to mad."'

'You can't seriously think he's talking about me?' Chapman was aghast.

'How did you get on with Mr Verdon, sir?' Williamson's question was innocuous enough, delivered with charm.

'I've already told you,' Chapman snapped. 'He was a colleague, a friend, a senior editor, a shareholder. What more can I say?'

'You can tell me why you killed him, sir.' Williamson leaned back in his chair as though he were discussing the weather.

'I . . .' the publisher was lost for words.

'What was the impossible thing he couldn't do for you?' Williamson asked. Then he leaned forward, his eyes flashing fire. 'And just how mad *are* you?'

Chapman was on his feet. 'This is as preposterous as it is outrageous,' he said, the words half strangled in his throat. 'Am I under arrest?'

'No, sir.' Williamson leaned back again.

'Then I am free to go.'

'You are.'

'Don't think you've heard the last of this,' Chapman stabbed the air with his finger. 'My solicitor will be in touch. You can't go round accusing people of murder, willy-nilly.'

'I look forward to it,' Williamson said. 'And actually, I can.'

Chapman would waste no more words on this moron. He spun on his heel and left.

A plainclothesman sidled into Williamson's office as the door was still rattling from Chapman's exit. 'Sir?'

'Follow him, Sergeant. Round the clock. If he so much as farts, I want to know about it.'

'Very good, sir.'

It was already the early hours when Grand and Batchelor sat with their brandies in the room in the attic. The skylight was open and the stars shone down on Alsatia.

'So, Williamson doesn't know that Verdon wrote Dickens.' Batchelor still had the bruised shin to prove it.

'No,' Grand said, 'but I get the distinct impression that there isn't all that much that Williamson doesn't know.'

'He's a shrewd customer, all right,' Batchelor conceded. 'Wonder if he's talked to Chapman yet.'

'Now.' Grand lit a cigar and ran his eyes over the fluttering notes again. 'Friend Chapman, what do we know about him?'

'He and Verdon go way back,' Batchelor said. 'As far back as Dickens and maybe even earlier.'

'But they didn't get on.' Grand was piecing it together.

'Latterly, apparently not.'

'Was that because Chapman found out that Verdon was really Dickens? Did they have a row that got out of hand?'

Batchelor chewed the end of his pencil stub. 'Chapman didn't strike me as the murderous type. We're looking for two murderers.'

'One for Dickens.' Grand took up the theme. 'One for Verdon.'

'And one for Arthur Clinton,' Batchelor threw in. 'Let's not forget dear Artie.'

'Right.' Grand blew his smoke up to the skylight where it skeined momentarily, making a milky way of the London stars until it thinned and disappeared. 'Clinton belongs to the Dickens category; both men were poisoned.'

'Yet Verdon *must* be connected. It's too much of a coincidence otherwise.'

'And we don't believe in those.'

'No, we don't.'

There was a silence.

'Let's go through it again,' was Grand's suggestion.

'Even if you're right,' Batchelor said, 'that Chapman found out that Verdon was Dickens – why kill him? He was an in-house golden goose and things could have gone on as before. There wasn't even a need for a row.'

'Unless,' Grand countered, 'Chapman felt betrayed. Let down by his old co-worker who had been lying to him for years.'

'Inside job, I think we agreed.' Batchelor was running with it. 'To be able to get at Verdon in his office; likely to be somebody with access.'

'Chapman,' Grand nodded. 'Half a dozen other editors, and we mustn't forget Henry Trollope – he'd known Dickens well since he was a boy.'

'Your dear old mum,' Batchelor sniggered. 'I wonder how the old besom's doing at Charing Cross?'

'Yes,' Grand muttered. 'I felt a bit bad about that, but subterfuge is a middle name in this business.'

'You can . . .' but James Batchelor never finished his sentence because Mrs Rackstraw had burst in.

'I'm not on a bit of string, you know,' she said, her hair a mass of curling papers, her slippers on the wrong feet. 'People calling at all hours of the day and night. Does he know what time it is? Do you?'

'What's the matter, Mrs Rackstraw?' Grand tried his smooth Northern style but she was having none of it.

'This bloke just rang the bell and left this card.' She thrust it at Grand.

'Chief Inspector Field would like a word.'

'At this hour?' Batchelor and Mrs Rackstraw chorused.

'He has a lead,' Grand said. 'Wants – and I quote – "to bury the hatchet".'

'Where?' Batchelor asked.

'St Mary Matfelon. Know it?'

St Mary Matfelon's clock was just striking four as Grand and Batchelor reached it. The cab had dropped them in the Whitechapel Road and they had continued on foot. Not far away lay Cable Street and Bluegate Fields and both men were on the lookout for Irishmen. This time, Grand was carrying his Colt .32 because they couldn't always rely on Charlie Field to arrive in the nick of time.

In any case, it was Field they had come to see, and there he was, under the pale dial of the clock, the tip of his cigar glowing in the half-light.

'Hello, boys,' he tipped his hat. 'Good of you to come.'

'Wouldn't have missed it for the world,' Grand said. 'Although, last time we met, I got the distinct impression it *was* for the last time.'

Field chuckled. 'I *was* a little hasty back then,' he said. 'Waiting in Maryannes' Park always makes me a little testy. There'll be a law against that sort of bloke one of these days, you mark my words.'

'I think we know your views, Mr Field,' Batchelor said. 'And I'm not sure being dragged all the way to the East End at four in the morning to hear them again is my idea of a good time.'

'No,' Field said. 'Something's come up, and in the interests of catching a killer, I thought we could pool resources.'

'What?' Grand asked. 'What's come up?'

'Breakfast?' Field suggested. 'Just to show there's no hard feelings, let me buy you both breakfast.'

Grand checked his hunter. '*Breakfast?*' he repeated. 'It's a *little* early for me.'

'Jellied eels, Mr Batchelor?' Field nudged the man in the ribs. 'Pie and mash, eh? What's your tipple?'

It had been a while since James Batchelor had sampled the fare of the rookeries where civilization ended in the Jews' burial ground. And he *did* have a secret hankering for jellied eels. 'Well . . .' he began.

'It's on me,' Field said, and led them north through a tangle of scummed streets where rotting buildings leaned towards each other, all but blotting out the dawn sky. The first of the costers were on the move already, scratching themselves and yawning as they straightened their flat caps and laced their boots. There was a rattle of wheels as the dray horses from the Eagle brewery took out their first load of the day. Consumptive coughs hacked in the morning and the largest city on earth was awake.

'Does the name John Forster mean anything to you?' Field asked them as they reached the eel and pie stall.

'It might.' Grand was cagey, especially after he saw the fare on offer in pails and bowls under a flaring lamp.

'Friend of Dickens's.' Batchelor was more forthcoming. The smell from those pails was unleashing his inner pig. 'How did he put it? Literary agent?'

The three men sat down at a greasy table on the pavement a few paces down from the stall. Sol, the purveyor, or so he was assuring the world in stentorian tones, of the best eels north, south, east or even west of Wapping, wiped it down with a rag which tended to increase the grease quotient, if anything.

'Gents?' he said, leaning on the table on his knuckles, shaking the drop off the end of his nose with some panache. 'What can I get you?'

'I'll be over in a minute, Solly,' Field said. 'Just taking my friends' orders.'

'Suit yourself,' the stall-holder said and went back to his pails.

Field watched until he was out of earshot, though it was hard to hear anything over Sol's cry of 'Eels. Get your lovely eels here. Whelks. Winkles. Bring your own pin.'

'Friends, my arse,' Field said, getting back to business. 'I've done some digging and this is how I see it. John Forster's a greedy bastard and he's tired of just getting his ten per cent of Dickens.'

'Standard, that, isn't it? Ten per cent.' Batchelor was eyeing the stall greedily. There wasn't exactly a queue at this time of the morning but, even so, jellied eels didn't grow on trees and he had his appetite honed now.

'Not if you're a greedy bastard, it's not.' Field followed Batchelor's eyeline and chuckled. 'Mr Batchelor,' he said, clapping him on the shoulder. 'I can see you're ready for your breakfast. Excuse me, both of you, while I go and get some dishes of Solly's finest.'

Grand leaned forward when he was gone, being careful not to touch the table. 'What's he bringing us, James?' he asked. 'Jelly? What kind of jelly?'

Batchelor did a translation. 'I know what you're thinking,' he said, 'and no, it isn't *jam*, as I keep reminding you we call it here. It's eels, you know, eels?' He mimed a swimming creature with one hand. 'Well, they cook them, then they chop them up and let them get cold. The cooking liquor turns into jelly and that's it. Jellied eels.'

Grand's expression became more and more horrified as Batchelor expounded, and then reached its zenith as Field returned, balancing three bowls and some spoons in his hands.

'There we are, gents,' he said, sitting down. 'This one's yours, Mr Batchelor. A nice big portion. This is yours, Mr Grand – a bit smaller; I wasn't sure whether you could manage a big pile of eels if you haven't had them before.' He spooned up a pile of what looked to Grand like grey and black slime encased in slime. 'Hmm,' he enthused, through the mouthful. 'Best in London, my opinion. What d'you think, Mr Batchelor?'

Batchelor just nodded. He was in heaven.

Grand looked down into his bowl. Although it was securely placed on a flat table-top on a London pavement, it nevertheless seemed to move slightly with an agenda of its own. The jelly shone with a glaucous gleam which didn't quite hide the horrors within. He cautiously took some of the slop on the very tip of his spoon, and almost had it to his mouth when the smell got to his nose and his nerve failed him. He who had dined on nothing but goober peas, back in the day. He swallowed hard and smiled at the guzzling pair. He decided to concentrate on the proper subject at hand. 'We've been told Dickens was generous,' he said. 'To a fault, almost. Threw it away.'

'But not in John Forster's direction, apparently. Yes, he was keeping that stuck-up tart in Nunhead and shelling out on foreign holidays, but Forster was out of pocket. Are you not eating your eels, Mr Grand?'

Grand shook his head and slid the bowl further away. 'Not really a breakfast man,' he said. 'Did Forster tell you he was out of pocket?'

'Not in so many words,' Field said, 'but I've got a nose for these things.' He glanced across at Batchelor, who was chasing the last piece of eel around the bowl. 'Would you like some bread with that, Mr Batchelor?'

'Umm, no,' Batchelor said, with a smothered burp. 'I think I've had enough. I feel a bit . . . queasy now.'

'I'm not surprised,' Grand said. He vowed never to take Batchelor's recommendation on a restaurant ever again.

Batchelor frowned to himself for a moment, patting his chest. 'This Forster,' he said, slowly, concentrating on something other than his stomach. 'Are we sure his first name is John?'

'What are you thinking, James?' Grand asked.

'We had a visit from Chief Inspector Williamson the other day,' Batchelor told Field.

'Dolly? How is he?'

'Difficult,' said Grand, almost screwing up his courage to try some bread, then deciding against it. It may have been caraway seeds in there but, on the other hand, it may not.

'He found Gabriel Verdon's diary,' Batchelor told Field.

'That's the bloke at Chapman and Hall, isn't it?' Field checked. 'Had his head stove in, something like that.'

'That's the one. Verdon was being threatened by somebody with the initials FC.'

Field thought for a moment, 'Frederic Chapman.' He clicked his fingers.

'Yes,' Batchelor said. 'But the diary was in a code, based on transposition of letters. What if I made a mistake? What if the C was a J?'

'I didn't see it that closely,' Grand admitted. Batchelor racked his memory. He'd give his eyeteeth about now to have that diary in his hands again.

'Well, that would make sense,' Field said. 'I don't have to remind you, gents, how easy it would be for Forster to come and go at Chapman and Hall. He could get any number of keys cut for himself. And, of course, it was open house at Gads Hill.'

'Why don't you go to the police with this, Mr Field?' Grand asked.

'Ah, well, that's where you boys come in. I'm afraid I've rather blotted my copybook with the Yard over the years. I'm not sure Dolly would exactly greet me with open arms. You boys now – that would be different.'

'You haven't given us much to go on,' Grand observed. 'James? James, are you well?'

James was not. He had gone, even in the eerie half-light of dawn, a funny colour. 'I'm fine,' Batchelor said, squaring his shoulders and taking a deep breath. 'It must be the eels.' He flashed a reproachful look at Sol, who reacted with indignation.

'Let's get you home,' Grand said. 'Mr Field, thank you for your tip. We'll talk to Forster again.'

'Right.' Field tipped his hat. 'And then go and see Williamson. Time we got a noose around somebody's neck. Er . . . fifty-fifty, by the way?'

'Excuse me?' Grand was absent-mindedly patting Batchelor's shoulder.

'The reward money,' Field beamed. 'There must be some. And we aren't in this business for laughs, are we?' He raised an arm and clicked his fingers. 'Sol,' he called, 'a pint of your excellent whelks, when you're ready, if you please.'

The cab had not reached the Strand before James Batchelor had collapsed. He was sweating and shivering at the same time, as if the ague had got him, and his eyes were rolling in his head. Grand hit the cab's roof with his fist. 'The nearest hospital, cabbie,' he shouted. 'And use your whip.'

SIXTEEN

The cabbie drew to a clattering halt at the front door of Charing Cross Hospital and jumped from his perch. He hadn't thought the gent had looked very well when he'd got in and he wanted him out before he threw up – it could take days to get rid of the smell and he had a living to earn. He knew of blokes who had had passengers die in their cabs and that never went down well. He helped Grand half carry the stricken Batchelor up the steps and into the echoing hall where a porter leaped to his feet.

'You can't bring that there here,' he said, holding up a hand.

'What? My friend needs a doctor,' Grand said, now taking all of Batchelor's weight as the cabbie let go to bite down on the sovereign Grand had accidentally handed over for the fare.

'He's dead,' the porter remarked, with an expert air.

'I am not dead,' Batchelor murmured. He knew he was no expert, but was pretty sure he would be able to tell. 'But I do feel very . . .' and with that, his eyes rolled up and Grand could no longer hold him as he slid to the floor.

The porter looked down, dispassionately. 'Now he's dead,' he said.

Grand knelt by Batchelor's side. He crouched over him and listened for his breath, looked for a pulse in the neck and felt for his heart. There was a flutter there, but it seemed to be getting weaker by the moment. He almost cried with frustration. He had been so well not an hour before. He heard a clacking of heels and there was a sudden, almost overwhelming smell of carbolic.

'What seems to be the trouble?' A clipped female voice came from above.

'It's my friend,' Grand said and, even as he said it, his heart lurched. Not colleague. Not acquaintance. Friend. He had lost enough of those already; this one just had to stay alive. He looked up into a large, well-meaning face he knew.

'Don't I know you?' the nurse said. 'Isn't your mother in the hospital?' She looked stern. 'I don't think I've noticed you visiting, have I?' Her toe tapped, unseen under her long skirts, but Grand could tell it was tapping even so.

'No, sorry, nurse,' he said, chastened. 'But my friend here . . . I don't know what it is. He . . . well, he seems to be hardly breathing.'

She looked at the porter who withered under her gaze. 'Don't just stand there, Jenkins,' she said. 'Fetch a stretcher and call for a doctor. Who is on call this morning? It doesn't matter. Just fetch him.' She turned back to Grand. 'Come with us,' she said. 'I shall need to take some details.'

Grand reluctantly got to his feet. He couldn't just leave Batchelor stretched out on this cold, unforgiving tiled floor. But before he was properly upright, two stretcher-bearers appeared at the trot, with Jenkins slouching along behind. They expertly lifted the prone detective on to the canvas and were gone through the double swing doors into the wards almost before Grand could blink.

'There,' the nurse said, taking him kindly by the arm. 'He's in good hands. Just come with me and we'll just take a few details, such as name, address, ability to pay, that kind of thing. I assume he isn't indigent?'

'Indigent? Oh, no, no, not at all. Whatever it costs . . .' Grand was still looking at the doors, swinging gradually to a stop.

'That's good,' she said. 'I know I shouldn't say it, but, well, it isn't too good to be indigent in here. The doctor will be with him by the time we've done our bit of ledger-filling, so the sooner we start, the sooner we're done.' She tugged gently at his arm. 'Come along, Mr . . .?'

'Grand. Matthew Grand.'

'Ah,' she said, understandingly. 'Not the same name as your dear old mum. That explains it. We did wonder.'

Grand thought briefly about explaining the whole Miss Jones debacle, but in the end decided that now was not the time. As he was led down a corridor, he heard running feet behind him. A voice was calling, urgent, loud.

'Doctor, doctor. In here!'

Another voice cut in. 'He's gone.'

The nurse stiffened at Grand's side and pulled him into a side room. 'Come on, Mr Grand,' she said. 'There's nothing we can do out there. Your friend is in God's hands now.'

James Batchelor felt better. He had felt really, really sick. His heart had been racing, pumping as though it would leap out of his chest, and his lungs didn't seem able to get the air in and out. He was hurting all over. His hair hurt. Was that even possible? There was a lot of shouting, which he didn't like, because it made the insides of his ears ache. There were hands, pulling him about, and that just wasn't nice. Not when he felt so sick and ill.

Then, suddenly, it all stopped. The pains all just went away and the horrible gnawing at his bowels stopped, as though someone had thrown a switch. There was still some shouting, but it was much further away. His heart had stopped hammering. His lungs were not fighting for air. A soft singing noise filled his head and he couldn't feel the lumpy bed beneath him. Could he be floating? It was a good place he was in, wherever it was . . .

'He's gone, Doctor.' The stretcher-bearer had no medical training, having been seconded from the adjacent workhouse to help earn his keep. But he was a bright youngster who, in other circumstances, might have stood where the doctor stood now. And even if he had been the dimmest denizen of St Martin-in-the-Fields, he would still have been able to tell that Batchelor was no longer in the land of men.

The doctor wasn't a quitter. He had been torn from his breakfast to attend this emergency and he was damned if he would let it be for a corpse. He barked to a hovering nurse. 'Sal volatile, nurse. Keep the vial in place until it takes effect.' He rolled up his sleeves. 'You,' he snapped to the attendant. 'Open his coat. I will massage his heart. Come on man – now, not when you feel like it!'

Grand was sitting in the nurse's office, his elbows on his knees, his face in his hands, his heart in his boots. The gentle scratch of the pen in the ledger was all that he could hear. He was concentrating on this room, this moment. He could feel the sharp pain of his elbows on his thighs. He could smell the sweat of fear that Batchelor had left on his jacket. He didn't want to think about any moment other than now. The soft flap of an enormous book closing brought him back.

'Mr Grand,' the nurse said, in gentle tones. 'I've filled in the register. I . . . I'm afraid there isn't anything else to be done at the minute. Mr Batchelor's . . . effects . . . will be available for collection later today. There will be other paperwork for you to complete in the fullness of time, but for now . . .' She came around the desk and put a strong arm around the man's shoulder. 'Mr Grand, do you have anyone at home?'

'Mrs Rackstraw,' he said, quietly. 'She's going to be devastated, you know. She was always moaning at James, spending all his time in the attic and making her go up and down all the time, but she is very fond of him, really . . . *was* very fond . . .'

The nurse said nothing. These two young men certainly lived unusual lives and the ending of one of them was already raising questions. That the police should be involved was a given. How Grand was going to deal with that was his problem but, apart from his neglect of his dear old mum, who was perhaps no better than she should be, he seemed nice enough and she was sorry. She stayed there, patting his shoulder gently until he felt better.

With a sigh, Grand got up and dusted off his hat. 'My apologies, nurse,' he said. 'This has brought back a lot of bad memories. From home, you know.'

He was foreign, so that probably explained that.

'How much do I owe you?'

'We have the address,' she said. 'We'll send in the bill when the doctor has finished . . .' Her voice died away.

Grand smiled at her, a rueful smile that broke her heart. 'I see. Well, thank you for all your kindness, nurse.' And, with heavy steps, he left the room, leaving her standing there with tears in her eyes.

James Batchelor was annoyed. He wasn't floating any more; he was leaning over the side of a lumpy bed, vomiting what felt like his very soul over the immaculate shoes of a man who seemed to be squeezing his heart out of his body. He had enjoyed the floating, whereas this new stage in his existence, he was not so keen on.

'Bugger me!' a young voice said from behind him. 'I had him for a goner.'

The nurse, standing well out of range of the flying sick, was thinking the same, but was too genteel to say so. 'Doctor,' she breathed instead. 'You're a miracle worker.'

The doctor, whose valet would not be pleased to see him when he went home to change, was feeling rather smug. He knew he was good – no one rose in the profession as he did without being good – but raising the dead was a new height, even for him. 'Oh, just lucky, nurse, just lucky. But not as lucky as this young man.'

Batchelor's stomach, indeed his whole inside, was empty at last, and he looked up to say thank you to his saviour. He had begun to realize, as the retching became less, that floating wasn't a patch on living after all. He wiped his mouth. 'Thank you, Doctor,' he began, then found himself in chorus with Doctor Beard. 'You!' they both said together.

Grand was passing the ward when a compulsion gripped him. He couldn't just go home, leaving James in the hands of strangers. He needed to know, for his own satisfaction, that he was being treated right. He had lost a lot of friends, God alone knew how many, cut down by the withering fire on some random hillside, and he hadn't often had the chance of a goodbye. And, even though it was too late this time, he could perhaps have the luxury of a few quiet moments, with the blood not yet cool, with the pallor of death not yet fixed. He opened the door softly and peered in. The serried ranks of beds he expected were missing. The room was small, with only two curtain-shrouded cubicles in it. One set of curtains was partly drawn back, showing a narrow cot, with a shrouded figure on it. A woman in black was hunched at the head, a crumpled handkerchief to her eyes. That was good service, Grand thought, a mourner arranged just like that. Batchelor didn't need that kind of thing, of course, he had his own family and friends to mourn him, but still . . . it was a thoughtful gesture. He made a move towards the body, which seemed small and somehow diminished under the sheet.

The curtains around the other bed were suddenly thrown back and a man in vomit-spattered trousers emerged, his pepper and salt hair on end and a stethoscope swinging wildly as he strode across the room, making for the door. A nurse trotted after him, hardly glancing at Grand as she passed. At the threshold, the man paused and turned back, speaking to the attendant.

'Clean him up, will you, Dawkins? Then get him to the public ward.'

'But,' the nurse interposed, 'he has money, Dr Beard. You can tell that by his clothes.'

'Even so,' Beard snapped. 'The public ward for him. Jump to it, man.' And with that, he swept out, almost catching the nurse a nasty one with the swinging door.

Dawkins turned to the man in the bed. 'He's got a down on you, all right,' he said. 'Good job he didn't recognize you right off, or you'd be a goner now. Come on, let's get these stinking clothes off you and we'll get you washed.'

'Thank you.' The man on the bed was too exhausted to say more, but the voice was still music to Grand's ears.

'James?' he said, hurrying over. 'James? I thought you were dead!'

'You ain't the only one, mate,' Dawkins said. 'I reckon he was dead, and all. Dr Beard, he brung him back to life. He's got a lot to thank Dr Beard for. Though he seems to have took against him. Met before, have they?'

'In a manner of speaking,' Grand said. 'Do you have to put him in the public ward? I can pay.'

Dawkins sucked his teeth and looked doubtful. A florin tucked into his top pocket seemed to make up his mind. 'I'll have a word with matron,' he said. 'You go home for half an hour and when you come back your friend will be all spick and span and in a nice room of his own, you'll see.' He peered at Grand. 'You don't look so chipper yourself. I hope you ain't coming down with what he's got.' He looked down at Batchelor, who had collapsed back on his pillows, exhausted. 'I don't reckon he's out of the woods yet. I never seen nobody throw up like that before.' He tittered. 'All over the doc's feet. Funny, that was, but it's more than your life's worth to laugh, o' course. Not at Doc Beard.' He shooed Grand off with a grimy hand. 'Off you go, then, mister.' It seemed pretty clear that no more money was going to be forthcoming and he had work to do. 'Come back in an hour and ask at the door. Jenkins'll let you know where your mate is, you can be sure.'

Grand knew he should go home. He should tell Mrs Rackstraw. But all he could find it in his heart to do was to pace the pavement outside the hospital. Flower sellers were setting up strategically along the street; undertakers were patrolling, in step with Grand and almost as gloomy. Death was in the air and it was impossible to think straight. As the end of the hour approached, the American stood on the bottom step approaching the front door and looked about him. Above the roofs of the houses, spires and steeples poked at the summer sky, hot and blue already. Cab horses pulled their loads, flies thick around the sweaty harness. Some shone like conkers, the brass fittings on their reins and bridles glinting in the sun. Others had coats like coconut matting, ribs like knives, their tails thick with grease and horse-shit, the filthy leather the same colour as their hides. The crossing sweeper leaned on his broom. Not much to sweep as yet, but the day was very young. The flower sellers called their wares, the undertakers' mutes, glycerine tears on their cheeks, paced behind their masters. Grand didn't need glycerine. If Batchelor did still die, he couldn't stay here. And he realized, with a lurch of his heart, that he loved this place, smells, noise and all. Shaking himself free of the black cloud around him, he turned and bounded up the steps. He had a friend to attend.

A nurse barred his way. She was younger than the one who had taken down Batchelor's details, shorter, prettier. But that there was iron under her starched front could not be in doubt.

'I cannot let you see your friend now,' she said. 'He needs his rest. He had been eating shellfish or something similar, I understand. Nasty stuff; I never touch it. He will need careful nursing for quite a while; there are often complications in cases of ptomaine poisoning.'

'Come across those often, have you?' Grand was in no mood to exchange pleasantries this morning, of all mornings.

'One or two,' she said, frostily, 'Mr . . .?'

Instinctively he passed over his card and watched her eyes

light up. 'Ooh, how exciting!' and she actually clapped her hands. 'You're a detective.'

'I am,' he said.

'And your friend . . . Mr Batchelor . . . he works with you, does he?'

'When he feels up to it,' Grand nodded.

'I've never met a detective before,' the nurse trilled. She was softer now, smiling. 'But I am something of a follower of grisly murders. I have newspaper cuttings. That's not peculiar, is it, Mr Grand? For a woman to be interested in such things?' She looked into his face, a little anxiously. She wanted to give a good impression; he was a detective, after all, and – apart from that – easily as handsome as any man she had ever met.

'Er . . . no,' Grand dithered, secretly finding it a *little* strange. 'No, not at all.'

'The James Greenacre case is my favourite. Dismemberment. Regent's Canal. Very gruesome.'

That rang bells for Grand, who sat down on the hard chair in the anteroom to where Batchelor lay dozing. 'One of Inspector Field's cases,' he remembered.

'Field?' The nurse blinked and the first detective she had ever met lost a little in her estimation. 'No, sir, you're mistaken. A sharp-eyed constable called Pegler solved that one.'

'Did he?' Grand asked. No surprises there, then; Field building up his part yet again. Still, just to be sure, 'What about Daniel Good?'

'Yes, he led the police a merry chase,' the nurse remembered the cutting, yellowing now in her scrapbook. 'A retired policeman caught him – Tom Rose, his name was.'

'What about Muller?' Grand was intrigued now. 'Was Field in on that one?'

'Lord love you, no, Mr Grand; that was Inspector Richard Tanner caught the Railway Murderer. An interesting case; the papers were full of it. Bludgeoning, though – very crass.'

'Tanner?' Grand was half out of his seat. 'When was this?'

'Ooh, let me see. Sixty-four, it would be. I hadn't even started my training then.'

In '64, Matthew Grand had been with General Sherman, marching to the sea.

'No, you're confused about Chief Inspector Field. The only famous case he worked on was the Bermondsey Horror. You know – the Mannings?'

Grand didn't. 'When was that?' he asked.

'Eighteen forty . . . now, was it forty-eight?' She thought for a moment, finger to her lips. 'No, I tell a lie. It was forty-nine.'

In 1849, Matthew Grand had still been at school.

'Dreadful hanging, it was. Horsemonger Lane Gaol. The late Mr Dickens witnessed it and wrote about it.'

'Did he now?' Grand wasn't so sure about that, but there was no reason to share that with the nurse. 'Tell me, what sort of crime was that? The weapon used, I mean?'

'Bludgeoning again.' The nurse beamed broadly. 'With a side order of quicklime. Very messy.'

Her smile vanished as Matthew Grand dashed for the door. 'Mr Grand,' she called after him. 'Mr Grand, you can see your friend for a minute now, Mr Grand.'

SEVENTEEN

G rand had waited for half a day, planning his moves, checking his strategy. He had even gone to Batchelor's usual domain, the hushed circle of the British Museum Library to check on the crimes that the nurse knew all about. And she had been right. There was no Inspector Field involved in any of them. Except . . .'

'Good evening, Chief Inspector.' Grand swept off his hat and perched on the end of the park bench. 'I'm sorry to bother you again so soon, but I hoped to pick your brains on the Manning murder. What did the Press call it? The Bermondsey Horror?'

'Mr Grand.' Field's smile was frozen. 'Good evening to you too, sir. How's Mr Batchelor?'

'Alive,' Grand told him. 'And although he would hate me for using this overworked cliché, it seems appropriate, so, "No thanks to you".'

'Me?' Field's eyes widened. 'You flatter me, Mr Grand. Old Solly has killed more people with his jellied eels than anybody I've seen hanged. The rumour is that he just mixes the leftovers from the day before in with his new batch; there are eels in there older than I am, or so I believe. It's just your good luck you don't like 'em, eh?'

'And your bad luck,' Grand said. He watched as Field threw his crusts of bread to the mallards, clucking and squawking in the waters of St James's again. 'These ducks of yours are better fed, I'll wager, than most people in the metropolis.'

Field laughed. 'I leave such social comments to Mr Mayhew,' he said. 'As for me, I find ducks more honest than people, don't you? They don't lie and cheat, they don't let you down, they don't commit immoral acts, they mate for life. Oh, they're greedy, I grant you, but they're honest about that, at least.'

'But this case has nothing to do with greed, has it, Mr Field?' Grand said.

'What case is that, then?' Field asked, all innocence.

'The poisoning of Charles Dickens. The poisoning of Arthur Clinton. The bludgeoning of Gabriel Verdon. Oh, and the attempted poisoning of James Batchelor. They might put you on the treadmill for the last one, but they'll surely hang you for all the others.'

Field's smile had gone. 'Why did you ask about the Bermondsey Horror a moment ago?'

'Because, when you were reeling off your successes as a cop, you cited various crimes you had no connection with. And the one you *did* crack, the Manning case, you didn't mention.'

'It slipped my mind,' Field said, rummaging for more bread in his box.

'It was your first brush with Charles Dickens, who was very critical of the whole case and the public hanging. It made me wonder whether you were such good friends after all, but I digress. Another case you didn't mention – because it was by no means a career-maker but which you were called in on – was the Bradford Poisonings. Dozens died from adulterated sweets and I believe that your investigations then gave you a lifelong interest in poison, making you something of an expert.'

'Oh,' Field looked down at his box, sorting out the best crusts for his favourite duck, who had left the water and had waddled over, quacking softly to herself. 'I wouldn't call myself an expert. An interested dabbler, that's the furthest I would care to go. And that was twenty-one dead, by the way. Trust a Yankee amateur to get that wrong.'

'Arsenic, I think it was, in the candy, wasn't it?'

Field nodded at the duck.

'And it got you thinking. Organic irritants, good old standbys like deadly nightshade and moonflower.'

'Angel's trumpet, yes,' Field almost purred. 'That's what did for Arthur Clinton. The smug, degenerate bastard. Well, it wouldn't have been right, Mr Grand, would it, for him to walk away from his abominable crime? They used to stone people like him to death, you know, in the good old days.'

'So, you became his jury, judge and executioner.'

'In a manner of speaking, yes. And anyway, it got back at Stella, too, and that wasn't a bad result.'

'Stella?' Grand raised his head sharply and the duck, startled, flapped back to the safety of the water. 'Ernest Boulton.'

Field laughed at the memory of it. 'You know that deranged misfit was going to appear in *Edwin Drood*? Him! Her! Whatever! I couldn't have that. I confronted Dickens in that bloody chalet of his and I told him straight.'

'What did you tell him?' Grand wanted to know.

Field looked at the man. Had he no soul at all? 'I don't suppose you've ever been in a book, have you?' he asked.

'Maybe the odd despatch from General Sherman,' Grand shrugged modestly.

'I'm talking about a *book*, man. A literary creation. A work of genius. Dickens was happy to put me in his earlier works. So was Wilkie Collins. I read the first few chapters of *Drood* and couldn't see myself at all. So I asked him outright. "When do I appear?" I said. "What's the sobriquet?" and so on.' He turned to look Grand up and down. 'Do you use that word in your country? Sobriquet?'

'I am comfortable with the word, yes,' Grand said. He could scarcely believe he was sitting on a park bench with a murderer, feeding ducks and discussing vocabulary.

'He said he didn't intend to put me in at all. Me. Charlie Field! Doyen of *Household Words*. Inspector Bucket. Well, you can imagine, Mr Grand, I was outraged.'

'So you killed him.'

'I gave him one more chance to be fair. In that last interview, do you know what he told me? He told me he didn't actually write any of his novels. All that was Gabriel Verdon. He said that a lesser talent like that might be happy to include me, but he was above such things.'

'But you didn't believe him?'

'Of course not. The very idea! A weak excuse from the world's greatest story teller, I thought. So, I just popped an extra large dose of angel's trumpet in his homeopathic cocoa. It wouldn't have taken long.'

'And you didn't go with him to Canton Kitty's, did you?'

'I certainly did!' Field was insistent. 'He didn't do anything like that without me by his side!'

'Lying's kinda pointless now, Mr Field,' Grand said. 'I know you didn't go to Bluegate Fields because you thought Canton Kitty was a Chinese lady and you didn't mention Nell Ternan or the Americans.'

'Charles and I were like *that*!' Field shouted, two entwined fingers in the air.

'Once, perhaps,' Grand said quietly. 'But not any more. And that's what this is all about, isn't it? You weren't famous any more and you couldn't handle it. You invented the crimes you'd solved, pretended to be a chief inspector years after you'd hung up your truncheon. You barked at rookie cops on their beat and when Dickens turned you down, you saw red and reached for the angel's trumpet.'

'Yes, I was the angel, all right. Angel of the Lord. Angel in the marble. Take your pick. And too right I saw red. And I'd do it again. Wilkie Collins is next.'

'What happened with Verdon?' Grand wanted to know.

'Ah, well, that was a mistake, I'll grant you. I didn't believe a word Dickens said about Verdon doing all the writing, but it stood to reason he might well finish *Drood*, so I went to see him. He did spend an awful lot of time down at Gads Hill at one time, so I wondered if there might not be something in it after all.'

'He was down at Gads Hill because he was rather enamoured of the gardener's wife. And the vicar's daughter. And any woman within a five-mile radius, from what I understand.'

Field clicked his tongue. 'No better than he should be, then,' he said. 'I had felt a bit guilty about losing my temper like that, but not so much, now. But how did you know it was me? You amateurs – have you never heard how a murderer always uses the same method? A poisoner never bludgeons, a stabber never poisons. That's the rule, that is.'

'It was when you let slip your little mistake about the keys,' Grand reminded him.

But Field was in full flow now. 'A locked-room mystery, eh? What a gem. And it would point suspicion at Chapman and Hall's people. Verdon laughed at me. He actually *laughed*, Mr Grand. Can you believe it? He said Dickens was writing *Drood* and I should have gone to see him while he was still alive. Well, of course I had. And of course, I had to kill Verdon. Red mist, yes, you're right. I just hit him and down he went. Skull cracked like an eggshell. I was the visiting angel again – avenging, this time.'

'But we were a problem,' Grand said, 'Batchelor and me.'

'Oh, Mr Grand, don't flatter yourselves. But yes, I needed to know what you knew. George Sala called you in, didn't he? Had to be him, big-nosed busybody. I pretended Catherine Dickens had engaged me – as she had, back when she discovered that bracelet that got her kicked out – and I told you that I too suspected foul play. And I followed you.'

'*You* did?'

'Not me personally. I've got a little private army of snoopers for that purpose. They told me your every move. You cost me a packet, you know, gadding off to Winchester and all over; train tickets don't grow on trees. I did try to warn you off, to be fair to me. I got my old mate Doncha and his blarney boys to rough you up. Then I arrived, like your cavalry, to save the day. Except that you were too bloody stupid to take the hint, weren't you?'

'So, Sol's for breakfast it had to be,' Grand said.

'That's about right,' Field said. 'I knew that nonsense about Forster would bring you running. And then a bit of the angel's brew.'

'But you didn't know about Verdon's diary.'

'No, I must admit that threw me. There I was, though, in a book again – "FC". I couldn't believe you and Batchelor missed it. Transposed letters indeed. Not Frederic Chapman but Charlie Field. Good old Charlie.'

He threw the last of his bread to the ducks. 'Well, what do you suppose is going to happen now?'

'Now,' Grand said, 'I'm going to take you to Scotland Yard. There's a *real* chief inspector waiting there for you.'

'Oh, I don't think so, Mr Grand,' Field smiled. 'You see, I've got unfinished business. There's Wilkie Collins, as I told you. Your friend Batchelor, apparently, he of the nine lives. But first of all, of course, there's you.'

Suddenly, there was a gun in Charlie Field's fist and it was pointing at Matthew Grand's forehead. 'And don't even think of reaching inside your coat, Mr Grand; a Tranter tops a Colt every time, I fancy. You know, you should be grateful. I can see the headlines now – "American found dead in London Park". Well, in our line of work, it's not too surprising, is it? And all these Maryannes prowling places like this: who's to say one of them didn't take advantage of you – good-looking, well-set-up bloke as you are. Maybe George Sala will write your obituary.'

'Mr Field?' a voice called from the shrubbery. 'Everything all right?'

Grand saw his chance and swung out with his left arm, sending Field's pistol flying. With his right, he smashed the man's nose and dragged him off the bench. A uniformed constable was running towards him, truncheon in hand. He pulled up short as he found himself staring down the muzzle of Grand's Colt.

'Nice of you to call, Constable,' he said. 'And who says there's never a cop around when you need one? Now, you be a nice bobby and put that shillelagh away.' He crossed to pick up Field's gun and stuffed it into his belt. 'And instead, how about using that rattle of yours? I think we could all do with some assistance about now.'

James Batchelor lay back on more cushions than one average-sized home should possess. Mrs Rackstraw had left no stone unturned when it came to making the invalid comfortable and a cooling bowl of calves'-foot broth stood on the nightstand along-side a glass of warming lemonade. Batchelor was at that stage of convalescence when he could take as much pampering as was thrown at him. Grand suspected, though, that his threshold was very near and Mrs Rackstraw was on the verge of being told where to put her nourishing broth. He made a mental note to make sure he was elsewhere when that happened.

'You were very lucky, though, Matthew,' he croaked. His throat was still sore from the vomiting, and from the stomach pump, which for some reason Dr Beard had prescribed three times daily for his week in hospital. 'That policeman might not have come along for hours.'

'Very true, James,' Grand said with a smile. 'But in fact it wasn't luck at all. Mrs Rackstraw was all of a doodah when she found you were in hospital. I more or less had to nail her to the floor to stop her hurtling round there to nurse you herself. Apparently, the nurses there are no better than they should be.'

'I didn't notice,' Batchelor said, with total accuracy.

'They're a bit starched, but . . .' Grand brought himself back to the point. 'So I told her that you weren't to be troubled. That I had had enough difficulty getting in and that she stood no chance. That it was an open police investigation . . . well, I just told her any old story I could lay tongue to, I suppose. In the end, she seemed to just give in.'

'That doesn't sound like her,' Batchelor remarked.

'And it isn't, thank God,' Grand laughed. 'If she couldn't get at you, she decided she had to look after me. So she followed me. All afternoon. That wasn't hard, I guess. I spent a lot of the time in the library . . .'

'You?' Batchelor was impressed. 'Which library?'

'That one you use. The British Museum library. I had to look up some cases. Anyway, that's not part of the story. Mrs Rackstraw tracked me there, waited outside – I gather she could have made a few pence if she had been willing to accede to a certain rather unchoosy gentleman's requests, but she declined. Eventually, I came out and then she almost lost me. I went down into the conveniences and she didn't know whether there was another exit. In fact, and don't tell her this,' Grand leaned closer and lowered his voice, 'she waited on one of those glass panes in the ceiling, which of course is just pavement outside. If she thought I had looked up her skirt, even accidentally, she would be mortified.'

Batchelor exploded with laughter, but clutched his midriff. 'Oh, please don't make me laugh. It hurts.'

'Sorry. It gets a bit exciting from here on in. She tracked me to the park and sat on a bench a few along from where I met Field. It occurred to me we had no idea where he actually lived, but St James's Park was a pretty safe bet. I did notice her, but didn't recognize her, which I suppose doesn't say much for my detective skills. She couldn't hear what we were saying, but she began to get worried. She saw Field waving his arms about and could tell he had raised his voice, though she couldn't actually make out what the words were. She heard just a few, though, and it was enough to have her beetling off to find a bobby.'

'Matthew,' Batchelor grated. 'You've gone native at last.'

Grand raised an interrogative eyebrow.

'Bobby. Not cop. You're coming along nicely.'

'Well, whatever we call them, she found one. She managed to convince him that he needed to intervene. She was lucky; apparently, she reminded him of his old mum, so he didn't run her in for being an itinerant mad person, what do you cusses call them – "a lunatic at large"? He came over as if everything was as natural as you like and there you are. Field in handcuffs before you could say . . . what is that bloke?'

'Bloke? Robert Peel?' Batchelor had dropped off briefly and thought they were still on the etymology of police nicknames.

'Robinson. Jack Robinson.'

Batchelor was confused, but let it go.

There was a gentle tap on the door and Mrs Rackstraw peered around, what she fondly thought was a caring expression on her face. 'There's that peeler again,' she said. 'You know. The big one with . . .'

There was an altercation in the hallway and her face abruptly disappeared, to be replaced by the not-insubstantial bulk of Dolly Williamson.

'That peeler?' He looked behind him and slammed the door with a foot. He was carrying a small sack and reached into it and brought out three bottles of ale. 'Present from Dick Tanner,' he said, handing them round. 'He thought you might need building up. How are you, anyway?' He sat on the foot of Batchelor's bed and the sudden weight nearly catapulted him across the room.

'I've felt better,' Batchelor said, as loudly as he could manage. 'I still feel a bit feeble sometimes and I can actually vomit if anyone mentions . . . well, snake-like water creatures in goo.'

Williamson thought for a minute, then raised a finger. 'Got it,' he said. 'I never cottoned to jellied eels much anyway. Sorry.'

Batchelor had gone green and Grand was reaching for a bowl. Batchelor raised a hand and they waited but all was well.

'I never had Charlie Field as a murderer,' Williamson continued, when all danger was past. 'He was a nuisance, of course. Used my name more than once, it turns out, when he wanted to question people who knew their rights. Couldn't let go, that was his trouble. Not like old Dick,' and he took a hefty swig from the bottle. 'Not a bad tipple, this.' He turned to Grand. 'You've been to his place, yes?'

Grand nodded. His head still ached sometimes, just thinking of it.

'I thought I might pop down there for a few days. Bit of a holiday.'

'You could take your wife,' Batchelor suggested helpfully.

'I could,' Williamson ruminated. 'Yes, I could do that.' He

looked at the bottle, held up to the light, then brightened. 'But it will be a while yet. I don't think poor old Charlie will be fit to plead. Mad as that wardrobe, if I tell the truth. But we'll have to go through the motions. Frederic Chapman isn't making my life any easier, for a start.' He sighed. 'I did try and blame you, Mr Batchelor, but he didn't seem convinced.'

'Blame me?' Batchelor strained up on his pillows. 'What for?'

'Well, telling me FC instead of CF. That's what set me off on the wrong direction.'

Batchelor was speechless.

Williamson clouted the man's knee in a manner not recommended for invalids and Batchelor jackknifed on his pillows. 'Just joking, Mr Batchelor,' he said. 'Just joking. We only questioned him for an hour or two and he hardly fell downstairs at all.' He drained his bottle and set it down alongside the cold calves'-foot broth and the room-temperature lemonade. He took a deep breath and stood up. 'I don't often say this,' he said, in a growl. 'But thank you. We already suspect that poor old Charlie has done a load of murders we will never get him for. I don't want to think how many more he would have added to his list if you hadn't caught him. So . . . thanks again.' And with that, he spun round and wrenched open the door, dragging Mrs Rackstraw, in a crouching position putting her ear approximately level with the keyhole, into the room. 'And, take my advice, get rid of this bloody woman!'

And with that he was gone.

Mrs Rackstraw drew herself up to her normal height and smoothed her apron with one hand and her hair with another. 'Can I get you gentlemen anything?' she said, in a voice so prim she was almost unrecognizable.

Grand looked at her, grimly, then smiled. 'Don't worry, Mrs R,' he said. 'We never take advice from Chief Inspector Williamson. If you happen to be heading to the kitchen, I could just murder some dripping on toast.'

A closed ambulance drew in through the gates of Colney Hatch Asylum. Some of the more ambulant inmates watched as it passed through, the iron bars eased aside to let it in, then locked again behind it. One in particular, a bright-eyed woman in a pinny and neat dress, smiled to watch it. She liked new inmates. Sometimes,

although not often enough, they might have a cat in their luggage.
She started to make her way to the door.

The woman helped out of the ambulance was quite the ugliest
woman that Mrs Manciple, late of Alsatia, had seen, but that
didn't mean she wasn't a cat lover. Mrs Manciple had learned
that it is hard to spot a cat person by outward appearance alone.
She drew nearer and smiled encouragingly at the woman, who
looked back at her with her tiny eyes, far too close together on
the bridge of her tremendous nose. Her lips worked above her
negligible chin but eventually she smiled back. She was held by
one of the burly asylum nurses, but she had one arm free and
beckoned Mrs Manciple nearer.

'It's Young Mr Frederic I worry about,' she said, confidingly.
'He has the wrong legs, you know.' The nurse pulled on her arm
and the woman went with her, uncomplainingly, into the dark
maw of the hall. Mrs Manciple gave a shudder. *That* was a close
escape; any cats in *her* luggage weren't going to be very nice
kitties, that was for sure.

But, wait. Another person was coming slowly down the steps
of the ambulance, a big man with piercing eyes which missed
nothing. He was shackled hand and foot and had an expression
which brooked no argument. He also beckoned to Mrs Manciple,
standing there hugging a phantom kitten to her chest.

'I'll get them, you know,' he snarled. 'Those bastards.'
Mrs Manciple blenched. 'That Grand. That Batchelor. When I get
out of here, it's curtains for them. A drop of the angel.' He winked
at Mrs Manciple. 'And Bob's your uncle. Oh, yes.'

Two more nurses came running down the steps and pinioned
the big man's arms to his side. 'Come on now, Mr Field,' one
of them said, crooningly. 'Let's get you inside, shall we?'

Mrs Manciple watched them go, her fingers deep in invisible
fur. Grand. Batchelor. She wasn't sure, but she thought she might
once have had kittens called that. It certainly seemed very familiar.
With a happy smile, Mrs Manciple wandered away, calling. 'Here,
kitty, kitty, kitty . . .'

Chief Inspector Dolly Williamson was not a vain man. He knew
that he was only ordinary to look at, that if he were special it
was because of his extraordinary skill in being able to winkle

out a bad 'un. Grand and Batchelor, he had long ago decided, were by far the best of a bad bunch and it would do no harm to keep in touch. They were nice lads, taken by and large. Dick Tanner had certainly had a soft spot for them, and Dick was known for his nose for a good character. He was smiling to himself as he strode off the final step and on to the pavement, but not really looking where he was going. He came to the moment with a jolt as he found himself suddenly enveloped in a tangle of silks, satins, parasols and furbelows as two extremely dressed young women crossed his path.

'Oh, I say,' trilled one. 'Sir, please watch your step. I bruise particularly easily and Mama checks me over every night for contusions.'

'Indeed, sir,' the other joined in and fetched Williamson a sharp one on the wrist with her intricately chased parasol handle. 'Please be careful, do.'

Williamson was covered in confusion. He blushed to the roots of his hair and backed away, only to find that a button on his sleeve had become snarled in the auburn hair of the slighter of the two women.

'Don't pull at it, idiot,' the larger growled, then coughed and trilled a laugh. 'Excuse me,' she said. 'A case of laryngitis. Don't pull, let me disentangle you.'

To Williamson's discomfiture, the street seemed suddenly full of cabs passing extremely slowly, policemen strolling past in pairs at the regulation speed and women out marketing, gossiping as they went. His lapel was dusted with powder, his hair was full of an exotic perfume which he knew he was going to have to explain to his wife. He stood stock still; it seemed to be the only way to get this embarrassing incident over and done. Finally, his arm was free and the auburn-haired beauty was patting her curls back into place.

Her friend was solicitous. 'Are you all right, dear?' she cooed, tweaking a ringlet behind a shell-like ear. 'Would you like to press charges?' She looked around at the backs of the passing policemen. 'Shall I call a copper?'

Williamson looked up suddenly at the use of the vernacular and the woman laughed.

'I think he's clocked us, Stella,' she said, in a light tenor.

'I do believe he has, Fan,' the redhead agreed. She leaned forward and patted Williamson's cheek with a gloved hand. 'Mind 'ow you go, Chief Inspector,' and, arm in arm, they sashayed off down the Strand, laughing like starlings, parting briefly to let a portly gent with a large nose pass between them.

'It's a sailor,' Mrs Rackstraw announced, flinging open the door of Batchelor's bedroom. She dumped a plate of toast and dripping down on the nightstand, tutted at the undrunk broth and lemonade and flounced out.

George Sala peered round the door. 'A sailor?' he asked, an eyebrow almost in his hair.

'Take no notice of Mrs Rackstraw,' Grand advised, his mouth already full of toast. 'She has a rather unusual world view, but I think it's fair to say she suits us. Wouldn't you agree, James?'

Batchelor nodded. His mouth was watering from the smell of the hot dripping, but toast was totally out of the question.

'Sorry to hear you are unwell, Batchelor,' Sala said, in full sick-room tones. 'I trust you are on the mend.' He proffered a bag to the man on the cushions. It contained grapes, only a trifle squashed.

'Thank you,' Batchelor said, putting them on the nightstand, which was becoming a little cluttered.

'I just came,' Sala said, 'to settle my bill and also to make sure that none of what you have discovered goes any further.'

'Discovered?' Grand asked.

'That Dickens didn't write Dickens. That he had a mistress in . . . That Arthur Clinton was murdered before he could be . . . could be . . . well, before he could be. That Gabriel Verdon . . .' Sala ground to a halt. There seemed hardly anything in this whole case that could be discussed, even in the company of Grand and Batchelor, let alone polite society.

Grand gestured with his toast and said nothing.

Batchelor was busy half choking on a grape.

Sala looked at them with a sardonic eye. 'Shall we say, gentlemen, that your lips are sealed?'

The detectives nodded and Sala saw himself out.

Lightning Source UK Ltd.
Milton Keynes UK
UKOW05f1020200617
303713UK00001B/52/P